GOLDILOCKS

Print Cover Design done by the incomparable Hang Le:
http://www.byhangle.com
Ebook Cover Design done by my friend Ali Hymer:
AliHymer@comcast.net
Editing and Formatting by: Elaine York, Allusion Publishing
http://www.allusionpublishing.com/
Copyediting by: Bethany Salminen, Bethany Edits
www.bethanyedits.net

GOLDILOCKS

JAY CROWNOVER

AUTHOR'S NOTE

Hello, friends.

Are you as excited as I am for a new year and new books?

I know I'm throwing a lot at you here in a short amount of time, but I feel like that balances out the veritable drought of content from me in 2020.

Now, *Goldilocks* may seem familiar. This book was written month-by-month for my newsletter subscribers. So, you may have followed along or caught a chapter here or there when the file was available.

I've written three books this way, and all have been super valuable learning experiences. It's always fun to share a rough draft with my readers, and I find the instant feedback enlightening. The other two books that I did this way are *Recovered* and *Downfall.* Both actually ended up being a couple of my bestselling titles, both here and overseas. Fingers crossed *Goldilocks* follows in their footsteps!

If this book does well, I'll wrack my brain for a new idea that can be the next newsletter book. Though, I may have to put that off until 2022 in order to stay on top of all the content I have planned for this year. If you read the sneak peek at the end of *A Righteous Man,* I'm sure you are anxiously awaiting my next big project. If you didn't... oh boy... you are gonna be BIG sad that you missed it.

This version of *Goldilocks* has been edited, copyedited, and proofread. Along with having an actual ending now, it is all polished up to be a more cohesive and professional story. You will notice some changes if you read the first draft, and hopefully, you'll find that they made the book better.

Regardless, if you read along while I was writing, thank you for powering through my terrible, often incomprehensible rough draft. And if you just picked up this title the minute it was published or somewhere down the road once it became a real book, thank you for honoring me and my words with your time and dollars.

These days both are so precious, and I appreciate you sharing any little bit you have.

Happy reading!

Love & Ink,
Jay

I'm not usually one who offers up trigger warnings in my books, because I don't ever consider the content I write taboo or that far outside expected events in real life. However, I'm sensitive enough to know this story does touch on emotional abuse, mild physical abuse, and a touch of suicidal ideation, and that's a lot of heavy material for one book. If you are a reader who struggles with any of those topics, you might wanna sit this one out. I'm a big believer in self-care in all forms. Do what you gotta do for you!

PROLOGUE

I was a girl born to be caught forever between two extremes. And between two brothers.

I grew up in a home that was opulent and over-the-top massive. Everything was accented in gold, and the artwork on the walls were originals from the masters. There were rugs and silverware that cost more than my mother made in a year as the head housekeeper of the sprawling estate. Before I could even talk, I was juxtaposed between outrageous wealth and abject poverty. I was never sure on which side of the coin I fell, because while I was privileged enough to attend the fancy private school where the homeowners sent their two sons, I was by far the poorest kid attending the academy. I received the best education money could buy, but it was no secret I was a kid bound for community college or trade school, not the Ivy League like the rest of my classmates.

I was also trapped in a bitter back and forth between good and evil throughout my entire existence. I grew

1

up in the shadow of two boys who were as different as night and day. My mom cared for both of them like they were her own...and treated all three of us the same. That couldn't be said for the rest of the adults who haunted the halls of the ostentatious mansion. Both boys were the same age, born mere weeks apart. One was the rightful heir to the family fortune, his mother the reigning society queen of the small, ritzy New England town where we lived. She called all the shots and was scary powerful in the right circles. Her child was the favored son. He could do no wrong in the eyes of the elite.

I knew better.

He might look like the prince of the castle, and the hero of every fairytale, but I knew he was the villain. He didn't look it with his blond hair and bright blue eyes. He hid it well behind a perfect, pearly white smile and carefully crafted charm. He looked like a dreamboat, but underneath the polished façade, he was a living, breathing nightmare.

The other son was always an afterthought. No one wanted him. Not the mother who had him in order to blackmail his father and had quickly abandoned him after she got paid. Not the father who couldn't be bothered to focus on either of his sons or care how hateful his wife was to his bastard child. He was gone for most of the boys' childhoods, and when he was around, it was never pleasant. I learned at a very young age it didn't matter how big your home was or how hefty your bank account was, you could never escape a fractured family by avoiding the problems that created the cracks in the first place.

The forgotten son didn't fit in with the rich kids and social climbers any better than I did. He was an outcast. A blemish on the image of one of the most well-respected families in the nation. He was a burden and a problem that couldn't simply be swept under the rug. I never understood why the father brought him home and promptly washed his hands of the boy, but as I got older and started to pick up on subtle clues, I wondered if he hated his wife. Forcing her to raise the dark-haired boy who looked exactly like him was his ultimate revenge on the bossy, demanding woman who took no joy in anything other than looking down on those she deemed beneath her.

The illegitimate son should've been bitter and angry that he'd been born into a family that only acknowledged him when they wanted to hurt each other. But unlike the golden child, he was easygoing and affable, not taking much of anything too seriously. He was a jokester and liked to play around. He was cute, and so much softer than his half brother. He looked for trouble and liked to cause a ruckus because he was bored in that fancy school and didn't care about gaining anyone's favor. He was the ultimate rebel and my very best friend in the whole wide world from the time I could walk until the moment I betrayed him.

He wasn't the kind of guy who popped up in fairytales very often. He was too goofy, and his unpredictable temper could be scary. He generally saved his anger for only one person, his brother, but when it was unleashed, he was like a whole different person. For me, he was always the hero in every situation and story. There wasn't a person with whom I wanted to spend all my time, or one I looked up to more than the second son. Next to my mother, he was my favorite part of my forever-conflicted life.

Much to the annoyance of the supposedly perfect son.

One treated me like a beloved little sister and watched out for me from the get-go.

The other treated me like a possession, like something that belonged to him and him alone.

I figured out the hard way that it was very possible to be caught between right and wrong. Anyone removed from obscene wealth would think those two things were absolute with no room for interpretation. When money was involved, right was more like a suggestion, and wrong was a judgment call. I lost count of how many times the second son was punished for outshining the first simply because it made the family look bad. It was predetermined who was supposed to shine and who was supposed to fade away, but the bastard child had nothing to lose, so he refused to play by the rules that were created against him. I grew immune to the legitimate son receiving praise for abhorrent behavior. He was a bully and a beast, and his mother encouraged the hell out of him, making everyone around him feel like they were less than.

Especially his half brother.

I was enamored with one boy and terrified of the other. I lived my life like a human ping pong ball bouncing back and forth between them. One was my savior, the other an enemy I couldn't escape. One tried to protect me with everything he had, while the other used my one and only weakness—my mother—to manipulate me and make me behave exactly the way he wanted.

If my life were a fairytale, when the second son promised me a life beyond everything I knew, I would have believed him. I would have waited and trusted that there was going to be a happily ever after for at least one of us.

But my life was more like a horror story. The golden child always got his way, and not only did I throw away my life and any chance at happiness, I also betrayed the only boy who ever made me feel like I belonged.

In the end, I was more of a villain than the perfect, wicked boy I hated with every fiber of my being ever was.

CHAPTER 1

Ollie

"**B**ut... you're a girl."

It wasn't the second or even third time the very cute boy who answered the door had muttered the exact same phrase. I had knocked and announced I was the new roommate moving in today. He looked adorably dumbfounded, and the other boy standing in the entrance to the living room with his arms over his wide, muscular chest looked very annoyed.

I'd expected pretty much this exact reaction since I'd gone out of my way to make sure the current residents of the house didn't know my gender when I filled out the rental application a few weeks ago. The ad clearly stated a male roommate was preferred, and it was common knowledge on campus that this particular house had a 'no girls allowed' rule. Apparently, it was how the boys who had all lived together in this house since they finished freshman year kept the peace and managed to remain friends rather than rivals all these years. One of the roommates had graduated an entire year early, leaving the other three boys behind, and left a vacant room in the converted Victorian a couple blocks away from campus. It was a highly coveted rental, so surely I wasn't the only female applicant hoping for a chance to get past their gender preference, but my reasons for pushing so hard to get picked had little to do with the location, and everything to do with one of the current occupants.

I sighed and cast a dramatic look down the length of my body.

"I *am* a girl. No matter how many times you say it, or how hard he glares at me," I hooked my thumb in the direction of the glowering football player hovering behind him, "that isn't going to change. The fact that I already signed the lease and put down a deposit, as well as the first and last month's rent, won't change either. I know the rental ad said you would prefer a male roommate, but the actual homeowner picked me as the best applicant and already took my money. This is a done deal."

Thank goodness.

The elderly landlord picked me, but only after I'd tracked him down and begged and pleaded with him to let me move into the house regardless of any objections the boys might raise. Luckily, he was a kind, decent man who wasn't immune to big ol' crocodile tears. He was also the father to several daughters, and a grandpa to a couple adorable little girls. I don't think the no-girls-allowed rule was ever his in the first place. I gave him the *CliffsNotes* version of why I *had*... no, why I *needed* to move into the Victorian, and promised I'd be the best tenant he'd ever had. The biggest selling point: I reminded him that the three boys currently occupying the property were going to be leaving soon after graduation, but I still had three years left of school, if not longer. I was undecided on my future plans and pretty much everything else in my life. The only thing I knew for certain was that I was exactly where I needed to be at the moment.

The big, unsmiling jock grunted and narrowed his eyes at me from behind the smaller guy in the doorway. It was a struggle to keep up a calm, cool front when the guy's stock in trade was being good at intimidation, both on and off the field.

"The old man must be going senile if he approved you. I'll call him right now and get this straightened out."

I lifted a dirty blond eyebrow back at the big guy and plastered on a fake, sickeningly sweet smile. I'd had a lot of practice playing nice with someone who wanted me to cower and walk away from confrontations. "Go right ahead. When you get off the phone with Mr. Peters, you can help me haul the heavy boxes on the porch up to my new room. I'll wait."

All I had going for me at the moment was false bravado... and a signed lease.

However, if I didn't put up an unbreakable façade, I knew I would cave and let these two send me running with my tail between my legs. And that just wouldn't do. I'd put everything on the line in order to stand exactly where I was right now. I was sick of scheming and sacrificing. Of lying and evading.

When things changed this summer and I finally found an inch of freedom, I took every risk imaginable to stand on this very doorstep. I hired a private investigator to track down these boys and get every bit of information on the three of him he could. I changed schools. I emptied secret bank accounts. I left behind the only home I'd ever known and escaped the crushing hold that nearly killed me. I hadn't put those things in motion without suffering a huge, tragic loss. Instead of spending my time grieving, I decided to take back control of my life. To do that, I needed to be here.

These two gatekeepers weren't even the ones I was worried about.

Oh no.

The biggest obstacle wasn't home yet, and I knew once he finally showed up, I was going to have the real fight on my hands. So, refusing to cave under the weight of the football player's glower was nothing more than practice. The big guy growled at me again and stormed off with his cell pressed against his ear. Once he was gone, I wanted to let out a sigh of relief, but I couldn't. Curious gray-green eyes were peering at me like I was some kind of scientific experiment, and he was ready to dissect me on the spot.

Harlen Danvers definitely had the brawn part of this friendship group covered. He was big and imposing in all the right ways. It was well known on campus and in college football circles that he took no shit from anyone. He was loyal to a fault and would gladly break the knees of anyone who crossed his friends. That went double for the young man standing in front of me.

If ever there was someone suited to the term 'pretty boy,' it was Vernon Banks. He also happened to be an actual genius. He was younger than I was, but just about to graduate from college. Vernon had the 'brains' in the friendship the three remaining boys in this house shared. He was so smart it was scary. He was also undeniably beautiful.

He was about an inch taller than I was, which would put him around five nine, give or take a few centimeters. He had lovely golden skin, and wide, dark eyes that lifted just slightly at the outside corners, hinting at a touch of Asian heritage somewhere in his lineage. He had thick, well-groomed eyebrows, one decorated with a silver barbell. His naturally dark hair was bleached a startling white, giving him an anime vibe that I knew the girls on campus went bananas over. They all wanted him to help them with their homework or to help them get naked. However, Vernon was known to be shy and reserved around the opposite sex and strangers in general. He was far more interested in video games and grades than dating.

Which was the exact opposite of the boy standing behind him. From what I knew, Harlen Danvers was a ladies' man through and through. He hadn't had a steady girlfriend since he started school here, but he never lacked for company. He wasn't the most talkative type. However, he didn't need words when his perfect smile was enough to have half the campus fall to their knees for him. Harlen was tall, way taller than me, and he carried his bulk well. He had dirty blond hair, which had a slight wave. He kept it longish, but it was a good look for him. It kept him from looking like a stereotypical college athlete. He had pale blue eyes that were responsible for making a hundred different girls hand over their hearts to him without question. He had a smattering of freckles across his nose, which were only visible if you got up close and personal. He was ridiculously good looking, but not pretty in the way Vernon was. They made a dynamic duo, and when the third Musketeer was around—oof—no one was safe from the impact of the three.

It was no wonder my private detective had found fan pages on the Internet dedicated to them. It was impossible to Google anything about this private college in this small, midwestern town without tumbling across these boys. I'd avoided it until recently because I'd always been scared of the repercussions. Not knowing anything was better than being informed and having that knowledge held against me at every single turn. It'd been safer to pretend the third and final roommate didn't exist, even though he was always and forever at the forefront of my mind.

"Mr. Peters called you Ollie. Did you lie about your name just so you could move in here? Are you some kind of stalker? You know there are laws against that, don't you?" Vernon's voice was soft and critical. I nervously cleared my throat and lifted a hand to twist one of my gold curls around my finger. It was a nervous habit I'd had since childhood that I couldn't seem to shake.

"My name is Olivia, but I've gone by Ollie since I was little. Mr. Peters has all my legal information. He knew exactly who I was when he agreed to let me move in here. Frankly, I don't know why you're making such a big deal about it. Girl or boy, you were getting a new roommate, regardless. You're only going to be stuck with me for a year. What's the big deal?"

Vernon hummed and lifted a finger, which had the nail painted black, to tap his full bottom lip. "It just seems weird. Mr. Peters never objected when we told him to find us a new *male* roommate. He actually seemed to appreciate that we weren't looking to change up our dynamic. And how come I've never seen you around campus? Even as big as this campus is, our paths were bound to cross at some point. I never forget a face."

I kept fiddling with my hair as I tried to calm my racing heart. One would think I would be a better liar by now, considering how often I did it. But I wasn't. My nervous energy always gave me away. I was simply hoping that since he didn't know me at all, Vernon wouldn't notice. Just because I knew pretty much everything about these boys didn't mean they had the first idea who I was or why I was so desperate to get close to them.

I didn't want to tell him I transferred over the summer with every intention of getting as close as possible to his missing roommate. I didn't want him to know it felt like a sign from above when I found out their other roommate was leaving, clearing the way for me to insert myself in their lives in the most inescapable way possible. It sounded desperate and creepy because it was.

"I keep to myself mostly." I was no dummy, but I also wasn't a savant. I was a couple of years behind all of them in terms of academics. "I transferred recently, so there's been no time to go out or make friends. I'm not exactly a social butterfly anyway, and I have a part-time job, so I keep busy away from school. It makes total sense that our paths haven't crossed before. As for

12

remembering my face," I flashed that fake smile once again, "mine isn't all that remarkable."

I was cute, at best. I knew how to work with what I had, for sure, but I was under no illusion that I had some kind of heart-stopping beauty. I did have pretty chocolate-colored eyes. I had strong, sharply angled brows that could look a little villainous if I wasn't careful about keeping them tamed. I was also blessed with good skin and a great head of hair, but all of it was just a step above average. If you didn't take into account the pink, slightly jagged scar that started below my left eye and zagged down my cheek until it disappeared underneath my chin, my face was all right. The scar was more memorable than all of my other features combined, and I knew it was what Vernon was referring to when he said he'd never forget my face if he'd seen it around campus.

Vernon didn't look convinced. However, whatever argument he was going to give died when Harlen made his way back into the living room. The football player didn't look happy, and it really took every ounce of control I had not to wilt to the floor under the weight of his irritated gaze.

"Mr. Peters said she's here to stay. He verified that Olivia Adams, who goes by the name Ollie, was the best candidate of all the applicants who applied to rent Fisher's old room. He even told me we better be nice to her or there will be hell to pay." He rubbed his temples as if he suddenly had a splitting headache. "Huck is going to lose his mind when he hears about this."

I thought I was prepared to hear his name after all this time pretending he didn't exist.

I wasn't.

A small gasp escaped before I could stop it. Luckily, Vernon was working himself into a state of panic, and his sounds of exasperation covered my own rising anxiety at the thought of dealing with Huck Snyder.

Huck was the whole reason I was here, after all.

The second son. The unwanted one. The boy I burned and betrayed because I had no other choice.

"Shit. You don't think he'll be mad enough to do something like move out, do you?" Vernon's voice rose, and his eyes widened.

The football player gave me a steady look and shrugged. "Maybe. Who knows what that unpredictable bastard will do?"

Vernon made a squeaky sound and twisted his hands together. "We can't let him leave. We already lost Fisher." I knew these boys were close, but I didn't realize exactly how close. The pretty genius sounded devastated at the thought of being separated.

"If Huck goes, we'll go with him, and she can keep the whole fucking house." Harlen said it so matter-of-factly that my heart immediately sank into my shoes. Having them all pack up and leave me alone in this rambling old house wasn't something I'd planned. It was actually the worst case scenario. I only wanted to be here because this was where Huck lived.

"Where am I going? And whose crap is scattered all over the front porch? What in the hell is going on right now?" Huck's voice was the same raspy rumble I remembered from childhood.

He always sounded like he smoked no less than a pack a day when he didn't even smoke at all. His voice never fit with his soft, pudgy face and jittery movements. The voice always sounded like it belonged to a man who'd been through hell and back, while Huck always looked like an excited kid on Christmas morning.

I froze, unsure if I wanted to run or melt into the ground. I knew getting in the door of this place was just the beginning and that the biggest challenge had yet to come. But I thought I'd have a chance to get more settled, with a moment to possibly win over the other boys before I had to face the big boss. I figured if I could unpack, it would be harder for Huck to throw me out, but my stuff was still in boxes at everyone's feet.

"Uh, it's her stuff." Harlen pointed a finger in my direction, much like I'd done at him earlier. I closed my eyes briefly and ordered myself to get my shit together. I knew what it meant to be scared of another human all the way down to your soul, but I'd never felt that way about Huck. I would hate to have to start now. "She says she's staying, and Mr. Peters agrees with her. V and I were just wondering what you were going to do about it. We know you don't want a female roommate."

Harlen was the brawn.

Vernon was the brain.

Fisher had been the quirky, irreverent one.

But there was no question that Huck was, hands down, the leader of their little gang of heathens and outcasts.

He was the one they followed. The one they looked to for guidance. He was the one who made the rules and made sure they were followed. All of that applied outside of this house and their tightly knit group as well.

Huck was at the top of the food chain when it came to the hierarchy on campus. He was infamous, and the sole reason I'd run away and transferred here.

I wasn't a stalker. Not really.

I just happened to know Huck Snyder almost as well as I knew myself. And I'd been dying for any information on him since he left home when he was sixteen. He always did everything first while I ached to follow. Including running away and leaving a really toxic environment behind. The enemy of my enemy had always been the best, and only, friend I'd ever had.

I slowly turned around to face the one person on the planet who could understand how hard it was for me to be here right now. Without winning Huck over, I had no hope of setting my life back to the way it was before someone else successfully took it over.

"Hi, Huck. Long time no see."

Everything seemed to fall deathly silent as I found myself pinned in place by a pair of eyes that were the same color as the world's purest, sweetest honey.

"Ollie."

It wasn't a question or a curse. It wasn't a greeting or a dismissal. As always, it was somewhere in between.

It was said flatly with little emotion. I went cold all over, and this plan that I'd spent weeks concocting suddenly seemed like the stupidest idea I'd ever had.

"Wait." Vernon's voice broke through the tense moment, as did his wildly waving hands. "You two know each other?"

Once upon a time, we were inseparable.

Now, we were further apart than most strangers.

16

The distance between us was confirmed when Huck growled, "Not anymore."

Just call me Goldilocks.

Not just because we had the same hair, but because I'd been bouncing around all the wrong places until I realized the only spot that was 'just right' was right next to the boy glaring at me like he wanted me to drop dead on the spot.

CHAPTER 2

Huck

Olivia Adams.

My little Ollie.

There was a time when we were inseparable. We were so in sync, I was convinced she could read my mind. We were conspirators. Twin troublemakers. Her wild spirit spoke to my soul in a way no one else had before or since. We were the odd ones out in our very affluent, entitled neighborhood, but it was never a problem to be on the outside looking in because we had each other.

Until we didn't.

Ollie looked the same, if not a little bit taller. It'd been five years since the last time I laid eyes on her, but I could've picked her out of a crowd if I was blindfolded. She was still cute and innocent looking with all that curly blond hair in every shade of gold, yellow, bronze, and white imaginable. Her wide brown eyes still looked warm and velvety soft, but where they'd once sparkled with unlimited humor and mirth, they now looked dull and flat. There was no shine, no life. This young woman was like the discount version of the one who'd followed me blindly, no matter where, or into whatever kind of trouble I was bound to find growing up. She was still pale, which made that scar on her cheek stand out even more. Despite myself, I felt my hands clench and my breath still when my gaze locked on the pink imperfection.

Five years later and looking at that scar still felt like a punch to the gut.

That mark was a constant reminder of the worst night of both of our lives. And that was saying something coming from a guy who'd pretty much been on his own since he was sixteen.

My family threw me to the wolves the minute I showed them my one and only weakness. I hated it with the passion of a thousand fiery suns that said weakness was now standing in front of me looking as unsophisticated and guileless as ever.

"What are you doing here, Ollie? How did you even find me?" It wasn't like I was in hiding or anything, but I knew my name and whereabouts were pretty much forbidden in the place she called home. It was unlikely she had the resources or the support to track me down.

Why hadn't she just stayed a distant memory?

A memory wasn't dangerous. It could be painful and hard to let go of, but overall, a memory didn't have the power to destroy the life I'd carefully and diligently rebuilt. A memory wasn't going to endanger the people who helped me heal and made sure I kept all my worst tendencies in check. I could turn my back on a memory and pretend like it no longer haunted me. I wasn't sure I had the strength to do that to the young woman standing in front of me more than once.

I'd done it before, and in the process, I'd lost a huge part of myself. The part of my heart and soul that attached themselves to hers had left giant, gaping wounds when I tore myself away from her and everything else I knew when I was just sixteen. I always figured she needed those pieces I left behind more than I did anyway. I had little use for a whole heart and a fully functioning soul back in the day. It was only as I got older and gained some perspective that I realized what I was missing and how hard it would be to live a totally successful life without reclaiming the pieces of myself I walked away from.

Ollie was frantically twisting one of her curls around her index finger, and she refused to meet my gaze. She was nervous. Outwardly, it would've been hard to tell if you weren't familiar with her mannerisms. But I used to know what every twitch, flinch, eyebrow lift, and eyelash flutter meant when it came to this girl. I could tell she was about two seconds away from crawling out of her skin. It was apparent that she wasn't surprised to see me. I figured that meant she was here because of me.

Ollie cleared her throat and shifted her weight. The soles of her black combat boots squeaked on the wood planks of the porch, and I saw her try and fight back a cringe.

"I go to school here now. I transferred for the upcoming semester. This rental is perfect, and one of the few I can afford. It's nothing more than a coincidence that you happen to live here too. I didn't know you were one of the tenants when I filled out the application."

Her voice was steady, but I could see that she was fighting hard to keep her tone and expression bland. She was a bad liar, which was why I ended up being such a good one. It always used to fall on me to spin tall tales to keep us out of trouble. I lied to protect her far more than I lied for my own gain.

"Is the fact you picked this school a coincidence as well?" I smirked and stared at her without blinking. It'd been a long time, but apparently, she thought I'd gotten stupid in the years we'd been apart.

Ollie flicked her gaze between me and Vernon. I could see my younger roommate was totally confused and slightly alarmed by my confrontation with the girl I never wanted to see again. Vernon was the best of us. He was totally innocent and too good to be influenced by me and the other boys who sheltered him after I rescued him and brought him into our circle. It was a full-time job keeping him focused, and if anyone in this room was going to have a bleeding heart toward the little liar standing in front of me, it would be him. He was still too soft, regardless of all the bullshit life had thrown at him.

My other roommate, Harlen, and I got along so well because we had a lot of similar qualities. Neither one of us trusted easily, and we were both hardwired to take absolutely zero shit from anybody. The big football player and I had butted heads a few times over the course of our friendship, and it never ended well. But I knew he would have my back without question, and if I asked him to toss this fragile interloper out on her admittedly fine ass, he would do it with no questions asked.

After a moment of awkward silence between us, Ollie sighed and dropped her hands to her sides.

"I found out this was where you go to school, and when I decided to transfer, I picked this college because I knew you were here." She looked down at the toes of her boots in a very guilty manner.

An uneasy grumble came from my roommates as the atmosphere shifted to one of alertness and alarm at her admission.

"You said you weren't a stalker!" Vernon's exclamation made me smile because the kid could really be clueless for being an actual genius.

"Do stalkers ever admit to stalking when asked, Vernon?" Vernon pouted at me after I asked the question and narrowed his eyes at Ollie. It took a lot to get on Vernon's bad side. Once you were there, good luck getting off of it.

Ollie sighed and nervously wiped her palms on her thighs. That was another give-away gesture. She really must be anxious and trying hard to hold it together.

"It wasn't hard to find you, Huck. Even though you don't have social media, you're all over everyone else's." She let out a rough laugh and put a shaking hand to her chest. "You have fan pages dedicated to you on pretty much every social media site."

I arched an eyebrow at her. "Excuse me?"

She sighed again and shook her head. "Never mind. Look, I signed a lease. I put down the deposit, and even though you may have posted that you prefer a male roommate, the Fair Housing Act prevents landlords from discriminating against renting to someone based on gender." She huffed an annoyed little breath and finally met my gaze. I'd forgotten that she could be a handful when she really dug her heels in about something. She'd had to be tough to hang with me and survive my seriously chaotic and toxic family. As annoying as it was in the moment, I was secretly glad to see she still had bits and pieces of her steel spine intact. I was worried my family, especially my half brother, were going to break her when I left her behind.

I grinned at her, but it wasn't nice. It was with lots of teeth and just enough threat to have her take a step backward.

"There are stalking laws that protect victims from having to share space with predators as well. You already admitted you came here because of me, that you've been tracking me on social media. I'm sure you know I'm pre-law, Ollie. Do you really want to go head-to-head with me? How often did that work out for you back in the day?" I cocked my head and regarded her coolly. If anyone knew just how ugly my temper could get, it was her. "There are plenty of other places for rent in this town. Something tells me you knew there wouldn't be a warm reception when you tracked me down, so you manipulated things so I couldn't turn you away exactly like you knew I would."

Vernon threw up his hands in obvious bewilderment at the situation. "Why do I feel like you two are suddenly speaking a foreign language? This seems like a private matter. Harlen and I are going to let you figure this out. We'll be in the kitchen." He spun on his heel and marched toward the glowering football player.

Normally it took a whole offensive line to move Harlen, but when we were home, he willingly let Vernon drag him around like he was an overgrown puppy. It was pretty cute and would totally ruin Harlen's tough-guy image if the truth ever got out.

Once we were alone, Ollie and I faced off like two opponents gearing up for an epic battle.

It used to be us against the world, and something felt incredibly wrong about it suddenly being us against each other.

She made a sound and clenched the hand resting on her chest as if she were trying to hold onto her heart. When she spoke, her words were shaky.

"You look good, Huck. Very grown up."

Where she hadn't changed much physically over the years, I sure as hell had.

I was always a runt and had been a little chubby when I was younger. It had taken years to finally grow into my larger-than-life personality and for my outward appearance to match all the attitude I was hauling around. I wasn't as tall or muscular as Harlen. But he still had to put a decent amount of effort to take me to the ground whenever our tempers turned to exchanging blows. Having a professional athlete as a best friend was good for keeping one in shape. Even on the days all I wanted to do was watch Netflix and drink beer, Harlen usually managed to get my ass in gear and drag me to do some kind of physical activity. My baby fat melted away once I hit my late teens, leaving behind a face full of sharp, angular features, and making my unusual light eyes stand out even more. My hair hung out somewhere between brown and black and could look darker or lighter depending on the day and lighting. I kept it fairly short and trendy. I put a lot more effort into my appearance when I got out into the world on my own. I'd learned that being attractive was just another tool one could use for survival.

I looked good.

I knew it.

And so did Ollie, if the look in her eyes was anything to go by. Soft appreciation for my obvious glow-up was the only sign of life I'd seen in those chocolatey eyes since she finally decided to look at me.

I sighed and dragged a hand down my face. I had no idea why she was suddenly here, trying to insert herself in my typically uneventful life. But I knew deep down to my bones that I wanted nothing to do with whatever she brought to my doorstep. Even if it was a long overdue apology. It bugged me that I couldn't look away from that scar on her cheek and that I couldn't forget the reasons it was there.

"You aren't moving into this house, Ollie. I don't want you here." I snorted and lowered my eyebrows into a ferocious scowl. "I don't want you at this school, or even in this state. I want you to go far, far away. Forget my name for good. If you aren't out of my sight in the next ten minutes, I'm calling the police. Get your damn stuff off my fucking porch." I let out a breath and practically growled in her face, "Don't make me get mean."

I watched as her bottom lip started to quiver as her dark eyes glazed over with a glossy sheen of tears. "I signed the lease." Her voice was tiny and weak. I used to hate it when she spoke to someone else that way. It made me feel a touch bad that I'd forced her to sound the same with me.

I shook my head. "I don't care. The boys and I have lived here for years. Mr. Peters loves us. We take care of all kinds of crap for him at his properties. If he has to pick between me and you, he's going to pick me."

Ollie might not expect that from the old man because no one ever picked me when we were younger... no one but her.

"I don't have anywhere else to go, Huck." This time, she wasn't lying. She sounded sad and scared and so very alone.

Refusing to be swayed, I shrugged. "Not my problem. Get gone before I make you go. I'm not playing around with you, Ollie. I don't want to see you ever again."

I heard her suck in a painful breath, but I didn't turn to look back at her as I stepped around her and out of the living room.

Unsurprisingly, Harlen and Vernon were waiting for me in the hallway. I locked gazes with Harlen, and without having to say a word, I knew he would make sure the girl was gone. Vernon looked torn between being pissed and curious.

"I'll call the old man and make sure he knows she absolutely cannot move in here. There were no less than a hundred *other* applicants. Even if I have to pay for her to break the lease, I will." I went to walk past both of them toward my room only to be brought up short by Vernon's hand on my arm.

I looked at the painted nails and perceptive eyes. "You know you need to explain this to us, right?"

I bit back a sigh and lowered my eyes. "Not now."

He didn't bother to hide his exasperation with me. "What if she really doesn't have anywhere to go? You can be cold and mean when you want, but I've never seen you be heartless. And to a girl at that."

He had no idea. Heartless was easy when it came to the girl I'd just turned my back on. She was the one who

26

taught what that word meant in the first place all those years ago.

I barked out a dry laugh. "She brings out the worst in me. Let's talk about everything later." Much later. I'd worked hard to put the past behind me.

I needed Ollie to be out of sight and out of mind like she'd been for the last five years. If she wasn't, she was going to consume my every waking thought and moment the same as she had when we were young.

I had too much to lose to let Ollie in my front door or back into my life.

I'd fight tooth and nail to keep her as far away from me and mine as possible.

And I had no intention of losing to her again.

CHAPTER 3

Ollie

"Went about as well as expected, huh?" I looked up and took the bottle of water my boss-slash-new-best friend was handing down to me. I was sitting on the stairs that led up to her funky vintage shop, which, like most businesses around campus, existed inside a converted Victorian.

I was so lucky when I stumbled on that Help Wanted sign a few weeks after I came to this small college town. When I got here, I had to scramble to put together anything resembling basic necessities because I left that too big house in such a rush. Luckily, this little shop had plenty of fun, funky secondhand offerings for really reasonable prices. Otherwise, I would have had to go to class in my bathrobe. I was also fortunate that Mercer McKay, the owner, and I clicked right away. When I saw that she was hiring and asked about the job, she didn't hesitate to offer me a part-time job, partly because she was nice, but more because she knew I was desperate to be here. I wouldn't bounce on her if schoolwork got overwhelming and intense. I was reliable, which I'd proven to her time and time again. Over the summer, she let me crash in one of the back rooms that she'd set up as a bedroom while I put my plan in place to move into Huck's fortress. The room was approximately the size of the walk-in closets back in that house I never thought I would escape, but it was infinitely more comfortable. Nothing at that house had been pleasant or homey. I hated that my mother refused to live anywhere else. We might not have been able to afford anything in that tiny New England town, but we could've lived elsewhere. My mom was too attached, too committed to serving a family that hers had worked for over generations. She felt she owed them, even more so when my father took off before I was born, leaving her alone and terrified. Huck's grandparents let her live in the small servants' quarters and paid for all her medical expenses, as well as my primary education, as long as she agreed to stay on staff and help with their son's children. She was a housekeeper and a nanny, but really, she acted like the only real mother those boys had. She practically raised all three of us on her own, and it wasn't until she was gone that I realized one of the main reasons she sacrificed her life and her own happiness and fulfillment was because she wanted to make sure I was guaranteed a better life than she had. She suffered so much solely so I could succeed.

I pulled at my curls with one hand and squeezed the bottle of water with the other as Mercer took a seat next to me. She had her hair pulled up in twin pigtails, and her bright, vibrant makeup always made her look like a kid playing dress-up. I knew she was nearly a decade older than I was, but she looked like she could be my younger sister. Her carefree and easygoing personality made her seem more youthful than I ever felt. I was honestly envious of her ability to see the good in everyone and the positives in any situation. Mercer wasn't really a hipster or a new-age hippy-type. She was simply someone who marched completely to the beat of her own drum and didn't care at all what others thought of her song and dance. She was quite possibly the happiest person I'd ever encountered, and I knew I wouldn't have made it when I showed up at this school without her to lean on and confide in.

"I mean, I got tossed out on my ass as expected, but Vernon was nice enough to let me leave my stuff in their garage." I didn't have much, but what I did have was precious to me, and I wasn't going to leave it behind.

"You knew he was the nice one going into this. You should've tried to work that angle even more." All of her stacked bracelets jangled and clicked together noisily as she reached out to pat my back in a conciliatory manner. "You knew it wasn't going to be easy, but you took the first step, and you need to give yourself credit for that. Now that Huck knows you're here in the same city and plan on going to the same school, things are going to get interesting."

I groaned and pulled harder on my hair. "I don't want interesting." I'd had that, and it had gone horribly wrong. "I want boring and safe." I wanted what normal was supposed to look like.

Mercer patted me a little bit harder and sighed. "So, what's the plan now? You're sort of at a legal stalemate.

You have a legal right to live there, and he has the right to go to the authorities and claim you're a stalker. His evidence that you may be a stalker is pretty weak, but your name goes in the legal system here regardless."

I closed my eyes and held the water bottle to my forehead. "Huck was always really good at backing people into a corner." Only, I'd never been one of the unfortunate ones before.

"He didn't seem even a little bit happy to see you after all this time?" Mercer kept her voice low like she knew she was tiptoeing across very dangerous territory.

Huck had looked as far from happy as one man could. He looked horrified. He looked angry. He looked traumatized. And he looked... so fucking handsome.

He was breathtaking these days. He'd grown up so well that he was almost unrecognizable. If I hadn't peeked at him on the Internet, there is no way I would've recognized him, even with those golden, glowing eyes of his. I'd always been the taller of the two of us, and now he practically towered over me. He looked slick and stylish and not at all like the boy I used to play in the dirt with and chase up trees. He no longer looked like a kid all our rich classmates would tease and torture to gain favor. He used to run around in torn t-shirts and faded jeans. The jeans and t-shirt were still there, but now they fit him perfectly and molded to muscle he hadn't had before. He'd also added scrolling artwork to his skin along with the bulk. The tattoos weren't all that surprising since Huck had always been rebellious and wild. I wasn't expecting the fancy haircut and expensive brand name clothes, though. The Huck I knew used to

31

mock the amount of money the people around us wasted to look just like everyone else. At one point in my life, I understood every single move he made; now, I had no clue what he was thinking and was surprised how easily he turned his back on me.

I knew I was a reminder of things better left forgotten, but I'd been sure that once we were face-to-face, all the good memories we'd made as two misunderstood kids would be enough to replace the biggest, baddest memory that tore us apart.

I was wrong.

So very wrong.

"No, he wasn't happy to see me. And he told me he never wanted to see me again. His roommates even mentioned he might be mad enough to move out if I pushed taking the room." I groaned. In my heart, I really thought things would go smoother than they had. But my head knew going up against a grown-up Huck who had a grudge against me wasn't going to be a walk in the park. I just hadn't expected him to look at me like he hated me and it hurt so much.

It'd been five years, but it seemed the wounds from my betrayal were still fresh and festering. Having the truth of his disdain and dismissal shoved in my face was one of the most painful things I'd ever gone through. My heart still felt bruised.

Mercer muttered a soft and sympathetic sound. "Maybe if you just give him some time, he'll come around."

I shook my head and tried to keep defeat from crushing my soul and the last vestiges of hope I held onto with a death grip. "He's the most stubborn person on the planet. I don't know if I can change his mind or get him to listen to me long enough to hear my apology."

"You risked everything to come here and apologize and right the wrongs from the past. You can't give up now." She dropped her hand and cocked her head to the side. "Maybe you should be honest. Think about being upfront with him and tell him why you tracked him down after all this time. Would it hurt to let him know you lost your mom and now you're all alone? Do you think he's going to be surprised that you turned on him because his brother threatened your mom and you had no other choice? It sounds to me like he knows what that guy is capable of. I think you should explain how you've been living and what you've gone through since he left. He needs to know what his brother put you through. It might give him a new perspective and at least get you in the front door."

I'd always walked lightly around the golden child. Huck's half brother was touchy on good days and downright evil on bad ones. I got really good at avoiding his wrath, right up until he figured out the one surefire way to get me to bend to his will was to turn his ire on my mother. If I pissed him off or ignored him, he would make my mom work in the garden all day with no protection from the heat and the sun. He would make her get on her hands and knees and scrub marble floors until her hands bled. He would force her to wash windows balanced precariously on ladders that always seemed unstable. He would call for her in the middle of the night, over and over again, making sure she was sleep deprived. None of it was outright torture, but considering my mom was never in the best health, they were all risky tasks that strained her weakened heart. He endlessly exploited my desire to keep her safe when he figured out I would always acquiesce to keep his attention off of her.

After the accident, it was a weakness that worsened, and one that he used to his full advantage.

I was so done with living in a state of constant fear that someone would show up and make me go back to that house. Sure, I'd always wanted to track Huck down and see how he was doing and how far he'd come, and offer an explanation for my actions the night everything changed. but it was the ever-present fear that finally forced me to uproot my life and follow him. I wanted to believe, even after everything we'd been through and how badly I hurt him, that he'd still protect me, that he would keep me safe from those trying to keep me prisoner in a world where I didn't belong.

At first, when my mom passed away, I hadn't known where I was going or what I was going to do with myself. It was like sleepwalking, and when I finally woke up, I found myself here. I suddenly knew the only way I would stop being scared and get a handle on my future was if I managed to get as close to him as I'd once been.

I hadn't known Huck was the buffer between me and absolute evil until he was gone.

I sighed. "I can't blame him for wanting to protect himself and those he cares about from me." He had every right not to trust me anymore.

"Those boys aren't just friends. They're family," Mercer stated this matter-of-factly. Huck and his boys

34

were almost celebrities in the small town. They made waves as freshmen for different reasons, but mostly because they became an inseparable force to be reckoned with. It was pretty well known amongst the student body that all four boys came from less-than-ideal homes. There wasn't a single outstanding parental figure between the four of them, which meant they raised themselves and helped each other figure out how to be good, upstanding young men all on their own.

She sighed again and told me, "You know you are welcome to keep the room in the shop through this semester if you need to. I know it isn't anything luxurious, but it's better than nothing."

It was way better than nothing. Other than not having a real kitchen, the little room was actually just fine. The only thing it lacked was Huck. I didn't want to live in the Victorian because of comfort or convenience. I wanted to live there so I could finally stop looking over my shoulder and live like a normal human for the first time in forever. I hardly slept when I was living in the back of the shop...not because it was cramped, but because every shadow that moved terrified me and had me ready to jump out of my skin. I wasn't willing to go back to my previous life, but I knew that wouldn't stop someone from trying to make me.

I tilted my head to the side and let it rest on Mercer's shoulder. She always smelled like wildflowers and vanilla. What I wouldn't give to be as centered and calm as she always was.

"You saved my life. You know that, don't you?" My voice cracked, and I realized today had been one of the longest in history. It was a miracle I managed to keep putting one foot in front of the other.

Mercer took my free hand in hers and squeezed. "No. You saved your own life. Don't forget that. I know you think Huck Snyder is the answer to all your problems, but you made it this far without him or the support of anyone else. You are strong, and you are capable. Never let anyone convince you differently." Keeping my hand in hers, she stood and tugged on the limb. "Enough for today. You aren't going to come up with a solution pouting on the front steps. Let's order a pizza and watch Netflix."

I got up and followed my only friend inside the eclectic store. She was right that I wasn't going to come up with a solution to get through to Huck by pouting and bemoaning everything that went wrong in my life. I had made it this far on my own, even though the choices I'd made to get this far had been more than slightly questionable.

I just didn't know how much more fight I had inside of me. I felt empty and drained. At least I had until I was face-to-face with Huck. When I met those glittering gold eyes of his, I finally felt alive again. I felt something inside of me, bubbling and trembling with tentative hope. He'd been a dangerous influence when I was young and stupid. He was something so much more than dangerous now that I was older and stupider than I had been.

I knew he wasn't going to be open to listen to anything I had to say, so all I could do was keep my fingers crossed that my plan to plead my case with Mr. Peters had worked. There weren't many people Huck and his boys respected, but the older landlord was one of them.

The last advocate I'd had was Huck. I never thought I'd need someone to advocate for me to him.

CHAPTER 4

Huck

"I 'll move out. And the boys will follow."

I faced Mr. Peters defiantly across his ornate dining room table, giving him a look that had quelled many men before him. Only, I forgot the old man was a veteran, had been married and divorced three times, and raised three daughters. All of whom were incredibly successful and powerful women. The old man didn't scare easily, and a threat from some punk college kid wasn't even going to get him to bat an eyelash.

"Move out then." My landlord looked at me over the rim of his coffee mug, and if I didn't know better, I would've sworn he was hiding a smile. The grouchy old man had never cracked a smile in all the years I'd rented from him. He was more of the scowling-while-barking-orders type. "But keep in mind, the semester is starting soon, and I'll have to immediately rent the place out. You'll also be responsible for paying to break your current lease." He arched a fuzzy gray eyebrow in my direction. "That's a whole year's worth of rent since you just renewed, on top of the five-hundred-dollar fee. Even if you somehow manage to come up with your portion, I doubt the other boys will. Harlen is on a scholarship, if memory serves me."

He set his mug down on the table and leaned forward. I didn't want to be intimidated, but I was. I looked up to very few people, and Mr. Peters was at the top of the list. The old man was one of the few adults who'd ever given me a chance without making me jump through a million hoops to prove myself first. This was the first time we'd ever really clashed.

Of course, it had to be because of Ollie.

"And if you do come up with the money to get out of the lease, do you think finding a place to rent if you plan on staying with Vernon will be easy? He's still got a while before he turns eighteen. No one will ignore that he's a minor, and even if they consider renting to you without him on the lease, they're going to ask questions. Do you want to put the kid through all that just because you don't want a female roommate?"

I growled in frustration and pounded the side of my fist on the tabletop. He was right, and it grated that he knew me well enough to know there was no way in hell I would ever abandon Vernon. The kid had almost cost us the Victorian when Harlen and I were finally able to leave the dorms. It was only after I begged, pleaded, and promised my life away to the old man that he agreed to rent to all of us, including an underage Vernon. He did so without questions at the time, but he now knew all the ugly reasons the rest of us were willing to do whatever it took to keep the kid safe. My violent reaction received a dirty look from the old man, and I reminded myself I was here to appeal to his soft spot for all of us, me in particular, and not to provoke him.

"You were the one who implemented the 'no co-ed-living-if-it-can-be-avoided' rule. I don't understand why you're going back on it now. Things have been smooth sailing so far with just us at the house. Why change something that's proven to be successful?" Why was everyone always willing to break the rules for Ollie?

Me included.

It was baffling and endlessly frustrating. What was it about Ollie Adams that made everyone who encountered her lose their damn mind?

"You've asked the same question twenty different ways, Huck. You're going to make a great lawyer one day. But it won't change my answer. If I've told you once, I've told you a hundred times, I didn't know she was a young woman until after all the paperwork was signed. Her name was misleading. Her lease to the room in the house is valid and legally binding. You had no right to run her off. She seems like a nice-enough girl. A little quiet and squirrely, but I don't think she'll be in your way or cause too much of a fuss. It's only one year. If you boys can't adapt to a change this close to graduation, I fear for your futures."

He smirked at me when I swore in aggravation under my breath. I shoved my hands through my hair and glared holes into the wood table between us.

"She tricked you by not using her legal name on the application. She lied. That should invalidate the lease. There are always legal loopholes, Old Man." I was getting desperate because it was becoming clear this would be one of the rare arguments in my life I was about to lose.

"And I told you, she didn't lie. I just did a cursory glance at the information. I'm the one who overlooked the fact Ollie is short for Olivia. Besides, your legal loophole could lead to a bigger legal headache for me down the road. You know one of my daughters is a lawyer. She's been telling me for years that my no co-ed living condition was going to get me in trouble. Just accept it. She's moving in, kiddo." He tapped his index finger on the table to get my attention. When our gazes locked, I could clearly see the old man had his mind made up, and there would be no persuading him. "And you and the boys aren't going to give her a hard time about it. You hear me, Huck?"

I bared my teeth slightly and didn't respond.

Mr. Peters slammed his palm on the wood and made me jump. I gulped slightly and forced myself to dip my chin in agreement. "I hear you, Old Man."

"I'm serious. If I hear you guys are making things difficult for her, you will be moving out and looking for a new place. It'll be impossible to find a place for the three of you this close to the start of school. If you put me in a position to give you a piss-poor reference, you won't ever find a place to rent again. I'm not threatening you. I'm telling you exactly how it is."

I let my head drop and felt my shoulders slump. It wasn't often I couldn't persuade someone to give me what I wanted, and it had been a very long time since I hadn't gotten my way. I guess I'd become spoiled since I left my old life behind.

Speaking of my old life, I quietly asked Mr. Peters, "Did Ollie tell you that we used to know each other when we were kids? Did she tell you she moved here because of me? She's stalking me. She might be dangerous. Aren't you worried about me at all, Old Man?"

I was actually a little hurt at how indifferent he seemed over the whole situation. I honestly thought our relationship had long since gone past the landlord-tenant stage. The boys and I considered him family, and it stung to think he didn't view us the same way.

A heavy sigh came from across the table, and when I looked at the man sitting across from me, I could see genuine sympathy on his craggy face.

"Huck, are you honestly worried this girl might have bad intentions toward you and your friends? Are you legitimately scared of her? Have you stopped to think why she's worked so hard to get close to you? You're a very smart guy, and you said you knew this girl from your childhood. You have to see there's more going on here than meets the eye." He gave me a pointed look. "If you are scared and truthfully believe she's stalking you, get a restraining order. I support your right to do so. I don't think it'll make you look weak. If you do that, I won't be able to uphold her lease. Legally I can break it. Bring me the paperwork, and I'll take care of the rest."

I was scared of her, but probably not for the reasons he suspected. "I don't want to know why she tracked me down after all this time. I don't want to know why she's so desperate to get close to me again." Back in the day, I protected her from everyone and everything. As a result, I lost all that mattered to me. "She attracts trouble like a magnet, and I don't have time for that anymore." Not when my life was finally on track and I was so close to making all my dreams come true.

"She's just a girl, Huck. A girl in a tough spot. I know you, kiddo. You aren't the type to turn your back on someone who's just looking for a way out of a shitty situation. And it sounds to me like the two of you might have some unfinished business to discuss. It's only a year. Suffer through and make amends before you graduate and start law school. It'll be good for you. That's the best option for everyone." He picked up his mug, looking overly satisfied with himself.

"It's the easiest option for you." Looking backward was quite possibly the hardest thing he could ask me to do.

I'd threatened her with a restraining order already. Mr. Peters was using that as my out, and yet, I hadn't reported her or gone to the police. The idea actually made my skin feel too tight, and I had a headache starting to throb behind my eyes. It was a simple solution, one I would be totally justified in doing. Only I couldn't do it. And not only because I had a healthy distrust of the police and was skeptical about a legal system that was easy to manipulate.

Ollie and I didn't have unfinished business. No, our business was dead and buried, just like any relationship we'd once had. I'd grieved and mourned the loss of what once was. I had no intention of being haunted by the ghosts of our pasts. Seeing Ollie's face every single day had once been a given; now, it was my worst nightmare. I wanted to seriously injure Fisher for moving out and moving on with his life, leaving the door open for this current disaster. I made a mental note to give him a piece of my mind the next time we met up for a drink.

I jolted when a heavy, gnarled hand landed on top of the fist I wasn't aware my hand had curled into on top of the table. I looked up and met the older man's concerned gaze.

"Huck." He paused for a long moment and sighed heavily. I hadn't even noticed when he got up and walked over to me, which was saying something because he had a distinct limp and didn't move quietly in the least. Ollie was already consuming all my thoughts and pulling my attention away from where it should be. Just like she had when we were younger. Mr. Peters had no idea how dangerous the girl could be. "I don't have sons, but you boys come as close as I'll ever get. I would never do anything to put you in danger. If I'm wrong about this girl, tell me. Be honest with me, and I'll see what I can do to find a suitable solution for everyone."

The words were on the tip of my tongue.

I wanted to tell him how I used to stand between Ollie and my family. How my half brother went out of his way to make my life a living hell because he was jealous she liked me more than she liked him. I wanted to explain how that demented kid killed my first dog, sabotaged my grades in school, got me kicked off the lacrosse team, and made sure I had nothing to enjoy in life just because he was bitter and couldn't handle anyone, but especially Ollie, putting me before him. I almost ended up in juvie because of him. I'd learned how to hate and hold a grudge early because of him.

I wanted Ollie gone so I didn't have to think about my brother, Sawyer, ever again.

I wanted to forget she existed like I'd been doing for so long.

I wanted to tell him she was dangerous and would bring nothing but harm to our household, but I couldn't get my mouth and my mind to cooperate. I couldn't actually say that Ollie was a bad person or that she meant to cause the kind of problems she inevitably did.

When it came down to it, the girl was just as desperate as I was. It was exactly what drew us together all those years ago.

We were desperate to be understood.

Desperate to be free.

Desperate to be loved... And we only managed to find any of that with each other.

Years had gone by, and I was sure she was as different a person as I was, so I couldn't be sure what her intentions were anymore. But I couldn't get myself to tell the old man I was scared that being around her was going to revive the old, altruistic feelings I'd tried my best to kill.

"You said she's in a tough spot. I don't suppose you want to elaborate on that?" I could only imagine what, or who, she was finally running from.

The old man squeezed my hand again and shuffled to the seat next to mine. "Nope. If you want to know, then ask her." He grunted and rubbed his bad knee. "Since you're here, how about making an old man some dinner. My knee has been acting up. I think the weather is gonna change in the next few days. We're probably looking at a storm moving our way."

I snorted and pushed away from the table. "You have no idea."

It wasn't a simple storm moving our way if Ollie was involved. No, if she was at the center of the tempest, it would be the kind of onslaught that leveled towns and upended homes. The kind of carnage that followed in her wake took years to clear and rebuild.

"What do you want to eat?" I was still mad at him, but I couldn't let him starve.

A gruff chuckle escaped his barrel chest. "I want hot dogs, but I know you won't let me have them."

He was right. He'd had some heart issues earlier last year, and ever since, I'd done my best to make sure he kept to a heart-healthy diet. I didn't want to lose him, and it had nothing to do with the difficulty of finding somewhere else to live if he kicked us out.

I gave him a dirty look as I moved toward his well-stocked kitchen. "Yeah, looks like neither of us is getting our way today, Old Man."

He chuckled as I walked away, and I wanted to stress that there was nothing funny about the fact I would be living under the same roof as Ollie Adams for the foreseeable future. However, I got a distinct feeling that my obvious annoyance over the situation would just delight him even further.

He had told me not to give Ollie a hard time and put her in a position that she wanted to move out. He didn't know that she was used to all my typical tricks.

If I wanted her gone without repercussions, I was going to have to come up with a new plan entirely. One she'd never see coming.

Let the games begin.

CHAPTER 5

Ollie

"So, you knew Huck when he was a kid? What was he like? He's always so serious, so intense. It's hard to picture him as a little kid. I like to think he was happier back then than he is now."

"He wasn't." I looked over at Vernon, who was manhandling the last box I'd left in their garage into the attic room that was now *officially* mine. I didn't believe Mr. Peters when he first called and told me he'd spoken with Huck and cleared the way for me to move in. He reminded me to give him a call if the boys gave me a hard time and promised to check up on me. When I showed up at the house, the only person home was Vernon, and he didn't seem shocked by my sudden arrival. In fact, he jumped right in with an offer to help me move my few meager belongings up the two flights of stairs into the room with the drastically sloped ceiling and small windows. "He wasn't happier, I mean. But he was less intense than he seems now."

Vernon informed me that he and Harlen shared the second floor, and that Huck had the master bedroom on the main level. He also said that since the house was old, every step made the floorboards creak and that the pipes rattled nonstop, so everyone could hear everyone else moving around in the morning or late at night. He suggested I invest in a good set of noise-canceling earplugs because when the weather got cold, they turned on the old-fashioned radiators, and they sounded like war machines when they started up and turned off. He'd rattled off other tips like not to touch any of Harlen's weird protein powders or supplements unless I wanted an hour-long lecture on nutrition and muscle mass. He stated that none of them were great at grocery shopping, but they shared food when the fridge was stocked. Apparently, Huck had turned into somewhat of a health nut since I'd last seen him, which would explain the ripped body and loss of his adorable baby fat. I assured Vernon I wouldn't intrude and told him I usually just grabbed something to eat between classes. I barely made enough money to pay my portion of the rent each month. No way was I in a place to feed three boys, two of whom were built like professional athletes.

After I set down a box, I puffed out a breath and looked around the room. Fisher left behind a full-size bed, a battered wooden desk, and a set of bookshelves that looked like they had seen better days. It was minimal, but exactly what I needed. I would have to hit up Mercer for some bedding and maybe some curtains, but it was the perfect little alcove for me to hide away in. I didn't even mind that I was going to have to crouch down or scoot around on my knees to navigate the portion of the room that was designated as the closet. The slanted ceiling left no doubt this used to be an attic.

"Huck was a jokester when he was a kid. He liked to play pranks and cause trouble. He was fearless and tried to make things fun." I absently touched the scar on my cheek. It was a habit I had when I thought about the past. When I remembered what my life was like before the constant reminder of the night everything had gone wrong was etched onto my face. "I followed him everywhere because my mom worked for his family and we lived on their property. It had been like that for generations before my mother was born. Neither of us ever fit in, so we stuck together to make life easier. When Huck and I got older and into our teens, I thought he would get sick of me shadowing him all the time. When he started to notice other girls and they started to notice him back, I expected him to tell me to get lost. But he never did." He was always there when I needed him. Always protecting me from the rest of the world. I smiled slightly and noticed Vernon was watching me intently. "He was also chubby and clumsy back then. Nothing like he is now."

Vernon's lips lifted in a slight grin. "No. None of that sounds like the Huck I know."

I tucked a handful of curls behind my ear and asked, knowing very well I might not get an answer, "How did you meet Huck?"

He cocked his head, his unusual eyes glinting as he considered me silently for a long moment. When he finally spoke, I wasn't prepared for the impact his words were going to have.

"He saved me. He saved all of us in our little group one way or another." He watched as I inhaled a sharp breath and shifted my gaze away. He'd been nice... well, nicer than the other two, but Vernon was making it clear that Huck came first, no matter what, so I better not let myself be lured into a false sense of security around him. "I ran away from home when I was twelve."

I couldn't hold back a shocked gasp at his flat admission. Huck was sent away when he was only sixteen, which was bad, but it seemed ancient compared to Vernon's age when he ventured out on his own.

"I was on the streets for about a year when I bumped into Huck. Literally." He snorted and got a faraway look in his eyes as he recalled the past. "I was trying to pickpocket him. I wanted his phone and his wallet. Only, Huck knew what it was like to be on the streets and saw me coming from a mile away. He was never a mark or a sucker for anyone. He told me he would feed me and find me a place to sleep that night instead of calling the cops or kicking my ass."

Vernon shook his head slightly, making his white hair fall into his eyes. "He found a shelter that would take an unaccompanied minor for a little while, and when he figured out how smart I was, he found me an education program and a scholarship for gifted kids that got me off the streets for good until I graduated high school. I was in every accelerated program he could find. He got my family to sign the paperwork to get me into the programs when I told him they wouldn't. He also got them to sign my emancipation papers. I have no idea how he did it, but he makes miracles happen regularly. Kind of like you, I came to this school because Huck was here. Starting college so young wasn't easy, but the guys made it easier. Harlen helped me find my footing; he was my first real friend I ever had. Huck always kept an eye on me, and Fisher was like the father figure I never knew I needed." He pointed a finger at the shocked expression on my face. "Do you know why I'm telling you about my history with Huck?"

I shifted uneasily under his intense scrutiny before responding. "Because you want to make it clear how important he is to you." It wasn't a question. I knew exactly why.

Vernon nodded slowly, and I realized under his ethereal appearance, he could be just as scary, if not more so, than the other two young men I now lived with.

"I owe Huck *everything*. So do Harlen and Fisher. There is nothing, and I mean *nothing,* we wouldn't do to protect him. If you're going to fuck up his life, if you're going to make him miserable or hurt him in any way, none of us will let you live in peace. We will make it so you spend every single second regretting the moment you walked back into his life. You seem determined to be in this house and in Huck's way. I just hope you understand the full ramifications of whatever it is you're doing."

It was on the tip of my tongue that I had no goddamn clue what I was doing, that I'd been operating on instinct and fear lately, so I'd forgotten what it was like to have any direction other than running away from the monster who was constantly chasing me. Had I considered Huck's consequences of crash landing back in his life? Not enough. Honestly, I was glad these guys had Huck's back. He'd always thought he could take on the entire world by himself. Now he had a very capable group of like-minded misfits to help him bear the weight of the endless battles he was bound to wade into.

Before I could get a word in edgewise, a deep voice rumbled from the doorway. "Don't try and scare her, Vernon."

Both our heads whipped around at the sound of Huck's voice. He had an arm lifted, resting on the door jamb. He was dressed in nylon shorts and a faded shirt that had big gaps where the sleeves should be, showing off the fact the ink on his arms wasn't the only place he'd modified his body since he'd been gone. He had on sneakers and his hair was damp, looking close to black with what I assumed was sweat. My guess was he'd come from the gym, and Vernon and I had been so engrossed in our conversation, we hadn't heard him come up the stairs.

Huck glared at me with his golden eyes, his expression hard and completely unwelcoming. "Trying to scare her won't do any good. She grew up nipping at the heels of a madman, so your threats are just child's play to her. She knows what she's doing and that she's not wanted here. It doesn't matter. She pushed and pushed until she got her way. I wonder who you learned that from, Ollie."

I wanted to apologize. I wanted to tell him if there was any other way to break free, I would've done it. I wanted to promise to stay out of his way and out of his life as long as he let me make amends, but the words wouldn't come. Those weren't promises I could keep at this point in my life.

Vernon clearly wanted to ask about the madman comment, but paused when Huck suddenly moved.

All thought flew out the window, and words that were already difficult became impossible when he pushed away from the door, muscle and ink shifting enticingly as he grabbed his shirt by the collar and pulled it off over his head.

He had tattoos on each side of his ribcage: one was low on his cut, corded abdomen that disappeared into the waistband of his shorts. He had twin silver hoops decorating his nipples. He didn't look like any lawyer I'd ever seen, prospective or not.

Nope.

This definitely was not the cute, chubby kid who played in the dirt and snuck forbidden sweets with me.

Huck was a man.

A beautiful, but clearly dangerous, man.

The look in his eyes told me that he knew exactly what I was thinking. I pulled my gaze away from him and lifted a hand to tug nervously on my lower lip. In my lifetime, I'd felt a lot of ways about Huck Snyder. However, the slippery, slithering heat that worked through my blood after seeing him half-naked was entirely new. Our relationship was already ridiculously complicated and tangled with the ghosts from before. The last thing it needed was another layer to define and navigate.

"Come on, kid. Let her get settled in and leave her alone. As long as she keeps to herself, we should all be fine. Like the old man keeps telling me, it's only for a year. We've survived worse." There was a warning in

Huck's tone and something else I couldn't quite put my finger on. I felt the weight of his stare, but I refused to look in his direction while he was dressed—or rather, undressed—the way he was. It was too much to process.

Vernon made a distressed noise and went to move past me.

Before I could think better of it, I reached out a hand and let my fingers skim his forearm. He paused and looked at me with curious eyes.

"Thank you." I let the hand near my face drop and tried to force a smile. "Thanks for keeping an eye on my stuff while it was stashed here, and thank you for helping me move it all up the stairs." He didn't have to offer the slightest hint of kindness, but he had.

He was a good kid, and I was glad to know that Huck had seen something worth saving in him. It gave me a slight sliver of hope that Huck might eventually see that same thing in me.

Vernon tilted his head like a puppy and gave me a genuine grin. "No problem. I'm the only one around here willing to give anyone the benefit of the doubt, so don't make me look dumb." Did he ever look dumb? He was a genius, after all. "I have a couple of extra blankets stashed somewhere. I'll dig them up, and you can use them until you get your room setup."

He waved me off when I was going to protest, and used the back of his hand to smack Huck's sharply defined abs when he walked by his friend. He haughtily told him, "A year can go by in the blink of an eye or feel like it's going to last forever depending on the circumstances. Let's all keep that in mind since we're stuck with each other." Vernon wrinkled his nose as Huck turned to follow him out of my room. "You stink. Go take a shower. Also, how did you make it up those noisy stairs without making a sound?"

Huck's answer was lost as Vernon pulled the door closed behind them and they left me alone with my whirling thoughts.

I walked to the bare bed and flopped down face first. It squeaked under my weight but settled quickly. I closed my eyes and told myself to breathe.

I would get through this. This wasn't the end of the road, regardless of how hostile and difficult Huck decided to be. I told myself I was prepared for whatever he would throw at me to get me to leave, because even though it'd been a while since we were together, I still believed I knew Huck better than anyone else. He wasn't going to let me slide into the safe space under his roof without a fight. He wasn't going to simply let me have my way when he wanted something completely different. I needed to be ready for anything because the boy didn't play fair back in the day, and I doubted that had changed.

CHAPTER 6

Huck

I was rubbing a fluffy towel vigorously over my head and had a face full of wet hair in my eyes, so I couldn't see Vernon and Harlen, but I knew they were in my room regardless. And since they weren't waiting for me out in the living room or the kitchen, I knew they wanted to talk to me about our new roommate, or rather, the way I behaved toward our new roommate.

I tossed the wet towel in the direction of my bed and heard Vernon make a disgusted sound as it inadvertently hit one of the unwelcome targets. Chuckling under my breath, I shoved my wet hair out of my face and looked at my two best friends, both of whom were staring at me like we'd never met before.

I put my hands on my hips, shifting the other towel I had wrapped around my waist precariously low. Not that I was worried about these two getting an eyeful. Honestly, one of the best parts of the 'no-girls-allowed' rule was the option to wander around in as little clothing as possible and not worry about offending anyone.

That was also why we tended to keep overnight visitors to a minimum. When Fisher still lived with us, he was notorious for walking around in the buff at all hours. More than one unsuspecting girl had gotten more than she asked for after spending the night.

"Stop stalling. Just spit out whatever it is you wanna say." I shook my head like a wet dog and sprayed both of them with castoff. Vernon squealed and put up his hands, and Harlen swore and told me to watch it or get my ass beat. "I have to get ready for work, so I don't have time for you to circle around the subject."

I wasn't using the excuse to rush them. I really did have to get ready and leave shortly.

Vernon rolled over onto his stomach and kicked his feet up behind him. He propped his chin on one of his hands and gave me a hard look.

"What are you playing at with Ollie? You were the one who said Mr. Peters will kick us all out if we mess with her or make her life miserable while she lives here. You're plotting something, and don't try and tell me otherwise. That little striptease outside her room yesterday was very deliberate."

I snorted and moved to pick through my closet for a black t-shirt. Sometimes living with a genius was a real pain in the ass. There was very little Vernon missed. It would be nice if he applied that insight to himself and wasn't blind to the little hints relating to his own situation right in front of him.

"I'm not going to make her miserable." I pulled the shirt on over my head, which sent my hair standing up in every imaginable direction. "In fact, I'm going to make her feel better than she ever has before."

I dropped the towel and rummaged around for a clean pair of black jeans. I needed to do laundry. It looked like it was going to be a no underwear kind of night. Once I was covered up, I turned back to face my friends. Vernon looked confused. Harlen looked slightly pissed.

The athlete growled and narrowed his eyes at me. "You're going to sleep with her, aren't you?"

"What?" Vernon's head snapped up, and his unusual eyes widened to almost comical proportions. "No. You can't do that, Huck. You're a jerk, but sleeping with her and then ignoring her pushes you to another level of asshole you might not be able to come back from. Don't turn into that kind of irredeemable guy just because you can't get your way this one time."

Harlen made another irritated sound and dragged a hand down his face. "Seriously. That's crossing a dangerous moral line, Snyder."

I walked over to the bed and reached out to mess up Vernon's frosty white hair. "You guys are worrying too much. I've known Ollie a long time. There's only a fifty-fifty chance she'll let me seduce her anyway. I always treated her like a kid sister, which is probably the same relationship she's searching for now. If she does choose to sleep with me, then she knows there will be consequences for her actions better than anyone. Why not let nature take its course and see if things work out in my favor?" I shrugged. "I honestly know her better than most of the women I currently sleep with. She doesn't have any delusions about the kind of guy I really am."

Vernon sighed and flipped his body around so he was sitting cross-legged in the middle of the bed. "But you're going to try and sleep with her with an ulterior motive. That's not nice, and it isn't like you. I know you don't want her here, but what you're planning is a bad idea." He pointed at me. "I can see the wheels turning in your head. You're thinking about her reaction, and hurting her and embarrassing her enough that she leaves, but you aren't thinking about how you're going to feel when you become an actual villain." He shook his head. "I know that's a fine line you've gotten comfortable walking over the years, but I can't stand by and watch you turn into an actual bad guy, Huck."

"If you ghost her after fucking her, there is a good chance she's going to run right to Mr. Peters and tell him what you did. Then we'll all be out of a place to live, and you'll have added yet another black spot to your soul for no damn reason. Your head might be telling you this is the only way to win this standoff, but I refuse to believe your heart is on board with this scheme."

I moved away from the bed toward the mirror that was attached to the wall. The outfit was basic, but it looked good, and my tips tripled on any shift where I showed up wearing something that showed off my ink and was tight enough to make out the nipple rings under the fabric visible. I needed to dry my hair and brush my teeth, so I walked into the bathroom, hoping it would end the conversation.

I appreciated they were concerned for my moral wellbeing, but when I was backed into a corner, there was no end to how dangerous and defiant I could be. I thought they knew me better than that, but it seemed like even after all this time and the hardships we'd faced together, there were still secrets for us to uncover about one another. And neither of them knew just how sweet revenge sounded now that I let myself remember all the ways Ollie had let me down back when we were best friends.

I watched in the mirror as Vernon came into the cramped bathroom. He closed the lid to the toilet and sat down, his sharp eyes unblinking as I watched him in the mirror as I finger combed my hair. Huffing out an annoyed breath, I reached for the blow dryer and told him, "I know you kind of like her and think you can be friends with her, but you can't trust her, kid. You have no idea what she's really like. Everyone who comes in contact with her is compelled to take care of her, to worry about her, to protect her. She'll eat you up and spit you out before you know what happened. Don't get close to her. Don't let her hurt you. Trust me when I tell you that she won't feel bad about it when she inevitably does. If it comes down to you or her, she will pick herself each and every time."

Vernon rubbed his hands along his thighs. "What's the story with you and this girl? And what did you mean when you said she grew up with a madman? You and she grew up together, didn't you? So, you would've been close to this man, too? We can't help you if we don't know what we're dealing with, Huck."

I swore under my breath and switched on the hairdryer. It was all so complicated and hard to explain. It was also the last thing I wanted to try to explain to anyone. Sawyer was like a character out of a comic book or a thriller. It was hard for someone normal to understand how he operated. Shouting to be heard over the noise, I asked, "You've had girls obsessed with you before, right? Ones who are convinced that you're their one and only? Ones who say they can't be happy unless you love them back?"

He nodded and made a face. "Girls and boys."

I laughed because I didn't doubt it. He was pretty enough to be irresistible to all.

"Growing up, Ollie had someone like that in her life. Someone who watched every move she made. Someone who was there every single time she turned around. Someone who infiltrated every corner of her days and nights, and who tried to influence every decision she made. It was more than an obsession. It was oppression. And bit by bit, this person started to take parts and pieces of the Ollie I knew, the one who was my best friend in the whole world, and corrupted every last bit. The way she started thinking changed. All the ways she tried to fight back and rebel against the control everyone had over her started to fade away. I felt like I was watching her turn into a shell of who she was as time went on. No one around her—not her mother, not her teachers, or her classmates, none of her friends, aside from me—seemed too concerned about what was happening, because this bad guy has the face of an angel. He seems too good to be true, because he fucking is."

I blinked as dark, heavy memories started to swirl in my mind.

It was one thing to fight a monster from a distance, but I'd had to do battle daily while the beast lived under the same roof. I'd done my best to insulate Ollie and be the barrier between her and the insanity that was seeping into every aspect of her life. But I was just a kid. A hotheaded, smart-mouthed kid, and back then, when even the adults in our lives kept saying there was nothing wrong, that the infatuation was 'cute' and 'sweet,' I didn't know how to do anything more than I was already doing to keep Ollie safe.

"That sounds so scary for her." Vernon breathed out the words as I finished with my hair and moved on to slap on some deodorant and cologne.

I met his worried eyes in the mirror and dipped my chin in a nod. "It was. And it was terrifying for anyone who cared about her. I don't know why she finally decided to leave. I don't know how she got away. But I do know that wherever she is, the person who thinks she belongs to him, the person who is obsessed with her, won't be far behind. And I know there is *nothing* he won't do to get her back."

Vernon was quiet while I hooked a silver hoop in my earlobe and put a big silver ring on my thumb. When he finally spoke, his voice was soft and serious.

"Who is this person, Huck? Who are they to you? Why are we just finding out all of this now? You know every single dirty secret Harlen, Fisher, and I have. You've seen us at our worst, and yet, you're holding onto something like this, something this big, all to yourself. It doesn't seem fair, does it?"

I knew the question was coming, but I still didn't want to answer it. However, if I didn't, I knew Vernon would get on his computer and go digging into every single aspect of my past. He would find a lot of information. I didn't need him picking at old wounds unnecessarily.

I turned around and leaned against the antique vanity. I crossed my arms over my chest and met his gaze with an unflinching one of my own.

"The person obsessed with Ollie is my half brother, Sawyer." Vernon gasped at the bombshell, and Harlen swore loudly from where he'd propped himself up against the doorjamb.

"Since when do you have a brother?" The question was bitten out as Harlen glared at me. "We're your brothers."

I grinned at him because the statement was true. The four of us who'd found each other at our lowest moments had a bond that often felt like it went beyond brotherhood. They had been my family from the moment I met them, and they had done more for me than the people I shared blood with from the beginning.

"Sawyer is my older brother for all intents and purposes." A shocked silence descended on the small space. "Same dad, different mothers. Mine was a criminal who got pregnant for a paycheck. His is the heiress to a multimillion-dollar real estate fortune who was pretty much betrothed to my dad from birth." I shrugged. "My dad's affairs were the worst-kept secret in the town where I grew up. It has always been Sawyer's misfortune that I look just like our old man, so no one could ever deny I was his kid. Ollie's mom was the head housekeeper at the estate. She took care of me and Sawyer, and then Ollie when she came along a little bit later. The minute Sawyer saw Ollie, he decided that she belonged to him. It was instant and intense before she could even talk or walk. Something in his wiring was always off, but his mother coddled him and let him do whatever he wanted. Her mom was stuck between a rock and a hard place; she tried to rein Sawyer in but didn't want to risk being tossed out on her ass with a baby. I was the only one Ollie had to protect her from him."

I pushed off the sink and stepped around a silent, sulking Harlen so I could put on a pair of boots and grab my wallet and leather jacket before heading to the bar.

"Sawyer hated me for a lot of reasons from the start, but his biggest issue was that I was the only person who managed to get Ollie to question why he had so much control over her. If it wasn't for me, she would've more than likely been meek and mild. She would've accepted her place as his toy without question. But since she followed me around like a lost puppy and clung to me like a koala our entire childhood, I managed to convince her there was something wrong with Sawyer, especially with how he fixated on her. I was a bad influence, but I was the only reason she had any freedom. In return, Sawyer made my life a living hell every chance he got." And ultimately managed to get me to turn my back on the girl forever.

Harlen plowed a hand through his unruly hair and looked down at the ground. "Did your own family run you out of town, Huck?"

I shook my head. "Not really. But they forced me to pick between spending two years in a juvenile detention center or a boarding school for troubled boys after something really bad happened between all three of us kids. I don't have time to get into it all right now, but I'll give you the details later. That scar on Ollie's cheek, it's from that night. Jail, or reform school, was a great option, but it was out of sight, out of mind, which is what Sawyer always wanted when it came to me. I don't talk about my past because Sawyer is still insane. I don't want anything to do with him, and I don't want him anywhere near the people I care about." I gave them both a hard look. "Which is why it's best if Ollie is far, far away from us. It's been years, but I finally stopped looking over my shoulder every time I walked out of the house, thinking he might pop up to sabotage me. I'm not about to go back to living under the constant threat of an attack." I reached out and clapped a hand on Vernon's shoulder because he looked like he might throw up. "Look, I'm glad Ollie finally got away from him and slipped the leash, but the first place Sawyer is going to look for her is wherever I am."

Back in the day, I was the one person in the entire world Sawyer Richman was afraid of. He got to keep our father's last name, while I didn't. I was the only one who stood up to him, and I was the only one who dared to turn Ollie against him. He was a lunatic, but he wasn't stupid. I was certain he would figure where I was now that Ollie was missing. He would immediately assume she had run directly to me. Exactly like she always had back in the day.

"I need to go to work. I understand your concerns, and I really appreciate you both worrying about the state of my tainted soul. I've got this. You guys don't have the first clue what we might have to deal with if Ollie stays. I need you to believe me when I tell you that it's better for everyone if she goes."

I'd sacrifice myself to save them any day of the week. Not that sleeping with Ollie was much of a sacrifice. She was still cute as hell, even with that tiny imperfection on her face that would haunt me until the day I died. Taking her to bed wouldn't be a hardship and would, in fact, kill a long, lingering curiosity I'd always had once we started to get older. I walked away from girls I fucked all the time without a backward glance. She wouldn't be any different.

At least that's what I tried to tell myself as a nagging voice in the back of my mind warned me I was about to make a *huge* mistake.

CHAPTER 7

Ollie

I did my best not to scream when the attic room illuminated an eerie blue as lightning zipped through the sky, followed by a crack of thunder so loud it made my ears ring. I placed a pillow over my head and tried to breathe through the waves of panic washing over me. The sound of the rain against the old roof and as it pounded at the ancient windows was loud enough to drown out the thump of my racing heart and ragged breathing. But the next *boom* of thunder made me yelp like a wild animal as I sat up on the bed and threw the pillow across the room. There was another blinding bolt of light outside, and I squeezed my eyes shut as the room was suddenly sent into complete darkness. It was the middle of the night, but I'd had every single lamp on in the tiny room. I hadn't always been scared of storms, but ever since the night everything went as wrong as it possibly could, I found myself facing panic attacks and the kind of anxiety that was strong enough to make me cry and throw up whenever the weather got bad enough.

Usually, I could power through the irrational fear if the lights were on and thunder was just a distant rumble. I just hid under the covers and tried to breathe through it.

It seemed nothing like that was going to cut it as a coping method for tonight. To make matters worse, the wind outside started to howl, making the old house creak and groan in a million different, eerie ways. I was almost tempted to go downstairs and see if any of the boys were home. But I'd been doing my best to be as unobtrusive and as invisible as possible. I figured it was better to stay out of Huck's way, and even though Vernon seemed like he might be an ally, I didn't want to rock the boat now that I was finally aboard.

I had exactly one year to figure out how to get Huck to forgive me. One year until he graduated and moved on to the next phase of his life. One year where I was going to feel relatively safe and have a mostly normal life. I would walk on eggshells indefinitely to avoid riling the household up any more than I already had. Which meant I was going to have to get through this storm, the one outside the window and the one constantly whipping through my life, alone.

Crawling across the bed, I felt for my phone in the inky darkness and breathed a sigh of relief when I clicked on the flashlight app. I climbed off the bed, taking the quilt and remaining pillow with me as I carefully found my way into the bathroom. It only took a second to make a sloppy nest in the ancient clawfoot tub. I curled into a little ball and reminded myself to breathe slow and deep. I sent a few text messages to Mercer, hoping she would answer me so I could have a distraction until the storm was over, but I got no response. She wasn't the best at replying in normal circumstances, and last time we talked, she mentioned that she'd met a new guy and was in the early stages of infatuation. When she was dating, she was even worse about getting back to me. No one knew about my crippling fear when the weather was bad... well, no one but Huck. I doubted he cared that I was on the verge of losing my mind as Mother Nature continued to rage.

I don't think he wasn't even home from his bartending job yet. I had no clue how he managed to remain at the top of his class and earn perfect grades when he was up all hours of the night. I swore he only slept about four hours a night, because regardless of how late, or rather how early, he came in from his shift, he was always up to go running with Harlen the next day. Even though I was a floor above the other rooms and the front door, I still heard it squeak every time it opened and closed. I'd gotten into the habit of peeking out the window to steal glances at Huck before they started their run. Both boys were in really good shape and absolute heartthrobs, but there was something magnetic and compelling about Huck that made it hard to look away. When it was warm enough, he often started his routine without his shirt on, which made me wonder if I was the only one stealing glances at him through the shutters. A few times, I swore that Huck looked up at the attic before taking off, like he knew I was watching him. When I caught sight of that smirk I knew as well as I knew my own face, it made the thought of running into him randomly in the house we now shared totally intimidating. I felt like he was up to something that wasn't going to end well for me.

As a young boy, he'd always been tricky. As a grown man, he was cunning and slick.

Another crack of thunder had me pulling the blanket over my head and counting backward from one hundred as I tried to slow my racing heart and calm the fear that was rising in my throat, threatening to choke me.

All big storms were the same in my mind.

They took me back to another night in another place and shoved memories I'd much rather forget to the forefront of my exhausted, slightly broken mind.

Hidden under the flimsy fortress of the quilt, I could clearly recall slick, slippery roads. White lightning bolts zipping through the summer sky as windshield wipers struggled fruitlessly to keep up with the deluge outside the sports car I had no business driving.

It was the perfect recipe for disaster.

I remembered the flicker of illuminated eyes outside the windshield. I never found out if it was a deer, or a dog, or some other animal that suddenly darted in front of the car, that caused me to lose control and send the car careening off the road, down a steep embankment and into a huge tree off the side of the road. I could still hear the sound of metal crumpling like a tin can around me, and the screech of tires as they lost traction on the wet road. The memory of the tinkling sound of glass cracking and then imploding into a shower of painful shards still had the power to pull me out of a sound sleep. It was the soundtrack to each and every one of my nightmares.

I usually woke up with tears on my face and shaking fingers tracing over my scar. It was always a deeply visceral reaction.

Mixed in with the echo of the car breaking apart, I also heard Huck's voice calling my name. And another voice, the one I was constantly running from both when I was awake and asleep, laughing hysterically as if the horrible accident was some wild ride at an amusement park. It was never a good situation when Huck and Sawyer were near one another, but that night had been the worst of the worst-case scenarios.

If I'd known that night would result in losing Huck and becoming even more entangled in Sawyer's games than I already was, I never would've left the house. Back then, I'd been unable to say no to either boy. One by choice, the other through force. So when they both ordered me to play designated driver that night, even though I was underage and had only driven Sawyer's fancy car in an empty parking lot when he insisted I needed to learn how to drive, instead of doing the smart thing, I did what was expected of me by both of them. I went to pick up Huck because I was worried, and Sawyer convinced me I should take him and his car rather than borrowing my mother's old junker.

Lost in the past memories, I absently lifted a hand to touch the slightly lifted mark on my face. Sawyer wanted me to get plastic surgery to get it fixed. He also wanted me to forget all about Huck and seamlessly settle into the role he decided I was supposed to play.

I refused to get it fixed.

It was a constant reminder that the accident could've been prevented if I'd been smarter, faster, better than the boy who wanted to own me, and if I'd been more aware of just how dangerous caring about Huck really was. It forced me to remember that everything that followed the accident could also have been prevented if I'd been braver. If I'd been more honest—with everyone, and with myself.

But I'd lied, and it cost me close to everything. I hadn't even managed to save the only person I wanted to keep safe. I mean, the lie kept my mom alive a little longer than anticipated after she suffered a massive heart attack the night of the accident, but it wasn't enough to bring her home or help her recover fully. She passed away regardless of the sacrifices I'd made and everything I put Huck through as a result.

I had a hard time convincing myself those few years she gained, attached to machines, remaining almost totally bedridden, had been worth selling my soul and losing my friendship with Huck.

I was still breathing hard and sweating profusely curled up in the old tub. My hands were shaking where I held onto the blanket, and I could hear the blood rushing loudly between my ears. I felt like I was going to pass out, and honestly, being unconscious was preferable to feeling like I was going to come out of my skin at any moment.

I couldn't hold back a shriek of terror when the next clap of thunder rumbled through the night and rattled the whole house. I put my hands over my ears and tried to keep both the past and the present at bay.

Since most sounds were muffled by my hands on the blanket over my head, I didn't hear the noisy stairs to the attic pop and creak. And because I had my eyes closed as tightly as possible underneath the protective shroud, I missed the flickering light of a camp lantern as it entered the bathroom, held in the hand of the very last person I thought would come to check on me.

When the blanket was suddenly yanked off my head and a shadowy figure materialized in front of me, there was no more holding it together. I screamed at the top of my lungs, my arms and legs flailed about wildly. I hit the back of my head on the edge of the tub, and tears immediately started to creep out of my eyes and roll down my cheeks. My chest felt like it was going to cave in, and every breath I managed to take burned on its way into my lungs.

"Whoa. Calm down, Ollie." There was a thump as Huck hit the tiled floor, kneeling down and holding the lantern in front of his face. "The lights go out all the time when the weather is bad because this house is so old. There are camp lights and candles stashed everywhere. I was going to have Vernon bring you one when he messaged me that the power was out, but I figured having him pop up in the dark would scare you even more than the storm."

I was shivering so hard that my teeth were chattering, and I couldn't hold onto the blanket any longer. Huck sighed and reached out to yank the fabric back up to my chin. The faint light from my phone and the lantern cast weird shadows over his starkly handsome face, giving him an almost sinister look.

He cocked his head to the side and asked, "Are you going to spend the night in the bathtub if it doesn't stop raining?"

I nodded and curled my fingers around the blanket to keep it secured so that only my eyes and nose were showing above the edge.

Huck heaved a sigh and shifted so that he was sitting on the bathroom floor with his knees pulled up. He rested the wrist of one hand on his bent knee and tapped the fingers of the other on the edge of the tub. I couldn't tell if he was impatient or frustrated, but it was obvious he was having a hard time sitting still while I cowered and quaked a few feet away.

"I got off work early because of the storm. The bar lost power as well." One of his dark eyebrows lifted. "I wondered if you were going to have a hard time. I'm not surprised you're still this shaken up when it storms."

After the night of the accident, the weather had stayed really crappy for weeks. It fit the mood that descended upon the people in my life since I was hospitalized for several days, and so was Huck. I would never forget the first night I was alone in the hospital, and it started to thunder and lightning. If I hadn't had IVs poked into the back of my hands, I would've climbed out of the bed and found a place to hide. Luckily, Huck was in a room close enough to hear me screaming and had come to find me. He sat with me the whole night, much like he was doing now. Only, when the next big squall rolled around, Huck was gone, and I had learned I had bigger and scarier things to fear than the weather.

I anxiously cleared my throat. "I'll be fine. You don't have to sit in here." I tugged the blanket down so I could frown at him. "I know the door was locked. How did you even get in?"

He shrugged his broad shoulders and gave me a bored look. "I have the master key to all the rooms in the house. When we were younger, it wasn't an unheard-of occurrence that one of us would get wasted and accidentally lock ourselves out of our room or the bathroom. The old man got tired of having to come let us back in, so he gave me the keys to all the different locks."

I held out a shaky hand and told him, "You can give me mine. You don't need a key to this room while I'm living here."

Both his eyebrows lifted, and his mouth quirked upward. "Not gonna happen. Not unless the old man tells me to hand it over."

I made a mental note to call Mr. Peters in the morning. I wasn't up to having a fight with Huck over anything at the moment. I closed my eyes and rubbed my forehead where I could feel the beginning of a headache starting to pound.

"Really. I'm fine. I appreciate you checking on me since you've made it abundantly clear you don't want me here. If you don't mind leaving the light, I'll power through in here until the power comes back on."

Huck snorted and lifted a hand to run through his artfully styled hair. When he lifted his hand away from his head, the dark strands were sort of sticking up everywhere. It was kind of cute, or it would be if he didn't have such a hard, unyielding look on his face.

"Ollie, you're huddled in the bathtub. You are far from fine." His frown turned fierce as he quietly asked, "Why are you still holding onto that night? So much time has passed. What's done is done." He let out an ugly laugh. "It's not like we can go back and redo everything."

I sat up like I'd been electrocuted. I turned and grabbed the side of the tub. I was startled that he sounded so pragmatic and almost conciliatory. Neither of which fit with the way things had gone down back then.

"But I was the one driving, and I'm the one who lost control of the car." I huffed out a breath and gave him an aggravated look. "No matter what anyone believes, I know the truth, and so do you. I'm so sorry I lied and told everyone you were driving that night. I'm so sorry I told them you were drunk and lost control of the car. I didn't want to blame you. I had no choice. I've wanted to apologize for so long."

While I'd been unconscious with a serious concussion in the days after the accident, my mom nearly died from the stress of nearly losing her only child. While I was weak and vulnerable, Sawyer took it upon himself to tell anyone who would listen that Huck had been driving. Since we'd all been injured severely and thrown from the car, all the authorities had to go on was our retelling of the events. As soon as I woke up, I was ready to take the fall, until Sawyer's mom told me, in no uncertain terms, that their family would stop paying for my mom's medical care if I didn't back up her son's fabricated story.

At the time I really felt like I had no choice. I was only fourteen and my only family was hanging onto life by a thread. I didn't know they were going to use my words to send Huck away, or that Sawyer was going to get even more unhinged and demanding as time went on.

It drove me crazy how easily everyone accepted without question that Huck was the bad guy, that he

76

was the one who was careless and reckless with our lives that night. And it nearly made me lose my mind when Sawyer's mother started to aggressively hint that Huck had purposely caused the crash to injure me and Sawyer when it was revealed her son had suffered spinal damage and may never be able to walk again.

The writing was on the wall. Huck was in big trouble with no way out and no one coming to save him. He made a deal with his father and Sawyer's mom to go away. If he disappeared for good and gave up his share of the inheritance, and agreed to attend some military boarding school all the way across the country until graduation, no charges would be pressed against him. He was just a kid, and I was terrified for him. Plus, the guilt I felt over the fact that no one knew if Sawyer was ever going to be able to walk again was close to unbearable. So was the frustration that Huck was being punished in my place, and the terror of not knowing if my mom was ever going to get better. I was an emotional wreck and had no one to lean on or turn to. It felt like I was getting what I deserved for being dishonest.

Huck made a noise low in his throat and looked at me with an expression I couldn't read as he told me flatly, "An apology isn't as important as the person giving it or the person on the receiving end."

He reached out and knocked on the rim of the tub before hauling himself to his feet. He looked down at where I was still curled up in a protective ball.

"Don't spend the night in there, Ollie. You're old enough to know it's not the storm that was going to hurt you that night. Go back to bed. I'm sure the lights will be on any minute, and if you can't stand being alone until then, go hang out with Vernon. The kid plays video games until the sun comes up. I'm sure he wouldn't mind the company."

Huck left the bathroom without a backward glance, leaving the lantern behind.

I slumped back down in the tub and pulled the blanket back over my head.

I was afraid—of so many things.

I regretted so much from before.

I wished things could be different; that I had made better choices all around back then.

It didn't escape my notice that he didn't accept my apology... or that he'd had no interest in hearing it.

I couldn't blame him. Not when I was too busy blaming myself for everything that had gone wrong.

CHAPTER 8

Huck

Usually, when I went running with Harlen in the morning, I put in AirPods and shut out the outside world for an hour or two. Today I was so tired it felt like my sneakers were made of cement and each of my legs weighed one-hundred pounds. I was typically less than alert when we ran since my shifts at the bar ended so late at night, and we ran so early in the morning, but last night I'd come home early and then hadn't slept a wink. It was impossible to close out the noise in my head then and now.

When we rounded a corner and the college came into view, I slowed the pounding pace I'd been struggling to keep and eventually stopped, bending over and putting my hands on my knees as I wheezed to catch my breath, while Harlen jogged in a slow circle around me.

"I don't get you, man."

I looked up at him from under a sweaty brow, irritated for more than one reason. "What do you mean?"

Harlen huffed out an aggravated sound and stopped moving. He put his hands on his hips and glared at me as I stayed hunched over and exhausted.

"If you want the girl gone, why did you rush to her rescue last night? I practically had to sit on top of Vernon to keep him from running upstairs the minute the lights went out. He was dying to go check on her. It's an old house. It's creepy when the weather is bad. You obviously knew she was going to have a tough time in the storm. Why not make her tough it out or suffer alone? Maybe she would've decided to leave if it got bad enough. If she was scared enough. Even Fisher used to complain about how awful that attic room was when it rained—and nothing rattled him."

I frowned and shifted my gaze downward.

It'd been a long time since I'd had anything to do with Ollie, but one of the things that was impossible to forget was her near-total breakdown when it stormed after the accident. She looked like she was going to come out of her skin. She looked terrified and broken at the same time. I couldn't help but want to comfort her back then... and again last night. When it started raining, and then the thunder and lightning started, I wasn't able to concentrate on anything at work. It was so bad, my boss eventually told me to go home because I was useless and spilling more drinks than I was selling. I didn't tell her that, though. I lied about the power going out at the bar when I found her huddled in the bathtub.

I pushed upward and reached to shove my hands through my sweat-dampened hair. The air was still muggy from the rain last night, but that wasn't why I felt like I couldn't breathe.

"I told you I'd tell you about the scar on Ollie's cheek, right?" I lifted an eyebrow as Harlen rolled his shoulders and hopped up and down to keep his muscles loose.

"Hard to miss it."

"I'm the reason she has it." I blew out a breath and tossed my head back to look up at the clear early morning sky. "When I was sixteen, I partied a little hard with some kids from a town over I wasn't supposed to hang out with. I was drunk, probably high at the time, and not thinking straight. I was in no shape to drive myself home, and the weather was horrible that night. I called Ollie to come get me. I told her to borrow her mom's car and sneak out. I didn't want to deal with the shit I'd get from Sawyer's mom if I came home drunk, or not at all. And it wasn't like I could put Ollie's mom in a bind by asking her to pick me up. Sawyer insisted Ollie learn how to drive because he had this dumb sports car he wanted to show off, so I knew she could do it." I sighed. "I should've realized he was going to catch her sneaking out and insist on going with her. He watched her like a hawk, and I'm sure he was looking for any way he could find to get me in trouble."

I gritted my teeth, remembering the way he weaseled his way into nearly every aspect of Ollie's life, and how easily everyone had trusted him with her back then.

"I don't remember a lot of what happened that night because I was wasted. I know Ollie showed up with him, and I was pissed. I hated him and it bugged me when they were together. I know I threw a fit and refused to get in if he was the one driving." I scoffed at how stupid and shortsighted I'd been. "I played right into his hands."

Harlen stopped moving and looked at me with confused eyes. "What do you mean?"

I grunted and continued the trip down memory lane. "Ollie manhandled me into the backseat of the car and got behind the wheel after a big fight. I think I made her pick me over him, had her say she liked me better, or something else totally immature that wouldn't normally matter, but to Sawyer..." It was pretty much a declaration of war. "I must've passed out, because the next thing I remember is Ollie screaming loud enough to wake the dead; the car was skidding sideways with enough force that it threw me to the floor. I swear Sawyer had his hands on the steering wheel from across the car for some reason. The car spun out of control, went off the road, and slammed into a tree. It was completely totaled, and all three of us were seriously injured. Ollie's face was all cut up and she broke her arm. She was unconscious for nearly a week. Sawyer was ejected; they said he broke his back. Last I heard he ended up in a wheelchair. Because I was in the backseat and nearly asleep, I escaped mostly unscathed. To this day, I swear to God, Sawyer did something to cause the accident in the first place."

I didn't care that the roads were shitty or that Ollie was inexperienced behind the wheel. Even in my stupor, I knew what I saw, and that was Sawyer messing with Ollie while she drove. Of course, I knew no one would believe me if I tried to explain what happened. Sawyer was the golden boy, and I was the unwanted bastard.

I sighed and looked at my friend, who was staring at me like I was a stranger. "I took the fall for the accident. Sawyer told everyone, our families, the police, anyone who asked, that I was driving and lost control because of the road conditions and because I was fucked up that night. When she was awake, Ollie backed his story up. She lied for him."

For a minute, it really seemed like I would spend the rest of my teens in juvie. Fortunately, my father, who'd never been much of one, stepped up for the first and last time. "My dad offered to send me away before things got really bad." I snorted out a bitter laugh and shook my head.

I put my hands on my hips and shifted my gaze away from Harlen's shocked face. "She blames herself for Sawyer ending up in a wheelchair. She said the whole accident was her fault and she couldn't leave him to fend for himself. She was ready to be the martyr for the whole incident. I was mad at her, and so hurt by her betrayal, I left without a fight. Last night she said she always wanted to apologize, but I didn't want to hear it."

Harlen made a strangled sound in his throat and started pacing back and forth in front of me in an agitated manner. "And you've been out here collecting other lost souls ever since you were disowned and sent away?"

It was as close to the truth as anything else. "I knew what it was like to be abandoned and alone. Didn't sit right with me when I came across others who knew how hard it was to make it with no support system and no family."

I stopped the heavy conversation as a couple of very cute co-eds suddenly jogged by. I lifted my chin in response when they giggled and waved in our direction, obviously hoping we'd pick our run back up and follow after them.

Harlen rolled his eyes, tapped me on the shoulder, and muttered that we needed to get moving because he still had practice this morning. We didn't follow the flirty girls, and this time the pace he set didn't make me feel like my lungs were on fire. We'd been moving for a few minutes when my friend suddenly asked, "If the guy Ollie's running from is in a wheelchair, why is she so scared of him? Seems like it'd be pretty easy to avoid him if she wanted to."

I shook my head and moved to keep up with him. "Nothing with Sawyer is that easy. He's sneaky and manipulative. He doesn't get his hands dirty unless there is no other choice. While Ollie is here, there is no telling who or what he's got his claws into to make life miserable for her and anyone around her. And if he wants her back, he'll do anything to make that happen. He's got a mom who doesn't tell him no and a father with a deep-ass wallet. Wheelchair or not, he's dangerous and evil, and I know there is no way in hell he just let Ollie walk away from him. He'd rather we all die than admit he doesn't have complete control over her. You think I want you and Vernon anywhere near someone like that? What if he goes after you guys to get at me, or to get Ollie to do whatever it is he wants? He knows she's soft, and that eventually you guys will matter to her. For him, there is no difference between love and war."

I had no doubt that death had been Sawyer's intent that fateful night. I was sure he hadn't planned on anyone escaping the accident alive. He was demented, and it didn't matter that I was the only one who'd ever kept him in check. He still scared the piss out of me, which is why I wanted Ollie gone.

I sighed. However, there was no way I'd been able to ignore the pull to check on her when I got home last night as the storm raged outside. I knew I was going to find her huddled in a ball and scared out of her skin. I knew she was going to be so pale that she was almost white. I knew she was going to have tears in her eyes and be shaking so hard I could hear her teeth clicking together. I knew the dark was going to seem large and looming in a new place, especially one as old as ours. Harlen was right. I should've let her suffer and hope that she was freaked out enough to leave my house, but I just couldn't. Which was an even bigger reason I needed her out of my life once and for all.

I didn't want her regrets or her remorse.

I wanted her, and the heartbreak in her eyes, gone for good.

The fact that I knew better but still found myself drawn to her when she was at her most vulnerable was almost as scary as the prospect of whatever demented fuckery Sawyer might bring my way.

CHAPTER 9

Ollie

"You're cute. Can I get your number?"

I stumbled to a stop, precariously juggling my phone in one hand and a frothy Starbucks drink in the other. A tote bag full of books and my laptop swung from my shoulder and down my arm when I was suddenly intercepted between classes.

I blinked stupidly at the young man standing in front of me, noticing his gaze seemed locked on my scar despite his throwaway compliment about my appearance. If he hadn't said something to me, I would've walked right into him and he would be wearing my drink.

"Excuse me?"

My mumbled words brought his eyes toward mine, and he flashed me a grin so perfect that I was sure he had practiced the exact curl of his lips in the mirror regularly. I didn't know why I was his target or what made him think I was open for conversation, friendly or otherwise. I knew there was nothing about my demeanor that was approachable or welcoming. I had walls erected a mile high, and I liked it that way. I no longer wanted to be an easy mark for anyone.

"Your number. Can I have it? I think you're cute. I like your curly hair."

I wasn't in the habit of interacting with strangers. I didn't trust them. I didn't trust anyone aside from Huck. At least with him, I knew exactly where I stood, even if I was pissing him off.

"Ummm..." I didn't want to cause a scene or get involved in an awkward situation. I was trying to blend in, not stick out. He wasn't the first student to ask me out once I'd transferred here, but there was something about the aggressive way he'd blocked my path and the direct way he was staring at me that made me super uncomfortable. It had me seriously doubting the authenticity of his intent.

The guy shoved his iPhone in my direction, lifting an eyebrow when I didn't shuffle the things in my hands to take it.

"Just put in your number, and I'll call it right now." He smirked at me as I continued to blink stupidly. "I want to make sure you don't give me a fake number. I hate it when girls do that."

If this was his usual tactic when trying to pick someone up, no wonder he got fake numbers often enough to have a plan to avoid it from happening. I fought back the urge to roll my eyes as I tried to figure out the easiest way to slip out of this situation. Rejection shouldn't be something that made me fear for my life, but after everything that went down with Sawyer, I knew just how dangerous saying no to the wrong person could be. It sucked and was totally unfair that I was far from the only female to learn that lesson the hard way.

I could tell the guy was getting annoyed as I remained silent and still, his phone dangling from his fingers between the two of us. I was about to lie and tell him I had a boyfriend who would be very upset if I gave him my number, when suddenly a heavy arm landed on my shoulders, and warm lips landed on my temple.

I gasped in surprise but didn't pull away, because even without looking at the tall, toned body pressing against my side, I knew it was Huck. He used to feel all soft and squishy when I leaned against him for comfort and support. There was no give in the body next to mine now. He was all hard muscle and threatening aura as he stared down the guy standing across from me.

"I thought we agreed to meet at the coffee shop. I was wondering where you got off to." His statement was innocent enough, but the way he said it, there was no missing the warning in his tone. "Who's your friend?"

My overly aggressive suitor fell back a step and held up his hands in front of him. "I was just asking her for directions. I just transferred here, and I'm a little turned around." He gave me another smile; this one showed too many teeth, making my skin crawl as he finally put his phone away. "Sorry to bother you."

Something close to a growl rumbled from the center of Huck's broad chest as we watched the other guy hurry away. When he let his arm fall from my shoulders, I took a second to adjust the things I was juggling and looked at the dark-haired boy out of the corner of my eye. I hadn't seen much of him since the night of the storm and the start of the semester. I took his disappearance as a good sign, because if I didn't have to face him, I didn't have to listen to him tell me how I ruined his life, and how I was his least favorite person on the planet. I didn't have to remember how he ignored my apology and dashed my hopes of smoothing things over.

"Where did you come from?" I took a sip of the sweet coffee drink and moved to put my phone in my pocket. I was still trying to get ahold of Mercer. She never returned my texts the night of the storm and hadn't messaged me back when I reached out about my work schedule now that school had started. I'd also called her a few times and gotten no response.

Huck made a face. He took a step away from me and shook his hand like it was dirty before slipping it inside the front pocket of his jeans. "I saw you when I was over by the library. I was going to go to class and leave you to fend for yourself, but I recognized that guy from my bar. He's a prick and has a hard time hearing no."

I lifted the fingers of my free hand to touch my temple where I could still feel the imprint of Huck's lips. That kiss was a familiar gesture, one he'd done often when we were kids.

I cleared my throat and shifted my heavy bag. "I had it under control. I don't let bossy men order me around or intimidate me anymore." I'd moved and taken solace in his home for that very reason. "But thank you for intervening. It made getting rid of him much easier."

Huck grunted in response. And looked past me toward the brick buildings of the college. "I have to get to my next class. I'll talk to you later."

Before he could walk away from me, I reached out a hand and grabbed his muscled, tattooed forearm. He stopped mid-step and looked down at my fingers like he wanted to peel them off of his skin one by one.

"Uh... I just wanted to thank you for the other night. I haven't really seen you since then, but I know that I owe you one. I wouldn't have made it through that storm without you." There were too many situations in my life to count where I wouldn't have come out the other side without him. I often wondered if he had any clue just how important he'd always been to me.

Huck shook his arm free and lifted his hand to wave at a group of girls who called his name. He motioned that he would just be a minute before turning his attention back to me.

"If you feel like you owe me, then do us both a favor and disappear. Get out of my house, and get out of my life before you force me to do something we'll both regret." He sounded deadly serious, and I couldn't stop a sharp chill from racing up and down my spine.

I forced a wobbly grin and told him, "I don't care how much time has passed. The Huck I know would never hurt me or do anything to me that either of us would regret."

I refused to believe he'd changed that much, and in such horrible ways, since we'd been apart.

He moved before I could react.

I gasped in shock when he was suddenly right in front of me, one of his rough hands holding my jaw tight enough that it hurt. His amber eyes glowed like they were lit from within by the fires of hell. His voice was low and scary as he moved his face alarmingly close to mine, his fingers holding my face hard enough to leave bruises.

"You don't know anything, Olivia. You never did. Don't make the mistake of thinking I'm the same kid you walked all over, who let you have your way no matter the circumstances. I'm not him anymore. I'm not someone you should underestimate."

I dropped my drink on the ground in surprise. It splattered across his black and white sneakers and my battered combat boots. He never called me by my full name. Not ever. I lifted a hand to his wrist, to pull him away or hold him closer, I wasn't sure. I felt his pulse kick under my fingertips.

I could feel his breath as he practically spat out the words. I could feel the tension in his big body as he nearly shook with restraint. If either one of us moved in the slightest, our lips would touch, and I was totally stunned by how much I wanted to lean forward. Our relationship had never been one of a romantic nature, but now that he was all grown up and pretty much the only person in the entire world I felt like I could rely on, something had shifted. My mind understood that he meant the move as a threat, but the rest of me didn't seem interested in reading the signs he was sending loud and clear.

Huck dropped his hold and shook loose from my hold once again. He turned and walked away without another word or backward glance.

It took me a second to get my breathing back under control as I looked forlornly down at the mess by my feet. I didn't have a ton of extra cash on hand most days, so the sweet drink had been a splurge to celebrate safely making it long enough to see my second semester and the start of a new school, one that I picked and wasn't forced upon me. For a good long while, I'd been convinced I wasn't ever going to get to decide any of life's basic choices. Where I lived, what I wore, what I ate, who I interacted with, where I went to school, what I was studying, all of those things were decided for me after the accident. If I dared dissent, Sawyer would threaten to stop paying for my mom's medical treatment, so I toed the line until it became clear she couldn't hold on. It wasn't until she passed that I learned she'd been squirreling money away for me, that she put every single dime into a secret savings account I couldn't access until she was gone. It wasn't a ton of money, but it was just enough to get away from that mansion and the people in it. It was enough I could get the education she wanted for me as long as I didn't have hopes for a top-tier college. She was doing her best to make sure I was cared for even after she was gone. It was like she knew I needed a way out, and the only way to get it was if she stopped being my biggest weakness.

I shook my foot in irritation and started toward my next class. I was almost to the building when my phone suddenly rang. Only a couple of people had the number, and since I'd been blowing Mercer up for days. I knew it was probably her.

"Hello." I nodded a slight apology as I nearly ran into a girl rushing through the doors. "I have class in a couple of minutes, so I can't talk long."

Mercer giggled in my ear as she apologized for not calling me back for days on end. "I'm in loooooooooove, Ollie."

The sing-song tone was nothing unusual. Neither was her over-the-top declaration. She'd been in loooooooooove at least five times since I'd known her.

"I'm happy to hear that, but I need to know if you are still planning on letting me work weekends for you now that I'm back at school." I needed the minimal hours at Mercer's shop for spending money so I could splurge on things like my spilled coffee.

Mercer laughed again, and I could almost see her tossing her rainbow hair over her shoulder. "You can work whenever you want. The other girl I had covering nights decided to quit suddenly, so there are extra hours available. I'd happily cover them as usual, but now that I have a man," she sighed in such a dreamy manner, it was hard not to laugh at her. "I can't wait for you to meet him. He's not my normal type, but he's so handsome and charming."

I paused outside the doorway to my classroom. "Just text me when you need me to be there. I gotta go, but don't ignore my calls for so long. I worry."

She was too nice for her own good. She would never see any of those guys whom she fell in love at first sight with as a threat. That's all I ever saw.

"Okay, okay. I'm really sorry that my head has been in the clouds lately. Love does that to me. How are things at the house? Did you and that boy call a truce yet?"

Typical Mercer. She wouldn't call me back when I had nothing but time on my hands and needed to hear a friendly voice, but as soon as I had somewhere else to be, she was super chatty and curious about what was going on in my life.

"Not even close. I think he's actually declared war, but I have too much to lose if I let him run me off. I'll talk to you later. Don't forget to send me those shifts I can cover."

I clicked off the call before she could launch into more details about her love life and slid into the full classroom. Luckily, the professor had yet to arrive. I slid into a remaining seat that was somewhere in the middle and pulled out my laptop. I scowled at the brown spots that had dried on the toes of my boots and absently hoped I hadn't ruined Huck's shoes.

It was a change from when we were younger. When we weren't in our school uniforms, we used to live in secondhand stuff and whatever my mom could get us from one of the big box stores. It was weird that his father hadn't protested Huck dressing the same as the help's kid since he was so concerned about image, but I was sure it all came down to keeping up appearances. There was no way Sawyer's mom would let the unwanted son look as put together as her own child, especially when they were in the same grade at the same school. I still lived in hand-me-downs and thrift store finds, while he was rocking stuff I knew cost more than the average, broke college kid could afford. He must be a really, really good bartender. He must've figured out how to leverage making money off that pretty face and ripped body of his. Which would explain how he kept the motivation to get up so early each day and tackle a workout with Harlen.

Lost in thought, I jolted when the girl sitting next to me suddenly nudged me with her elbow. My whole laptop shook in front of me, and I had to reach for it so it didn't slide to the ground.

"Are you friends with Huck Snyder? I saw the two of you talking outside before class." The girl looked at me with eager eyes, and I could see that her cheeks were flushed in excitement.

I was familiar with her expression and her question. When I was younger, it felt like my entire identity was tied to knowing Huck and Sawyer. It was almost as if no one had any use for me beyond using me as a stepping stone to get to the brothers. For a while, I tried to pretend I didn't know either one of them, but neither boy let it slide. We were all tied together for better or worse, which meant I was often the go-between for enamored suitors.

Giving her a bland smile, I played dumb. "Who?"

Some of her enthusiasm visibly dimmed at my response, but undeterred, she forged onward. "The tall, dark-haired guy you were talking to outside. His name is Huck. He's a bartender at one of the most popular bars near campus. Everyone knows who he is, and everyone knows his group of friends. They're all really popular, but they tend to keep to themselves. I thought it was different that he was talking to you since you're new around here, and I've never seen him act so familiar with a girl on campus like that before."

Good Lord, just how close was she watching him to notice something like that? The thought was fleeting because I belatedly remembered the boy had entire social media pages dedicated to tracking his every move.

"Sorry. I don't know what you're talking about."

I could deny with the best of them, even with the girl looking at me like I'd lost my mind. Plus, the truth was, after that little encounter and the way Huck had jostled me, I really might not know Huck Snyder like I thought I did. He was trying to scare me and he almost succeeded.

CHAPTER 10

Huck

My plan to be the great seducer was failing epically because I'd done too good of a job convincing Ollie to stay out of my way. If I walked into a room she was in, she immediately walked out. If I found a reason for our paths to cross either at the house or on campus, she would almost immediately find an excuse to switch gears and go the other way. Not to mention, we were both working and bogged down with schoolwork. Since the beginning of the semester several weeks ago, I would guess I'd seen her less than ten times, and each encounter had lasted less than a few minutes. She was really relying hard on the idea that if she was out of sight, she would be out of mind. However, like I told her when I saved her from the creeper who was hitting on her at the start of the semester, it was like something was buzzing under my skin, and I couldn't stop the sensation. Even without putting my eyes on her, I knew she was there.

I could feel her. I could smell her. I could hear her. It was as if her presence was seeping into every nook and

97

cranny of the old house. I didn't have to see her face to know that she was still under my roof, making me more unsettled than I wanted to admit. I would rather have all my teeth plucked out with rusty pliers than fess up to the fact that when I pulled her to my side and touched my lips to her temple the other day, I'd felt the impact of the simple gesture all the way down to my soul. They were familiar gestures that reminded me of a simpler time. But there was a new element there when I touched her, a new awareness of her that made my blood hot and my skin tingle. There was new awareness when I felt how soft her skin was and how silky her hair felt that lingered long after she was gone. All of those new sensations made my dick hard. I would die before I listened to the tiny voice warning me that I was attracted to her because she was my Ollie, not just a cute girl in close proximity. No, I was drawn to her on a much deeper level, and it scared the shit out of me. So, I didn't exactly mind that we'd been two ships passing in the night the last few weeks.

However, all of that aside, I still wanted her gone and any threats from Sawyer off the table. I didn't owe Ollie a single thing. But, I owed Harlen and Vernon pretty much everything. I needed to suck it up and charm the pants off of her so I could get her to fall for me, or at the least fall into bed with me. It was my experience that the quickest way to break someone's heart was to make them think they were special—then show them that they weren't.

I remembered how much it hurt when Ollie turned on me after the accident. I never thought I was in love with her. We were just kids, after all, and our lives were already beyond messed up, but I was crushed when she picked Sawyer over me. It didn't matter to me that she felt responsible and guilty for the fact my half brother could no longer walk. All I could focus on was that she told the authorities I was responsible, and it made me feel like I was suddenly her second choice when I'd always come first. I intended to get rid of her for my own peace of mind, but I would be lying if I didn't acknowledge there was a pretty big piece of me that wanted her to hurt in the exact same way that she'd hurt me.

When she agreed that I caused the accident on purpose, that I tried to hurt her when all I'd ever done was protect her, it crushed me and made me question everything I thought I knew. That uncertainty followed me for a long time and forced me to keep nearly everyone I encountered at bay. I didn't let anyone get close enough to hurt me like that, so I was very much alone for most of my life. It wasn't until the boys came along and I realized they needed someone as much as I did that I finally lowered my guard enough to let them in.

After I got home from a shift that felt like it would never end, I was getting ready for bed when I heard the stairs from the attic creak and groan. Whenever we ran a special at the bar where ladies drank for free, it was a madhouse. If they weren't shifts that were guaranteed to make such good money, I would've asked for the night off. It was well past midnight and the skies were clear, so there wasn't a reason for Ollie to be creeping around the house so late. But whatever her reason was, it gave me a good opportunity to bump into her and finally start to throw some of my well-practiced game her way. It was rare for a woman to turn me down when I put my mind to getting to know her, and Ollie was already predisposed to appreciate some of my finer qualities. She already knew the kind of guy I was deep down inside, even if I kept telling her how much I'd changed. She was the opposite of most girls. I needed her to fall for what I had to offer on the outside now that I was no longer a clumsy, chubby kid. I needed her to be superficial and shallow, like most of the girls I picked up at the bar for a one-night stand.

I stripped off my shirt, kicked off my shoes, tugged the waistband of my jeans down so that they were hanging precariously low on my hips, and dragged my hands through my hair so it was an attractive mess. I looked like I had just crawled out of someone's bed after a round of very rowdy sex, which was exactly what I was going for.

Let's see if Ollie could blatantly walk away from me now.

When I entered the kitchen, where I followed the faint sounds Ollie was making, the only light in the room came from the open fridge. Ollie's curly blonde head was bent inside as she rummaged through one of the drawers. I'd yet to see her eat a meal at the house, and I hadn't seen her bring groceries in, but that didn't mean much since I really hadn't seen her at all in several days. And if I knew Vernon, there was no way the kid would let our new housemate starve. I could almost bet on the fact he asked Ollie what she liked and stocked up when he went to the store. He was a good kid with a soft heart, and he knew all too well what it was like to go hungry. He would never let that happen to someone else on his watch. Especially someone he was fond of. Despite all my warnings, there was no missing that our youngest really liked the unwelcome blast from my past.

Since I was barefoot, I barely made a sound as I moved behind her. When she turned around, she had an apple in her mouth and a bottle of water in her hand. With the faint hint of light behind her, and her wild and unruly hair practically glowing, she reminded me of an old Renaissance painting.

She made a strangled sound when her eyes landed on me, but her teeth were locked on the piece of fruit, so the noise was muffled. I lifted an eyebrow at her and reached past her shoulder to shut the fridge, which brought our bodies very close together.

"What are you doing up so late?" I'd told myself to keep my tone friendly and flirty, but it still came out slightly accusatory.

She crunched down on the apple, chewing slowly, and narrowed her eyes at me in the darkness. It seemed like it took forever for her to swallow so she could answer. "I have a quiz tomorrow. I wanted to study before bed but lost track of time. I didn't even realize how late it was until I heard you come home. I'm headed to bed now. I'll get out of your way."

I shifted my weight just slightly to keep her from moving around me. "You've been busy lately."

She cleared her throat and pulled her gaze away from mine. "I'm surprised you noticed. I'm trying to be as inconspicuous as possible. I know you don't want me in this house, so I'm doing my best to make it seem like I'm not even here."

I leaned closer to her, forcing her to lean back against the fridge in the dark. "I thought you worked so hard to get under the same roof as me because you wanted to show me how sorry you are for what you did to me. How does that work if you're never around?"

She made a face and nervously fiddled with the apple in her hand. "You made it pretty clear you don't want to hear any excuses for why I did what I did. I fought a losing battle for most of my life, Huck. If I learned anything, it's when to know it's time to cut your losses."

When she put the apple back to her mouth for another bite, I moved quickly and grabbed her wrist so she couldn't pull the piece of fruit away. I bent down and bit the other side. I heard her gasp as I got close enough that our noses almost touched. She went still as stone as I put a hand on her hip and guided her body even closer to mine. I pulled back after taking a sizable chunk from the opposite side of the apple and grinned at her after chomping it down.

"It's too sweet." My voice was twice as raspy as it normally was, and I couldn't stop a shiver when I felt her body quake underneath my hand.

When I let go of her wrist, the apple fell to the ground with a thump and rolled away. Ollie lifted shaking hands to her open mouth and blinked wide eyes at me.

"What are you doing?" She sounded completely bewildered and baffled, but even in the dark, I could see the way her gaze locked on me, skimming my face and the rest of my barely dressed body. It was about damn time she realized I was missing most of my clothes while standing close enough to touch.

I lifted a hand to my mouth and used my thumb to wipe my bottom lip. "I just wanted a bite. I was curious how it would taste."

The double entendre was cheesy and as thick as maple syrup, but Ollie didn't seem fazed by it in the slightest. Instead of saying something sassy or silly back, she scurried away, chasing after the fallen apple and muttering that it was past time for her to go to bed.

I didn't stop her when she ran away, but I did grin at how fast she fled. I took it as a good sign that she was far from unaffected, even if she didn't respond in the way I'd hoped. I supposed there was simply too much history between us for her to fall fast and hard, no matter how high I turned up the charm. It was bound to take some time to get her to stop seeing me as her childhood friend and protector and make her see me as something... someone else.

If she was going to run from me now, I was going to have to chase her.

It was anyone's guess what kind of disaster was going to happen when I finally caught her.

I was egotistical enough to want to believe I could walk away unmoved after I ran Ollie off. I'd learned how to live without her once before. Only, the way my heart was currently racing, and the way my entire body felt tight and overly alert from being too close to her, were huge red flags that I was getting in over my head where this complicated girl was concerned.

It was unfortunate that I'd never been the type to abide by those pesky little warning signs. If I had, maybe

I could've stopped Sawyer from ruining all our lives with his selfishness.

I didn't pay attention all those years ago, and the monster nearly ate me alive.

I wouldn't make that same mistake this time.

CHAPTER 11

Ollie

"Do you think he was going to kiss you? It sounds like he was coming onto you, which is weird since all I've heard from the moment you moved to town is how much he hates you. Are you sure you didn't misread the situation? It's not like you have a ton of dating experience."

Mercer stirred her straw around her second margarita. She'd finally appeared out of nowhere and asked me if I wanted to meet for lunch. She immediately shrugged off my concern about her whereabouts and sudden attachment to her new boyfriend. She told me repeatedly that I was blowing the situation out of proportion and once again rubbed my innocence in my face. I was sure she didn't do it to be hurtful, but on top of Huck's weirdly forward behavior out of the blue, I didn't have a solid hold on my emotions, and I was overly sensitive about everything.

I traced a falling drop of water on the side of my glass and looked down at the table as I muttered, "I might not know much about dating, but I know everything there is to know about Huck. He wouldn't try to get close to me all of a sudden without a reason." And without acknowledging my apology or discussing what happened between us in the past.

He wouldn't get close physically or emotionally without a purpose. When we were younger, it was because he wanted to protect me and he liked the added benefit of pissing off Sawyer and Sawyer's mother. Now, I knew all the way down to my bones that he was scheming something. He was playing a game and I didn't know the rules, but I knew he intended for me to be the loser no matter what.

He'd grown up a lot in the years we'd been apart. Back in the day, his tricks and pranks had been mostly harmless and rarely hurt anyone. It didn't seem like that would be the case now. He'd grown up adjacent to evil, but always seemed to be unaffected by the darker influences around him. The adult version of Huck made me question that childish belief. There were times he was just as cold, calculating, and unscrupulous as Sawyer.

"So, what's his reason for suddenly being so flirty if you know him so well?" The second margarita was gone as quickly as the first, and Mercer signaled the waitress for a refill. While it wasn't uncommon for her to have a cocktail during lunch, full-on day-drinking was something new, and the worry that had been eating at me while she went quiet started to tingle along my senses once again.

I frowned at her as I aimlessly picked at the chips and salsa sitting between us. "I think he's going to try and get me into bed."

And I knew if I succumbed, he would immediately flip the script and freeze me out. He wanted to betray me the way I'd betrayed him. He wanted me disappointed and disillusioned the way he'd been. He wanted me to feel ashamed and embarrassed enough to leave the house on my own without dragging the landlord into our situation. He wanted to destroy any lingering infatuation I might have for the boy he'd once been.

Mercer sipped on her drink and lifted her eyebrows. "Well, that sounds like fun, not a threat." She continued to look at me questioningly as I sighed heavily.

It might sound like fun to someone else, but for me, I knew it would only end badly if I let myself fall into his trap.

She cocked her head and asked, "Why don't you give it a shot? If you know what his intentions are, why can't you have a little fun? If anyone deserves a couple of mind-blowing orgasms and some thoroughly distracting sex, it's you. Maybe he's got a magical dick and it can heal all that's wrong in your world at the moment."

I tossed a chip at her but she just batted it away, unbothered and possibly a little buzzed, if her terrible coordination was any indication. "Really, though. If he wants to sleep with you for his own end, why not play his game but make your own rules? You can't tell me you aren't attracted to him. Your entire face changes when you talk about him. And it has since you first stumbled into my store all lost and alone. He's like your magnetic north. No matter what direction you're spinning, your needle always points back to Huck."

Mercer wasn't wrong. I could spin and spin until I was so dizzy I made myself sick, but as soon as the world stopped being a blur, the first thing I saw clearly was Huck. Maybe she was right, and I should give in, even if the reasons were far from ideal. It wasn't like I viewed sex as something sacred and pure. I knew it could be used just as quickly as a weapon as it was a form of affection. My emotions were so shredded and worn after years of being used against me, I was confident I could have sex and keep what little feeling I had left separate from the act itself. The tricky part was, the few remaining bits of softness and sentiment that remained inside my heart all happened to be tied to Huck. If I was contemplating emotionless sex with anyone else to prove a point, it would be no problem. Since it was him, I worried my walls would never be high enough—or thick enough—to keep me safe and him at a distance.

"You're telling me to sleep with him and show him that it means nothing to me so he won't even bother to ghost me afterward?" It sounded so ugly, but it might be the only way I could keep my dignity as well as a roof over my head.

"You keep saying you know him inside and out, but he doesn't know you, Ollie. He has no clue what you've been through or how tough you had to become once he was gone. He's trying to provoke you to get his own way. He doesn't care if he hurts you. I think it is fair you hurt him first." She took a long sip of her frozen drink and clumsily reached for the bowl of chips. She was typically all about peace and love; it was weird to hear her be so ruthless out of nowhere.

"Isn't your usual advice to hug it out and hope for the best?" Plus, I already hurt him first. When he thought

I picked Sawyer over him, I would never forget the look of absolute heartbreak on his face. Uncomfortable with those memories, I quickly changed the subject. "What's going on with you lately? First, you disappear for days on end, and then when you resurface, you seem totally on edge." I motioned to the nearly empty glass in front of her. "You're also drinking more than normal. Are you sure you're okay?"

Mercer stared at her lime green drink for a long moment, her rainbow hair falling in front of her face. "I'm fine. I just really like this new guy I'm seeing. I like him more than he likes me, I think." She sighed dramatically and stirred her straw around her drink. "I want to see him and talk to him all day every day, but he's more reserved and kind of distant. Sometimes I get the feeling I'm annoying him." She pushed her drink to the side and folded her arms on the table, leaning closer so she could talk in a quieter voice. "And he's nowhere near as touchy-feely and affectionate as I am. He barely lets me hold his hand or hug him. And..." she trailed off as her eyebrows furrowed. "We haven't had sex yet. I mean, no judgment, everyone moves at their own pace, but we've been hanging out for a while now, and he hasn't tried to initiate anything. When I try, he always finds an excuse to pull away. If he wasn't so sweet and shy, I'd think he was playing the opposite game with me that Huck is playing with you. I'm frustrated, and it's starting to hurt my feelings. It has me wondering what's wrong with me."

She pouted prettily, so I reached across the table and patted her on the arm. She was the one person who'd been there for me without question when I was at my lowest. She had an untainted heart that was pure gold. I hated the idea of anyone not appreciating how special she was. Mercer flitted from flower to flower like a busy bee, so it was odd to see her so hung up on a guy who she said wasn't her type. Maybe he was playing hard to get on purpose so that she spent more time thinking about him and trying to win him over than she would on someone more accommodating.

"You were the one who kept telling me to stay persistent and not give up on getting into Huck's house. And you mentioned this new guy is shy. His relationship pace might not match yours, so you'll have to slow down to stay with him. If you really like him, all you can do is try and find common ground." I was the last person alive who should be giving relationship advice, but I hated seeing her look so sad or questioning her own worth.

She sat up as our food finally arrived, and we dug in hungrily. She pointed the end of her taco in my direction and told me, "He actually tried to tag along on this lunch date. I was tempted to let him come since it's the first thing he's seemed interested in about my life in days, but I knew you were upset with me since I have been so bad about getting back to you lately. He was honestly a little bit rude when I refused to let him come." She shrugged her shoulders and took a big bite.

I tried not to panic as I asked, "He doesn't know who I am or where I'm from, right?"

I was still anxiously waiting to see what Sawyer would do next. It was entirely possible he hired a minion to do his bidding, and the easiest way to get close to me would be to get close to Mercer. I trusted her and wanted to protect her. It was a weakness I was well aware of. One that Sawyer would absolutely use against me if he knew about it.

"Don't worry. I only told him I was meeting with a co-worker. I keep your secrets close. You know you can trust me." I nodded slightly, hoping I could indeed trust her even though she was acting somewhat strange since this new guy had entered the picture.

She was the one who changed the topic now that the atmosphere was heavy with worry between the two of us. "So, what are you going to do about Huck? Are you going to sleep with him?"

"If you're being technical, I've slept with him plenty." When we were little, and even into our teens, having a secret sleepover wasn't uncommon. We were inseparable in all ways, and I didn't realize until he was gone that my attachment to him might read as something else to those looking in from the outside. It wasn't until Sawyer started showing his true colors and accused me of some really perverse things that I understood why clinging to Huck might not appear as innocent to others as it always was to us. "If you're asking if I'm going to have fuck him before he fucks me, then yes."

I had too much to lose to not at least consider it.

Mercer made a humming sound and gave me a look I couldn't fully decipher. "Or you could just have sex together. Maybe it'll be so damn good you'll both forget there are ulterior motives."

I bit down harder on my fork than I meant to, my teeth clicking against the metal angrily. I cleared my throat and reached for my drink.

"Huck has plenty of experience, so I'm sure he'll be fine if I strike first. You know my story. I've only been with one other person, and it didn't end well." And that single time had also been rife with reasons other than love and affection, or even teenage curiosity.

The first boy I'd ever been with was more of an experiment than anything else. I knew Sawyer was interfering in my life in unmanageable ways. I knew he had his fingers in everything I did and that he was maneuvering and manipulating anyone who dared get close to me. I couldn't prove it. No one listened to me when I told them he'd gone too far. My last desperate attempt to have any kind of control was to sleep with a seemingly nice guy I met my freshman year of college. I never wanted to be at that hoity-toity school in the first place. I went because Sawyer made me. I went because he made me feel like my mom would die if I didn't. I knew my education played into some greater plan Sawyer and his mom had for me, like down the road if I was forced to mingle in their social circles, they wanted to make sure I had a pedigree that held up. I was being groomed, and I was achingly aware of it.

I was also aware it was risky to get close to someone new with the threat of Sawyer always hovering in the background. Regardless, I wanted one thing in my life to seem normal, to be in my control, so I let a boy in one of my classes chat me up and flirt with me while I was at school. I wanted to see how long the friendship would last. I wanted to know how far Sawyer would go to keep me isolated and alone. The answer was horrifying when I let things with the boy from school go a little too far and pushed Sawyer past a point of no return.

I went into the friendship knowing that the guy was bait more than anything else, but still, I couldn't but feel a little dirty and slightly ruined by the way I used him when it was all said and done. I set him up to see exactly what would happen if I went against the rules and pushed back against the path laid out clearly in front of me. I lost my virginity to a boy I didn't care about or have any real interest in because I wanted to see what would happen afterward. It wasn't about me and him. It had nothing to do with pleasure or feeling good and making a connection. My first time was about me and Sawyer and power and control. Not my fondest memory by a long shot, and I still felt bad about ditching the guy whom I hooked up with almost as soon as it was over.

"I still can't get over the fact that that guy you lived with had hidden cameras in your room. He has to be some kind of sick bastard to spy on you that way." Mercer sounded as horrified now as she did months ago when I told her how I'd brought that boy home only to find out we were being watched, and that Sawyer never had any intention of sharing me with anyone.

Bringing the stranger home sent Sawyer into a rage no one could have predicted. He flipped out to the point that he threatened me with a hidden video of me and my classmate in a compromising position. He wanted to humiliate me, to bring me to heel. However, his obsession finally gave me a bit of leverage to push back. We lived in a state that was one of the few to adopt laws about revenge porn, so I could finally turn Sawyer's threats back on him. I told him if he did anything to harm my mother, I was going to press charges against him and would urge my poor, innocent classmate to do the same. I might not have the name and clout to be a threat, but the kid from school did. And his parents were almost as scary as Sawyer's mom. I felt like I finally had a way to get him to leave me alone, at least for a little while.

His mother was furious when she found out about the cameras and ordered him to stop watching me, but she also warned me what would happen if I bought another boy home and provoked her son. She promised she would find a way to make me pay, and I believed her. Sawyer slipped, and it was finally out in the open just how bizarre and dangerous his obsession with me and controlling everything in my life was. No one knew when he put remote cameras in my room, if it was before or after the accident. But there was no denying he'd been watching me in my most private moments, which was a whole new level of violation.

It was a turning point for me. It showed me I was going to have to do anything to get out of that house and away from Sawyer as soon as I had an opportunity to escape.

Mercer interrupted my unwelcome trip down memory lane. "You deserve to be with someone you have feelings for and with someone who has feelings for you. Even if those feelings are blurry and undefined. Not all your experiences with Huck have to be so combative and complicated. After all, the two of you used to be best friends. That usually takes some of the pressure off of the sex having to be all perfect and romantic. It makes it more real."

She made it sound so simple, but it was anything other than that—the days when he considered me a friend felt forgotten.

I mean, I'd felt like I was going to pass out when he got close enough to bite the other side of the apple, and I was far from immune from his new habit of wearing as few clothes as possible whenever we happened to bump into one another. I couldn't deny I was alarmingly attracted to all that Huck had become. How could I not be? He was hot. He was smart. He had a dangerous edge that had only been sharpened and honed over time. There were also hints of the boy who was my whole world that shone through his hard exterior, and those were the bits I liked best about him.

CHAPTER 12

Huck

"**W**hat are you doing?"

I didn't expect Ollie to suddenly jump up from where she'd been kneeling on her hands and knees, peering underneath the couch in the living room. Her rapid burst of action drove the top of her head into the bottom of my chin. My head snapped back as white spots of pain popped in my vision. I swore loudly while Ollie gasped. She reached out a hand as I stumbled backward and lifted one to the crown of her head.

Almost as if we were caught in a pivotal scene in a terrible rom-com, just as Ollie reached for me while I was backing up, my feet somehow got tangled up in her giant tote bag. Her fist tightened on the fabric of my shirt just as I went down. It wasn't clear if she was dizzy and off-balance, or if I just outweighed her enough that my falling momentum was enough to pull her down with me. Either way, a moment later, we were both sprawled on the living room floor, her body landing fully on top of mine as we both let out sounds of discomfort and surprise. My elbow connected with the hardwood hard enough to make my eyes water, and Ollie must've landed on something the wrong way because her yelp of pain was loud enough to have my ears ringing.

Instinctively, I lifted a hand and cupped the back of her head, feeling for a lump or anything amongst the wild tangle of curls. She flinched slightly, but I didn't notice anything that shouldn't be there.

"Are you okay? Why were you crawling around on the floor in the first place?"

I was running late for class and thought I was home alone. I didn't expect her when I walked into the living room. And I really didn't expect the reaction I had when my eyes inadvertently locked on her ass pointed up in the air while she wiggled around on the ground. It wasn't seductive or sexual in the slightest, but for some reason, my body hardened, and my heart started beating like I was watching the most triple X-rated porn.

She moaned slightly and shifted on top of me.

"My earring fell out. The back must've come loose. I was looking for it, but I'm late, so I was distracted. I didn't even hear you." Her brows furrowed, and she wiggled some more. I had to bite my tongue to stop from moaning as her thigh rubbed against the hardness that was pressing painfully against the zipper of my jeans. I knew she wasn't purposely trying to be sexy or alluring, but she was doing it without any effort. "Don't you have class right now? Why are you here?"

How was she putting complete sentences together and acting so unaffected? I felt like my skin was on fire and I couldn't catch my breath. I was supposed to be luring her. I was supposed to be corrupting her and convincing her that I was a terrible person, but all I wanted to do was wrap my arms even more tightly around her and hold on for dear life.

This was not part of the plan.

I was not supposed to be so greatly affected by her nearness.

I was not planning on getting lost in her endlessly dark eyes.

I definitely didn't account for the fact that she felt both comfortably familiar and achingly new and unknown at the same time.

Holding her close sent a barrage of sensations shooting through me. All of them moved so quickly, I couldn't latch onto a single one to figure out how I really felt about all of me touching all of her.

"I was running late too. You surprised me." Which was not in the plan. I was supposed to surprise her. I was supposed to be shocking her with callousness and cruelty.

Instead, she took my breath away.

Literally.

Before I could get my hands somewhere safe and offer to help her up off the floor, she shifted just enough so our lips were aligned. For a split second, I thought maybe she was just playing with me to get me back for the stunt with the apple, that she was just teasing and trying to get a reaction out of me.

I wasn't ready for the soft brush of her mouth against mine. I didn't stand a chance against the whisper of a kiss, and how sweet she tasted as our lips slid together, almost as if they were made to fit against one another.

I liked kissing pretty girls as much as the next guy.

I enjoyed their reactions, knowing I was the one making them sigh and shake in pleasure. I got off on knowing a kiss was just the start, and that things tended to heat up rapidly the moment our lips parted. A good kiss was like pretty scenery on the way to the final destination. An enjoyable part of the journey, but kind of forgettable once you got wherever it was you were going.

This kiss wasn't like that at all. This kiss was the start and end. This kiss was where I wanted to be. It was the start and the finish. There was no blurry view passing by in a rush. Everything was crystal clear, and I knew every moment would be burned into my memory for eternity.

The way her mouth moved on mine. The way her hands shook against my face as her fingers timidly traced the line of my jaw. The way the tip of her tongue flicked against the tightly sealed seam of my lips until I let her in. I didn't mean to relent, but there really was no choice. In all the years I'd known her, I never imagined what it would be like to kiss her. Now that we were older, and there was so much hurt and history between us, I couldn't fathom that anything like this between us would feel so... special. So significant.

I was supposed to be an iceberg these days. She reminded me of the times when I was full of fire.

She murmured a sound of surprise against my mouth as our tongues twisted together. I forgot all about being sprawled on the floor in the living room and fell into all of her softness and warmth. I wasn't one who lost his head in the heat of the moment, but if anyone asked me my own name right now, I wouldn't be able to answer. I forgot about everything—everything but the way she squirmed sexily and deepened the kiss, asking for more, wordlessly, as my hand landed on the rounded curve of her backside. I wanted more than anything to have the annoying barrier of clothing out of the way. I wanted to know if her skin was as soft and supple as I thought it would be. I wanted to see if she had freckles in other places aside from the bridge of her nose and if she blushed a pretty pink all over when she was turned on.

Never in a million years did I think I would have such graphic, dirty thoughts about my childhood friend. I'd always wanted to protect her in the past. Now, I wanted to fuck her. But for the immediate future, I would take kissing her as my heart pounded so fast I was worried it might burst.

Her teeth dragged along my bottom lip, and this time when her leg moved between my legs, it felt much more deliberate and provocative. She was not nearly as fumbling and innocent as I thought she was before this kiss.

The palm of her other hand rested on my chest right above my heart. I wondered if she could feel my confusion and excitement through my skin.

After pulling away for the briefest of moments so we could catch our breath, she bent down and attacked my mouth anew. Our tongues tangled together in a thoroughly aggressive manner, and her teeth nipped and bit playfully. It was a kiss that went from hesitant and careful to one that was wet and wanton in seconds. I was holding onto the curve of her backside like it was a lifeline, and I could feel the way her breasts flattened against my chest, her nipples hard, making themselves known.

This was insanity in the best way. If I'd known how good it would feel to have even a little part of her, I wouldn't have been so cautious to get her into bed to prove a point and take a stance. The plan had been to ruin her, not to be ruined by her.

But here I was, on the verge of being very destroyed.

Just as I was about to tangle a hand in her hair and roll her over so that she was on the ground and I was able to grind and glide, she suddenly pulled away and scrambled off me like my skin had sprouted thorns. I was dumbfounded for a split second as she bolted to her feet and hurriedly grabbed her fallen bag. She was at the front door when I finally got to my feet, and when a sleepy Vernon rounded the corner carrying a laptop, I realized why she looked so spooked.

I had no idea how she could hear anything over the sound of our breathing or the pounding of my heart, but she must've known we were about to be interrupted and ran rather than bumble through an awkward explanation. At least, that was the only option I was willing to consider. I felt the way she responded to me. There was no way in hell she wasn't as into what we were doing as I was.

I rubbed my thumb over my bottom lip and looked at Vernon as his unusual eyes skipped between me and the front door that Ollie just slammed shut. He lifted a dark brow and asked, "Aren't you supposed to be in class right now?"

I grunted in response and lifted a hand to my chest to cover the spot where Ollie had been touching my heart. "Why does everyone have my damn schedule memorized? It's like living with three moms."

I was harsher than the situation called for, but Vernon was far tougher than he looked. He simply rolled his eyes and made his way to the couch. He made himself comfortable while he did whatever he did on his ever-present computer. Hell, he might be taking over a foreign government, or even our own government, for all I knew.

"I know your schedule because we're family, and we keep track of each other. If I don't know where you are, I worry. As for Ollie, I'm sure she knows when you're supposed to be coming and going so she can avoid your sneaky ass. She's smarter than you give her credit for. You want to burn her so badly; you aren't paying attention to the fact that the flames don't give a shit what they scorch. Fire is indiscriminate, my friend."

I shook my head and walked by the back of the couch so I could knock my knuckles on the top of his head on my way out the door. There was no point trying to make it to the class I'd already missed half of, but I didn't want to be late for my next one. "She was doing the very opposite of avoiding me. Which you were about two seconds away from walking in on."

I wasn't sure if I should thank him or curse him for interrupting what had been quickly getting out of control on the floor. Either way, I needed a minute to get my head around how I was feeling toward Ollie. Aside from turned on and hot as hell.

Vernon just laughed and muttered, "Some people can't wait to watch the world burn. Be sure to let me know how those flames feel when they finally catch up with you, Huck." He turned his head and gave me a crooked grin. "Also, you might wanna wipe the coral lipstick off your mouth before you head to class. It isn't your color at all."

I swore at him as I pulled the front door shut behind me, furiously scrubbing at my tender and slightly swollen lips as I pounded down the stairs. It was annoying that he was the youngest, and yet had a history of being right about pretty much everything. He saw more than I ever wanted anyone to see.

Besides, I figured my world was already ash and embers, that there wasn't anything left to burn.

I hated being wrong.

CHAPTER 13

Ollie

I was even more rattled than normal.

Trying to concentrate in class made me so tense I was sure my shoulders were never going to unlock. Not only had the kiss with Huck made me feel ready to crawl out of my skin, but the change in Mercer's behavior and the fact she was once again impossible to contact would cause me to grind my teeth to dust. The only time I saw her or spoke to her lately was in passing when I showed for my shifts at her store. She seemed even more distracted than she was previously, and she wouldn't listen to my concerns about her alarming actions. She refused to listen to my warning about her problematic relationship; she even got mean and snippy and reminded me how clueless I was about love and relationships.

I wasn't sleeping well on top of it all. I tried to force myself to go to bed at a reasonable hour after studying every night, but all I did was toss and turn, ears straining for the sound of the front door creaking open and the old floorboards squeaking to indicate Huck was home from the bar. Some nights, I caught myself holding my breath as the hours crept by into the early morning. The later he came home, the more graphic my imagination turned. Half the time, I envisioned him hooking up with any of the gorgeous girls on campus who made no secret about chasing him. The other half, I remembered his too-pretty face covered in blood like it had been the night of the accident, and I imagined all the terrible things that could befall him on his way home. Sleep remained elusive until I knew he was back under the same roof and that he was relatively safe.

Tonight was no different. I'd given up pretending to sleep a little over an hour ago and was lying in bed reading through an *Introduction to Programming* book I borrowed from Vernon. Since I was still in my first few years of college and mostly worried about staying alive and remaining one step ahead of Sawyer, I hadn't given a lot of thought to what I wanted to be when I grew up and was finally free. However, now that I was using everything my mother left me for my education, I needed to figure things out. I didn't want to let her down. I wasn't going to waste limited time and resources. Plus, the technical words and phrases in the book were far from exciting and helped make my eyes droopy when nothing else did the trick.

Vernon had asked if I had any interest in computers after he roped me into playing some online game with him the last time we'd been home alone together. While I didn't really have any curiosity about the actual guts and mechanisms of computers, when I started to think about all the ways Sawyer had spied on me through digital means, I realized cybersecurity intrigued me. I never wanted any other young girl to feel violated the way I had been.

Stifling a yawn, I glanced over at my phone to look at the time. It was closing in on three in the morning, which was the time Huck usually came home. He always made it back before it was time to go for his regular morning run with Harlen. I didn't want to acknowledge the fact that my anxiety about his whereabouts was tied directly to a steadily growing jealousy when I thought about who might be keeping him out so late at night. I'd kissed him so I could have the upper hand. It wasn't supposed to mean anything. It was supposed to be part of a bigger picture, but I couldn't deny that I'd been feeling some kind of way ever since I'd gotten a taste of him.

One quick kiss with Huck impacted me more than the entirely unremarkable sex I'd stumbled through before. It felt better. It lingered longer. It was a memory I would do my best to hold onto, instead of one I actively worked to forget. He kissed me the same way he treated me ever since I'd burst back into his life—like he wanted to punish me and pull me closer at the same time.

I yelped when I lost my grip on the heavy book, and it suddenly fell out of my hand, bonking me on the chin as it tumbled to the mattress. I swore and rubbed the tingling spot, sitting up so I could reach the small bedside lamp. The shift of my weight made the book and my phone slide to the floor with a loud thump. I sighed, throwing aside the covers and leaving my comfortable, warm cocoon so I could retrieve my phone from where it skidded under the bed. Luckily, my paranoia had me check underneath the bed pretty much every single day to make sure nothing had been in my space uninvited while I was at work and school. The area was just as clean as the rest of my room, so I didn't have to worry about putting my hand in a pile of dust bunnies or something worse.

Once I had my phone in my hand, I lifted it triumphantly and let out a victoriously little, "Ah-ha!"

My small win was quickly overshadowed by stark fear when I caught sight of a shadow moving across the far wall. It was definitely shaped like a person. I gasped in alarm and immediately whipped my head around to look at the one window in the room. All that was coming in through the old glass was pale moonlight, but I could see the outline of the giant tree that sat on the side of the house softly swaying. Scrambling across the floor on my hands and knees, I pressed up against the window to see if there were any signs of life in the yard. I pressed my nose up against the cool glass and tried to slow my racing heart, dreading what I might find.

The yard was empty. There was nothing that would cause any alarm. The tree moved lightly, the leaves rustling softly in the late night breeze. For anyone else, it would be a calm and serene sight, but I was freaking out. I was sure that shadow had been shaped like a human, and if it didn't come from outside, that left only one other option.

I whipped my head around, jumped to my feet, and frantically scanned all the nooks and crannies of the attic room. I'd felt inexplicably safe since I'd moved into this highly coveted space, but now I felt like I couldn't get out of the room fast enough. I wasn't even going to take the time to check the bathroom or any other good hiding places in the darkness.

Clutching my phone like a lifeline, I bolted from my room and hit the stairs at almost a full run. My plan was to pound on Vernon's door; he was probably awake and playing video games. He wouldn't be my first choice to check out what was going on upstairs, but at least I knew he would let me in. Harlen couldn't care less about the things that went bump in the night, and there was no way in hell he was going to go out of his way to help or comfort me. His dislike of me was only slightly less apparent than Huck's. However, since he was a stranger, I was still scared of him. With Huck, I couldn't erase the kid who'd cared for me and replace him with the man who loathed me.

Bare feet slapping loudly against the wooden floor, I was ready to hurl myself against Vernon's bedroom door. Only, my momentum was brought to a sudden stop as I barreled unsteadily into a warm body. Strong arms immediately locked around my waist as Huck stumbled back a step when the impact of my body slammed into his. I'd missed that Vernon's door was already open and that the small, blond boy was standing in the entryway with a phone charger in his hand. I hadn't heard Huck come home. If I had, it would've been his room I was running to.

"What's up with you? Are you okay?"

Huck's deep voice rumbled close to my ear while Vernon's softer one asked, "Why are you running around the house in the middle of the night with no pants on?"

I was too scared to stop and think about what I was or wasn't wearing when that shadow came to life on my wall. I'd been in bed trying to trick myself into sleep, so all I had on was an oversized, vintage t-shirt and a pair of cotton boy-short panties. I was covered enough that I shouldn't really be embarrassed, but the way Vernon asked the question made me blush anyway as I reluctantly pulled out of Huck's hold.

"I saw something in my room." My voice cracked, and my teeth started to chatter even though I wasn't cold.

Vernon blinked his odd-colored eyes and exchanged a look with Huck I couldn't decipher.

"You look like you've actually seen a ghost. Why don't you go sit in the kitchen, and I'll go upstairs with Huck and check things out? Make yourself a stiff drink while you're down there." Vernon reached out and patted me lightly on the side of my arm. "I'll grab you something to put on while I'm up there."

As much as I wanted reassurance that my safe haven hadn't been breached, there was no way I was stepping foot back in that bedroom tonight. I wasn't sleeping in the attic until I had the time to go over every baseboard and light fixture to see if hidden cameras were watching me. I was never turning a blind eye again.

Swallowing hard, I blinked pleadingly at Vernon and asked in a whisper, "Can I crash in your room tonight? I swear you won't even know I'm there." The thought of being alone until the sun came up turned my stomach.

Before Vernon could answer, Huck grabbed my wrist and pulled me closer to him. "Wake Harlen up if he isn't already and go see if you can find anything strange upstairs. Call me and let me know if anything seems out of place." His amber eyes gleamed with an unholy kind of light as he glared at me. "You can stay in my room tonight."

Oh man. That sounded like the worst idea in the history of ideas. Right now, I wasn't in any place to argue, so I just nodded meekly as Vernon smirked and held up the phone charger. "Can't call you. Your phone is dead, and your charger is still at the bar."

Huck swore and glared at his mischievous friend. "Then come knock on my door."

Vernon's eyebrows shot up, and he chuckled. "If you don't think I'll be interrupting anything, then fine. What did you see, Ollie? What am I looking for?"

I cleared my throat and shifted nervously on my bare feet. "I saw a shadow. It looked like a person. No one outside could have made it appear on my wall. That room is so high up."

Huck muttered something under his breath, and Vernon finally started to look slightly concerned. "Okay. I'll make sure no one is upstairs."

"Those stairs are so loud. You would've heard someone coming from a mile away." Huck's voice was gruff, and while he was trying to be reassuring, his logic didn't help.

"There might be someone watching." I whispered the words and put my hands to my face to hide from the reality of how fucked my life was no matter how hard I tried to turn it around. "There could be wireless cameras hidden in the room." And throughout the rest of the house.

I knew I sounded like one of those conspiracy theory nuts. I sounded beyond paranoid, but there was nothing I wouldn't do to prevent past mistakes from repeating. That included blindly following Huck into his room when we both knew it was the last place I should be.

Vernon's eyebrows lifted even higher, and a slight frown pulled at his pretty features. "Oooookayyyy." He drew the word out and again shared a long look with the dark-haired man who was holding me close. "Hidden cameras. Got it. You two go downstairs, and I'll let you know if I find anything suspicious. Give me a couple minutes. Harlen is a bear to wake up and he'll be grumpy that I'm asking him for a favor in the middle of the night."

"I'm sorry." The words felt like they were ripped out of me, and I could feel the scalding burn of tears at the back of my eyes. I barely held it together when Huck's wide palm settled on the back of my head and pushed my face toward the center of his chest.

"If someone has been in the house, it affects all of us. We'll all deal with it." He didn't sound nearly as angry at me as I thought he would be for bringing exactly what he feared right to his front door.

I was a terrible, selfish person, and I had no right to find comfort in his arms. I couldn't blame him for not accepting this apology either. I was starting to understand what he meant when he said it was more about the person giving the words than the words themselves.

Huck barked, "Follow me." And it was just like old times; that was exactly what I did. Followed him anywhere and everywhere and trusted that he would take care of me no matter what when I was too scared to think straight.

I found myself holding my breath as he pushed open the door to his room, tugging me along behind him when I faltered at the doorway. The room was pretty sparse in terms of decoration, but very much suited a single twenty-something guy. There were lots of dark colors and electronics, as well as a big bed that looked like it hadn't been made in a few days. It wasn't anything fancy, but I knew the space had to be special to him because it was his and his alone. It wasn't something he had to battle Sawyer for, or an area that he was sharing with a woman who hated him. It was a place he felt safe—until I showed up and threw all that serenity and security out the window.

I stood awkwardly next to the bed while Huck rummaged around in a dresser drawer. A moment later, a pair of faded black sweatpants came flying my way.

"Put those on." He practically growled the words as I clumsily moved to follow his demand. "Why do you think there might be hidden cameras in my house? Did Sawyer record you?"

I shoved my hands into my hair and looked down at my naked feet. "I didn't hear you come home tonight." It was a statement meant to change the subject, but I should've known Huck was like a dog with a bone when he latched onto something. He'd always been tenacious and determined.

"I got home right around the time you came running down the stairs. I asked Vernon for a charger and was going to come see what had you spooked, but you moved too fast. Now tell me why you're worried about cameras."

It was time to admit the truth to myself... and to him. "I honestly don't know that anything can stop Sawyer. Even if he isn't a physical threat, there is nothing wrong with his mind. He's perfectly capable of finding others to do his dirty work for him. And his mother will always be there ready to back him up. He has enough money to hire someone fearless to get what he wants, and that makes me very afraid. I didn't think things all the way through when I decided to run to you. If he's put a plan in place to force me to go back to him, he'll hurt whoever stands in his way. He used to be afraid of you, but now, I don't think he's afraid of anything." I didn't answer his question about the cameras because the truth was humiliating, and I didn't want to explain how I figured out I was being monitored.

I was covering my own ass by leaving that mansion the first opportunity I got, but now knowing his might be on the line swamped me with regret. He'd always put me first no matter how he suffered, and I did nothing but put him at risk.

"I have to get out of here." I said the words without thinking, but in my gut, I knew it was time to go. If anything happened to Huck and his friends because of me, I would never be able to forgive myself. There was already so much to apologize for, I couldn't keep stacking the deck. I couldn't keep forcing my feelings and regrets on him. It wasn't fair. I had to let him go. "You've wanted me gone, and I agree. It is probably past time for me to go."

I expected him to cheer.

To gloat.

To taunt me with my misguided and failed attempt to wiggle my way back into his life. I was ready for his relief and a swift farewell.

What I got instead was the shock of being thrown on the bed, and the surprise of having his well-built body crawling up over mine until I was completely caged in by him. He put a hand on my throat without applying any actual pressure and used his thumb to stroke along the length of my scar.

The spot on my face was mostly numb. However, I swore I could feel flames lick across my skin at his light caress.

"You aren't going anywhere, Ollie."

There was no mistaking that his words were a threat, and I should be very, very worried about whatever was going to happen next.

Interestingly enough, being worried wasn't at the forefront of my mind as he hovered over me.

CHAPTER 14

Huck

I recognized the look in Ollie's eyes when she declared it was time to go.

I was intimately acquainted with that special kind of tension that tightened your entire body and made your heart hurt when the person you cared most about might be in danger. I was sure I looked the same way back in the day when I realized exactly how crazy Sawyer was and how much danger Ollie was really in. She wanted to protect me.

I wasn't having it.

She'd pushed and pushed until I was forced to open the vault I'd locked all my affection for her in. I wasn't about to let her disappear into the dark. I'd been there and done that myself and knew how tough it was. I knew exactly how awful things could get when you took responsibility for a tragedy that wasn't your fault. It was a game of what-if that refused to end. It was confusion and conflict that took up more time and space than it should. It was regret that held me back and made me question important choices every step of the way toward my future. Holding onto blame that wasn't mine meant my hands were too full to grab other opportunities that came my way. It left me feeling frustrated and angry at the person for whom I was ultimately willing to risk everything.

A few weeks ago, I would say Ollie was getting exactly what she deserved. I convinced myself that I hated her. I started painting her and Sawyer with the same brush because that ugly night was tangled up in my mind. Regardless, I wanted her far, far away from me because I knew when I looked into her chocolate-colored eyes, I would have to face the truth.

I couldn't hate her no matter how badly I wanted to.

I braced an arm above her head and sighed at the feel of her soft hair brushing against my skin. I used my free hand to hold her face still so she couldn't look away as I slowly started to lower my head.

I always thought I would be the winner when it came to the games she and I had played since childhood... but it seemed like I didn't stand a chance against her.

I decided to cut off any argument she might have before it started. She kissed me out of the blue first. It was only fair I got a turn to kiss her back. After all, everything between us was about balance and a little bit of give and take, push and pull.

She gasped against my lips as they touched hers. Her hands curled into the fabric of my shirt, holding tight even though she was trying to convince me she wanted to get away a second ago. I didn't pretend to play nice or give her any time to adjust to the sudden onslaught.

Since her lips were parted, I dived in, immediately tasting every warm, wet corner of her mouth. The kiss was a little bit sloppy and totally uncoordinated. It was much more aggressive than the one we'd shared while rolling around on the floor. She'd been trying to tease and tempt me into giving her the upper hand.

I kissed her to warn her where we were going. There was no stopping. No going backward. No more looking at each other and seeing who we were. I kissed her to show her I was fully investing in who she was now. There were a lot of benefits of reconnecting now that we were older. Changing the way we spent our time in bed together was just one of them. Childish naps and innocent cuddling still had their place. But heated bodies rubbing against one another and soft gasps of surprised pleasure were so much better.

I kissed her breathless and used my teeth and tongue to make her squirm underneath me. I wanted her to have no doubt that I wanted her and that a stolen kiss was just the beginning. I no longer saw my playmate when I looked at her. I no longer thought of her as the silly, selfless girl who crushed my teenage heart when she let me go.

No. She was someone else entirely now that I knew how sweet she tasted and how eagerly and desperately she kissed me back.

I lifted my head and looked down at her. Her eyes were hooded and hidden by her long lashes. Her cheeks were flushed, making her freckles and scar stand out. Her mouth was damp and glistening. Her lips were plump and tinted red with a rush of blood. With her already wild hair spread out around her head in a thoroughly unruly halo, she looked like an entirely different girl than the one I'd been unable to forget.

Ollie sucked in a breath and looked like she was going to launch into a lecture. I put a finger over her lips and lowered my head once again. I kissed the pounding pulse point on the side of her neck and let the tip of my nose drag along the soft curve of her jawline. She wasn't the most stunning girl I'd gotten my hands on recently, but she would always be the most memorable. Unlike those other girls, this one knew me on more than a physical or intimate level. Every single part of her was imprinted somewhere inside of me, making her shine brighter and burn hotter in all my important places than anyone who had come before her.

Plus, she'd liked me a whole lot before I'd hit puberty and transformed into someone others took a second look at. She knew me inside and out before I'd had a six-pack and tattoos. She'd been charmed by me when I was the outcast and didn't fit in anywhere. She thought I was the best when I had nothing. She'd had my back when she couldn't watch her own, so in my eyes, she was always going to stand above even the most beautiful face that filtered in and out of my life temporarily.

In fact, I couldn't remember what the last girl I'd been with looked like. Her face was a hazy shadow with no definition, but even after years and years apart, I could recall Ollie exactly. And now I wanted to see the expression she made when she came apart in my hands. I wanted to know all her secrets and the sounds she made when she was ready to surrender.

Ollie's breath came in short, sharp bursts as it brushed against the fingers I had pressed to her swollen lips. I tilted my head so I could trace the prominent lines of her collarbone with my tongue. She had freckles there as well. They dotted her skin like a sexy constellation. I couldn't remember if she'd had them there when she was younger, but I really liked them. I followed the path they left for me as the little marks disappeared into the collar of her oversized shirt. I'd nearly grabbed her and shoved her behind me when she came barreling down the hallway half-naked. Not that I was worried about Vernon getting any ideas, but the flare of pure, possessive jealousy that hit me made me irrational. It explained why I liked seeing her in my too-big sweatpants practically as much as I liked seeing her in barely anything.

I shifted my weight so I could kiss my way across her chest. I only moved my hand when I was sure she wasn't going to tell me to stop and come up with an excuse to run. I dragged my fingertips over the curve of her breast and the tightened peak of her nipple that was super visible through the thin material of her t-shirt. Even if she could come up with words to argue why we should stop, her body told a very different story.

She was shivering every now and then, and her hold on my shirt had yet to loosen. Her legs shifted restlessly between mine, and I regretted giving her pants. If I hadn't, there would be a lot of soft, bare skin pressed against me right now. The thought was more than enough to have everything behind the zipper on my jeans tightening and lengthening to unmistakable proportions. There was no way she could miss that kind of reaction since our most private places were pressed so closely together.

I used the tips of my fingers to toy with the tip of her other breast and watched as indecision played clearly across her face. Ollie obviously liked how I made her feel, but her survival instincts were still raging hard in her dark eyes. She wanted to stay but felt like she should go. It was a good thing I planned on taking the choice out of her shaking hands. Before she could get her bearings, I dropped my mouth over the same eager peak, leaving a damp circle on her shirt as I used my tongue and teeth to torture her nipple.

She gasped loudly, and her back bowed up off the bed. Her eyes finally drifted shut, and I felt the bite of her fingernails in my skin through the fabric of my shirt. Her legs moved involuntarily, and while she was caught up in the initial wave of sensation, I quickly moved my free hand to her midsection. Her skin was soft and warm, and her bellybutton was a cute little indent that my fingers skated over as they swiftly found their way to the waistband of her borrowed pants. It was always sexy when I first explored all those places that were so responsive and sweet. But it was even better when I got to tug my clothes away from her private places no one else was allowed to see, let alone touch.

One of her hands landed on the back of my head, and I felt her fingers fist a handful of my hair. She made a noise that might've been a protest—or possibly a promise of retribution—either way, it quickly faded as my fingers dipped lower and my mouth moved with more purpose. I should've taken her shirt off before I started to feast on her, but I didn't want to give her even a moment to think things through. I wanted her as unsteady and unsure as I'd been since she showed up and turned everything upside down.

She didn't part her legs to give my questing fingers easy access. But it didn't matter. Her body was honest to a fault, and I could feel the way she got wet and slick to the touch the closer I got to that sweet spot between her legs. She quivered, and I felt her thighs tense as her delicate opening beckoned with welcoming heat.

It was hot.

She was so soft and slippery wet.

There was something about having the actual girl-next-door spread out shamelessly beneath me that made my head spin. She'd followed me everywhere I went, and this didn't feel that much different. Wherever I touched, wherever I tasted, her body responded as if it were hardwired to react in the most pleasing, desirable way. I'd always wanted to protect her, but now I wanted to devour her as well. She had all my baser instincts firing and pounding through my veins.

Because she kept her legs closed, it wasn't like I could dive into her heat and lose my head as she melted around my fingers. Instead, I had to skim as I slid my touch along her silky folds, using my thumb to barely dip inside. She shuddered anyway, and I wanted more than anything to know just how fast I could get her off. She acted like she'd never been touched intimately before. Her response was so unfiltered and pure. I didn't have to guess if she liked what I did to her or how I put my hands on her because she couldn't hide how she felt.

I finally lifted my head from her breast, taking an inexplicable amount of pleasure in how high and tight her nipple was through her sheer shirt. The material was wet enough, I could see the faint raspberry color, and just like the rest of her, I thought the tint was cute and unique to Ollie.

We stared at each other in strained silence for a long moment. I felt her fingernails dig into my scalp and watched as a million emotions played over her face. It was a toss-up if she would push me away or welcome me in. I thought I might die if she picked the former. I wasn't sure my dick had ever been this hard or that I'd ever wanted anyone more than I wanted her. I refused to think that my desire might be heightened because I knew she could slip through my fingers at any moment.

Without a word, she suddenly shifted her legs, and my thumb, which had been gently stroking along the slipper seam of her pussy, dipped inside and bumped against her clearly excited clit. We both groaned loudly at the contact, and Ollie's dark eyes slammed closed in surrender. Her hips lifted off the bed, and I had to undo the fastening on my jeans because it started to feel like my cock was being strangled.

We were both still mostly dressed, and the lights in my room were bright. Somehow both of those things just added to the atmosphere. It was like we were doing something we shouldn't and didn't care if we got caught.

I kissed her again, mouth moving hard on hers, and I let my fingers sink all the way into her heat. Her body shuddered, and I growled against her lips at the sensation. So soft. So warm. Every little flutter from inside had me chasing that response with my fingertips. I put my thumb back on her pebbled little clit and started to rub slow, erotic circles that had her entire body moving under mine.

"Huck."

Lost in a haze of sensation and desire, I wondered why my name sounded so weird when she said it.

"Huck." I paused abruptly when I realized it wasn't Ollie crying my name out in pleasure, but rather Vernon saying it through the door in annoyance.

Ollie's eyes popped open, and a look of sheer terror crossed her face. One of her hands locked around my wrist and tugged on it to remove my hand from her panties. I arched an eyebrow at her as I continued to move my fingers inside of her. She made a high-pitched sound and slammed both her hands over her mouth. She looked like she wanted to kill me, but not before I made her come.

Luckily Vernon was smarter than the average goofy teenager and didn't burst into my room like usual because I definitely hadn't locked the door.

"Did you guys find anything weird?" My voice was pretty steady, but I almost moaned out loud when Ollie once again locked her legs closed, only this time, my hand was trapped between them. There was no escape. I stroked her intimately, fingers moving and touching every single part of her I could reach. I never let up the pressure on her clit, watching as her eyes blazed with black fire, and her back arched while she tried to stay quiet. I smiled at her and tried to concentrate on what Vernon was yelling through the door.

"Doesn't look like there was anyone upstairs, and no spy cameras that I can find. I know someone from one of my classes who can do a more thorough scan. He's one of those weird conspiracy theory guys who thinks the deep state is watching everything we do through our webcams. I'm going to ask him to come over and check things out just to be sure."

I grunted as one of Ollie's legs lifted and her knee brushed against my dick. It wasn't obvious if she did it on purpose or not, but either way, I increased the pressure on her clit and moved my fingers deliberately in and out of her drenched opening. If Vernon walked in the room, there would be no missing the slick, sexy sounds coming from the bed. I wanted to bury myself inside of her so badly, I could feel it through every pore on my body.

"But..." Vernon paused, and I heard a thump like he knocked his hand against the door. "Did you work on the stairs recently?"

I stilled, frowning, and dropping my forehead down to rest against Ollie's as she suddenly started to quake from head to toe. A warm rush of wetness raced across my fingers, and a soft sigh slipped out from behind her clamped hands.

"No. I keep meaning to but haven't had the time or a weekend free." And I had more important things on my mind lately.

I looked down at the girl who was glaring up at me. The old man wouldn't like this turn of events at all. It was supposed to be hands off. The thought made me grin down at Ollie. I wasn't shocked when one of her fists knocked into my chest.

"Well, when Harlen and I went upstairs, there was no squeak. No creak. No noise at all. I even ran up and down the steps a couple of times. There was nothing." I heard him sigh, and there was another thump on the door like he was pushing away from the wood. "Anyway, I'm going to crawl into Harlen's bed. This was a weird night, and I have a bad feeling. Don't send Ollie back upstairs."

I looked at Ollie and told her more than him, "Don't worry; she isn't going anywhere."

And not just for tonight. I also had a bad feeling, that odd tingling at the back of my neck that indicated shit was about to get real, and I needed to be on high alert.

Before things went any further between us tonight, I tucked her head under my chin, and wrapped my arms around her tight enough she couldn't get away. I didn't want to rush her, or give her another excuse to use when she tried to put distance between us now that she thought I was in danger because of her. "Let's talk tomorrow. We can figure out some kind of plan and you can tell me the reason why you're worried someone is watching you. When you told me you didn't have a choice about what happened before, I wasn't ready to listen." I squeezed her until she squeaked. "Now I am."

She must've been lost in her own thoughts about the situation because for once she didn't argue and settled quietly inside the cage I created with my embrace.

Whether she was playing the role of friend or foe, I was keeping Ollie close.

So close it would be impossible to tell where I started and she ended.

CHAPTER 15

Ollie

Sneaking out of Huck's bed early in the morning was easier than I thought it was going to be. After all, we'd been up late, and as Vernon mentioned, it was a weird night. He was obviously exhausted and had faint shadows under his eyes, indicating he was worn out, even as he slept soundly. It was also a piece of cake to tip-toe up the stairs now that they no longer squeaked with each step. I didn't want to think about the why or how behind the suddenly silent steps. All I knew was that I now needed to get out of the house and far away from Huck, almost as badly as I wanted to get close to him not even a day ago.

My heart twisted painfully as I grabbed a stuffed duffel bag I kept packed and stored in a far corner of the room. I wanted the option to run as quickly as possible if I ever had proof that Sawyer was an immediate threat. Logically, I knew there was no way he could be creeping around in the dark and lurking around the house, fixing the noisy stairs while we were in class—

146

he was in a wheelchair, after all—but fear ruled out any kind of rational thinking where my forever nemesis was concerned.

Obviously, I needed to stop making the wrong choices where Huck and Sawyer were concerned.

I had to stop being selfish and putting my own thoughts and feelings first. Huck tried to tell me from the moment I trespassed into his resituated life that I would bring it all crashing down, and I hadn't cared. All I could see in my tunnel vision were scenes of my own redemption. All I could feel was the first easy breath I'd taken since he'd been so brutally ripped from my life. It wasn't until I saw how spooked Vernon was, or the sharp concern on Huck's handsome face, that I realized how right he'd been that I could possibly put other innocent people in the line of fire. I'd already done it once to that poor boy from college, but he'd been a stranger, so the guilt hadn't been nearly as bad as it was right now.

I finally understood Huck's resentment and all the reasons why he wanted nothing to do with me when I first showed up. I was always thinking of myself to the point I could barely see anyone else.

From the jump, I'd been wrong. Completely, inexplicably wrong.

I never should have let Sawyer use my mother as a weapon against me. And once he started, I should've been honest with her about what he was doing. Maybe she would've left to protect me, instead of having me suffer to protect her. It was such a convoluted mess.

And I never should've brought the past to Huck's front door after all he'd done to leave it behind.

I hurt him, and he'd healed. Then I'd popped back up, because I had nowhere else to go, and was still as clueless and clumsy as I'd been at fourteen, and tore his scars wide open.

I was a really bad person. Even more so because I knew I would never forget the way his hands felt moving over my skin last night. I had no doubt the way he tasted was going to be a memory that haunted me until I died.

Mercer was correct. There was no way to describe the difference between being with someone just because, and being with someone because you really wanted to. Honestly, it passed through my mind that Huck was the only one I ever *needed*, but now, he was also the only one I ever *wanted*. He was the only one I was starting to wonder if I could live without.

Which meant I had to do what he'd told me to do from the get-go.

I had to get as far away from him as possible. I needed to make sure Sawyer had no reason to mess with Huck's life. I'd been using Huck as a shield, but he'd already taken more than enough bullets for me. If I didn't do something now, there was no telling what his half brother might do to him, or how badly I could hurt him inadvertently.

And I couldn't bear the thought of that happening. I'd done enough damage already.

I'd been so messed up that he'd been disowned and effectively run out of town because of me that I let people who had zero consideration for me take over my entire life. If something tragic happened to Huck because of my dumb decisions and inability to fight for myself, I knew I would never get over it.

I tried to call Mercer as I left the house that no longer felt like an impenetrable shelter. Of course, she didn't answer. The bad thing about keeping to myself was that I had no one to rely on when I was in a bind. I knew I needed to get as far away from Huck and his friends as quickly as possible, but I also needed a minute to put an actual plan together. It wasn't like I had a ton of money on hand to flee with.

I needed someone to talk to.

Someone to share my fear with.

Since Huck was out of the question, and Mercer was clearly dealing with her own issues, that left the only other person I currently trusted.

Mr. Peters.

He didn't know everything about my past or how I was connected to Huck, but he knew enough. I told him I'd just lost my mother and that money was tight when I first begged him to move into the Victorian. And even without an explanation, he understood that I was afraid and needed help. Without question, he'd taken my side when Huck tried to send me away. He was the only person I could turn to right now, but again, I didn't want him to be in danger because of me, so I had to make some quick decisions and hope they didn't bite me in the ass down the road.

I walked the nearly three miles to the older man's house. I didn't want to spend what limited funds I had on an Uber or taxi, and I needed the vigorous exercise to help get my head on right. The early morning air was cool, and it smelled like it was going to rain, so my steps were fast and furious as I tried to beat the impending storm. I called to let Mr. Peters know I was stopping by to speak with him, and was relieved when he answered the call right away. I must've sounded as distressed as I felt because he asked me several times if I was okay. When I told him I sounded winded because I was walking to his place, he ordered me to stop and wait for him to come pick me up.

I hurriedly assured him I would be at his place in just a few minutes and hung up just as Huck tried to call through. When I didn't answer, he called again and again. He eventually switched to sending me a series of rapid-fire text messages. Worried that his words would weaken my resolve to do what was best for him for once, I shut my phone off and tucked it into the back pocket of my jeans.

I owed him a proper goodbye. And I still wanted to say sorry and have him accept it. I would go to my grave regretting what I'd put him through when my back was against the wall.

He made sure he gave me an unforgettable farewell before being forced out of my life in the worst way.

I needed to be brave enough to give him the same consideration, but not right this minute. My body was still sensitive, and my blood buzzed from being stroked and kissed by him for endless hours last night. It would take very little for Huck to convince me to stay. Which was silly since he'd put a helluva lot of effort into getting me to leave, and it hadn't even made a dent in my resolve.

It took about forty-five minutes to get to Mr. Peters. He was waiting for me on his front porch with a worried frown and a cup of coffee. It took every ounce of self-control I had not to burst into tears when he immediately wrapped me up in a hug and hustled me into the warmth of his house.

"Are those boys being mean to you, Ollie? If they are, I'll make them pay a heavy price." He sounded so fierce and protective, I wanted to cry all over again.

Why hadn't I had parents who could worry about me this way? It would have made all the difference in the world.

"No. I'm not here because of the guys." I curled my hands around the coffee mug he handed me and looked down at the dark liquid as I blinked back tears. "I know I made things difficult and asked for your help to get into Huck's house, but I made a mistake. I shouldn't be there. I need to leave as soon as possible. I need to leave the state. I was hoping you could help me figure out a way to go as far as I can on the limited amount of money I have." I gulped and gave him a pleading look under my lowered lashes. "I know there is no way to legally break the lease and get my money back, but if you'd consider letting me have some of the advance rent I paid back, I would be endlessly grateful."

The elderly man grunted and took a seat across from me at his long wooden dining table, pushing a plate piled high with bacon, eggs, and toast in my direction. I couldn't remember the last time someone cooked breakfast for me.

The tears started to fall despite my battle to hold them back as I gave my landlord the basic rundown as to why I needed to put as much distance between me and the boys as possible.

"Let me get this straight." Mr. Peters picked up his own coffee and watched me closely. "You wanted to live with Huck because you were childhood friends who had a falling out. Things ended on a sour note, and you wanted to make amends. You also had a stalker. And now you're worried they followed you from your hometown, or hired someone else to follow you, in order to bring you back home? And you think they'll hurt Huck and his friends to make this happen?"

I cleared my throat and tapped my nails on the ceramic cup in my hands. "More than a stalker. And I'm not afraid he followed me; he's not a physical threat per se. But he's very, very wealthy and doesn't understand the word no. If he manages to drag me back to his house, that's the same as being locked in prison for me. No exaggeration. He's Huck's half brother. He's the reason Huck and I turned against one another." I blew out a breath and pointed at the scar on my face. "I got this scar because Huck drunkenly asked me one night which one of them I liked better. I should've lied and said Sawyer, but I just wanted to get Huck in the car and go home because it was late and raining. I was driving because Sawyer made me, but I wrecked the car and injured all three of us. He altered the course of his whole life because he couldn't handle hearing he wasn't my favorite, that he didn't come first in my life. He has issues upon issues and enough money to be a real danger to anyone who crosses him."

The older man didn't seem alarmed at all, which I didn't understand since my heart was racing so fast, I had to put a hand to my chest to make sure it wasn't about to break free. I kept my eyes lowered and leaned forward to set down the drink. I kept falling forward until my forehead was resting on the table.

"I think someone came for me because last night; the stairs to the attic stopped squeaking all of a sudden. And there was a shadow on the wall that was definitely in the shape of a human. And I knew from the start, when I disappeared from my old life, it was only a matter of time before he tracked me down. I thought he would slow down after my mom died and he no longer had her health and wellbeing in the palm of his hand, but that was a delusional way of thinking. From the start, his obsession with me is all that matters to him."

Mr. Peters slapped a hand on the table and leaned toward me. "Okay, Ollie. Let's roll this back a bit. I want to help you, but you have to give me some more information. What do you mean he was holding your mother's health in the palm of his hand?"

I got a little choked up trying to get it all out. It was never easy to explain, and I hated how weak and powerless the explanation made me sound.

"My mom was chronically ill. She had a bad heart. She was easily overworked and exhausted. I think that's one of the reasons she was scared to leave the estate. She was a legacy employee, so they never pushed her too hard." I sighed heavily. "Until Sawyer figured out that the best way to make me behave was by punishing my mother. If I did something he didn't like, he took it out on her. She was always in the hospital because of something he made her do. The night of the accident, when she heard all three of us were hurt and I was unconscious, she had a heart attack. No one checks on the help, so it wasn't until she didn't show at the hospital that anyone performed a welfare check. She nearly died on the way to the same hospital where I was. By the time I woke up, Sawyer and Huck's father had moved her to a specialized cardiac center and had her under the care of the best doctors money could buy. At first, I was grateful, but not long after, Sawyer's mother let me know if I didn't corroborate Sawyer's story about the accident and say that Huck was driving and that he'd wrecked on purpose, all the medical care my mom was receiving would go away. She was kept alive by machines at that point, so I didn't have much of a choice but to agree." I knocked my head against the table again. "I've regretted the choice I made every single day. But how is any fourteen-year-old kid supposed to pick between their mom and their best friend?"

I turned my head to the side and pushed my hair out of my face as I kept talking.

"For a short while I convinced myself Sawyer got what he deserved after the accident. He was injured in such a way he won't ever walk again, but I had no idea once Huck was out of the picture how bad things were going to get with Sawyer. He was always overly possessive and bossy, but as soon as he knew I felt responsible for him and his situation, he took total advantage of it and of me. I wasn't allowed to talk to anyone he didn't approve of anymore. I had to pull out of high school and finish my last few years at home because he didn't want me to be out of his sight in case he needed me for something during the day. I became his chauffeur. His chef. His secretary. His full-time companion. I was at his beck and call twenty-four seven. It was exhausting, and he got more and more demanding as I got older. By the time I was ready to graduate high school, he'd taken over every single aspect of my life, including where I was going to college and who I was going to spend the rest of my life with. And none of the adults who should've intervened seemed to care. I had no one to ask for help, and my mom was barely hanging on."

I closed my eyes away and clenched my fist on the tabletop. "His behavior toward me also got more aggressive and sexually suggestive as I got older. He started to demand I help him change his clothes and that I bathe him. He started to touch me and grope me and tell me all the things he wanted to do to me when we were finally together. I didn't get a say in the matter. I was scared to death, and no one would help me or listen to me. Every single second of every day, I wished I still had Huck. I missed him so badly. I stopped eating and could hardly function for months and months. I found out that Sawyer was always watching me, that he installed surveillance equipment in my room and had hired people to follow me around when I was at school day in and day out. It got worse when I went to college."

I finally managed to meet Mr. Peters's gaze and realized he was the one who now looked like he was fighting back the tears.

"The last time I felt safe, or like anyone cared about me and what I wanted, was when I was with Huck, so I tracked him down to get as close to him as possible. But I didn't think about what would happen to him if Sawyer found out we were reunited, and I can't let him get hurt again because of me. At first, I thought I could. I thought I could sacrifice him again if it meant I was safe, but I can't. I've done a lot wrong in my life, but I can get this one thing right before it's too late, so please help me."

My voice cracked on the last words, and the sobs I'd been holding back broke free. It was a lot to wade through, but it'd been even more to live and survive with my sanity still somewhat intact. My shoulders shook, and so did my soul. This was the first time I'd laid it all bare for anyone or went into detail about just how bad things had gotten. Even Mercer didn't know the nitty-gritty because it made me feel pathetic, and there were days when I wondered if I deserved that treatment because I was the one who chased Huck away and put Sawyer in a wheelchair.

"You hear enough, kiddo?" Mr. Peters asked the question as he got up and made his way around the table. His withered, heavy hand fell on the top of my head as he stroked my hair in the most tender way possible.

I couldn't stop crying when Huck suddenly appeared in the doorway of the dining room.

His hair was standing on end, and he was dressed in the same jeans and shirt he'd tossed off before falling into bed with me a few hours ago. His big body was vibrating with so much rage I could practically feel the heat coming off of him. And his molten gold gaze was turbulent and dangerous.

"What are you doing here?" I hiccupped my way through the words as the sobs wracked my entire body. He was the last person I wanted to see, and the last one I wanted to know the full truth of what happened after he left. "How long have you been listening to our conversation?"

"Long enough." He stepped into the dining room, and the air changed. "I called the old man to ask him if he had any idea where you would run when something bad happened. He told me to come over because you were on your way and sounded really upset."

"How did you beat me here?" I was gasping for air and frantically trying to figure out what I should do.

He shouldn't be here. He shouldn't be this close to me or care about what happened to me.

He was right. I was nothing but trouble and would only bring bad shit directly to his door.

Why didn't I listen to him before it was too late? Both then and now.

"I didn't walk. I got a ride. I had plenty of time to make breakfast and talk to the old man about what we should do with you. We need to sit down and talk, Ollie. About a lot of things." Huck crossed his arms over his broad chest, and I could tell he was pissed all the way down to his bones.

I dragged my hand across my messy face and rose from the chair. I patted Mr. Peters on one frail hand and tried to give him a shaky smile. I knew he was only trying to help, but he'd made things infinitely worse by bringing Huck around while I was pouring out my heart and planning my escape.

I nodded like a bobblehead doll and shifted my eyes toward the front door. Huck was bigger and faster than I was, but desperation often granted people supernatural-level powers. There was no telling how far I would get if I ran.

Hell, there was no guarantee he would even try to chase me.

Without thinking things through, or really thinking at all, I suddenly bolted.

I blasted past a startled Mr. Peters, and hit the front door with enough force to rattle my teeth. I jumped down the front steps and dashed across the immaculately maintained lawn like the hounds of Hell were after me.

I made it about two blocks before my only other fear caught up with me before Huck did.

With a deafening crack, thunder and lightning rapidly filled the sky as dark clouds rolled over the morning sun. It started to sprinkle lightly, but the sky sounded as angry as Huck had looked a minute ago as boom after boom echoed in my ears. I dropped down in a crouch on the sidewalk and covered my head with my arms to block out the sound. I squeezed my eyes closed and tried to stop myself from hyperventilating. I was still crying and shaking from the conversation that turned me inside out, and now I'd raced blindly into this storm that was going to be the end me.

I felt strong, warm arms wrap around me just as it started to really rain. I heard Huck swear as we instantly got drenched. He picked me up like I weighed nothing, his eyes not looking any calmer or kinder than they had in the old man's house.

He took a few steps back toward our landlord's house, but I stopped him by pointing in the direction of Mercer's store. It was only a few blocks over, and I would settle down faster in the familiar back room. I didn't take my keys when I left, but I knew the combination code to the electronic lock on the back door where deliveries came in. I barely managed to get half-assed directions out, and told Huck how to get inside before my shallow, raspy breathing ultimately caused me to pass out in his arms as he was yelling at me for being a fool.

Things went black quickly. For once, I didn't worry about what was going to happen to me when I was unaware and out of control.

Because Huck was the one holding me.

CHAPTER 16

Huck

I juggled Ollie's limp body as she drifted in and out of awareness and my cell phone so I could let Mr. Peters know I had her and would take care of her. It was tricky. Add in the sudden deluge of rain, and I was lucky I didn't drop either of the fragile things I had in my hands.

The onslaught of cold water also made the short trek to the quirky secondhand store take longer than it should've. By the time I got to the back door in a wide alleyway, I was soaked, and Ollie's curly hair was clinging to her face and sticking to damp skin everywhere it could. I punched the code into the electronic lock, getting it wrong the first few tries because I was worried about dropping Ollie on her ass. She wasn't a large person, but she was no lightweight either. She was built like a normal nineteen-year-old girl. Just like the rest of her, the curves she had were cute and just enough to be an interesting handful when she let me grab a hold of her.

I'd passed by the cutesy vintage store a hundred different times on my way to and from various places in town. I'd never been inside, but I knew many of the girls in my classes liked to go here for vintage designer clothes and handbags. I had no idea Ollie worked there, or that she had lived in the back room of the small store for the summer while she waited for me to relent and let her move into the Victorian. She'd been waiting right under my nose for a long time. I felt like a fool for not realizing it much sooner. It seemed like the earth should've shifted as if we were tectonic plates grinding against one another, creating a natural disaster when we were finally near each other after such a long time apart. I couldn't fathom how her arrival had been so silent. Or how loud her attempt to leave was going to be.

The inside of the cozy shop was warm and smelled like vanilla and sugar. It was cluttered with boxes, bags, and racks of brightly colored clothes. It honestly looked like a costume store. The few items I could see clearly looked like they belonged in *The Great Gatsby* or on *Saturday Night Fever*. It was all unique for sure.

It took me a minute to find the back room with the bed in it. By the time I did, Ollie's eyes were open, and she seemed to be coming around. She demanded I put her down, but I was worried she would collapse again, so I tossed her on the narrow twin bed instead. She bounced a bit and swore as she lifted a hand to touch her dripping hair. Her face went from scarily pale to bright pink with embarrassment in a matter of seconds.

"We're drenched." She pushed a soggy curl out of her face and wrinkled her nose. "Let me find some towels and see if Mercer has anything laying around you can change into. She has a washer and dryer set up in the bathroom. I can throw our clothes in to dry while we wait out the storm."

As she muttered the words, a loud crack of thunder drowned the last couple of syllables. Ollie shrieked and put her hands over her ears. She started rocking back and forth on the edge of the bed, repeating over and over again, "It'll be okay. Everything is fine. It's just thunder. It can't hurt you." She sounded like a little kid. It was easy for me to forget how young she really was because I knew how unconventional her childhood had been.

Like me, she'd lived enough life in such a short amount of time; it made us seem older and more jaded than others our same age.

When she told the old man how everything went down with Sawyer, I had to physically hold onto something so I didn't put a fist through a wall. The way he'd treated her and the way all the adults around her had acquiesced while I'd been around had been bad enough. The rage that filled me when I heard how my half brother practically turned her into his own personal plaything once I was gone was hot enough to burn through all the resentment and disappointment I still carried toward her. I wanted to punish her for picking him over me all those years ago. As it turned out, she'd ended up punishing herself far more than I or anyone else would ever be able to.

I never liked or trusted Sawyer.

I hated him after the accident.

Now...I wanted to kill him, and I had no trouble at all finding forgiveness for her.

I should've tried to find answers before now, but I'd been blinded by my own sense of abandonment. That wasn't a feeling you got over quickly.

I wanted to make him pay for every single dirty, twisted thing he'd put Ollie through. I wanted to expose him as the monster he really was, and I wanted to make sure he never got close enough to hurt the forever scared girl who was falling apart in front of my eyes.

I was more certain than ever that he was the one responsible for the accident that night. The only way he could finally have complete control over Ollie was to make her completely indebted to him. I doubted he planned on injuring himself to the extent he had, but I was sure he knew she would feel responsible for the accident and stay by his side out of guilt. And there was a solid chance his messed-up mind believed I might die that night and be out of Ollie's life forever. To Sawyer, the risk would have been worth it.

Sighing, I walked over to stand in front of Ollie. I put a hand on the top of her head, her wet hair immediately clung to my fingers. The curls were cool to the touch but still soft and springy.

"It's just a storm. No matter how bad it is, it will pass." It was true. Even if they were destructive and ruined everything of value, the worst weather eventually died down and made way for sunnier days. "Come on, let's get you dried off."

I didn't think my heart could handle her fainting on me again. Back at the old man's place, my heart jumped right into my throat the minute she dashed for the front door. I knew I could catch her and that she wouldn't get far, but there was no reasoning with the blind panic that overtook me. I was terrified. I knew I wouldn't see her again if I let her out of my sight, so I was relieved when it started to rain and she began to falter. However, as soon as she toppled over into my arms, my heart dropped into my gut, and I felt like an asshole for causing her to run away in the first place. It felt like we were playing a perpetual game of tag. One of us was always running away from the other, and the other chased in a desperate, hopeless way for reasons beyond our understanding.

I reached up a hand and pulled my shirt off over my head. By now, a small puddle of water had gathered at my feet. I was sure under the bed was soaked where Ollie was sitting, but she didn't seem inclined to move. I stepped closer to her, moving between her legs so I could get ahold of her dripping shirt as well. I planned to pull it off and wrap the blanket on the bed around her until I could convince her to climb out of the rest of her clothing, but all rational thought fled when it became instantly apparent she'd snuck out of the house this morning with the bare basics, which did not include a bra under her oversized t-shirt.

I wasn't prepared for the sight of her naked breasts, with their cherry-colored nipples puckered tight from the chill of the rain, to hit me in the gut the way they did. I sucked in a breath and averted my eyes, but it did no good. The image was seared into my brain, and my mouth watered, remembering the way she tasted.

I cleared my throat and started to step back. I didn't get very far. A moment later, her hands were on my hips, and she was pulling me closer. Her fingers dug into the fabric of my track pants, and her chilly lips landed lightly above my belly button. A full-body shiver shook my entire body as my hand slid from the top of her head to her shoulder so I could push her back.

"You blacked out like ten minutes ago. I don't know what you need to make things better right now, but I'm pretty sure it's not sex." This would go down in history as the single time I could think straight when all the blood in my brain was rushing to my cock.

She shifted so that her forehead was resting against my abs, and her hands moved so that they were wrapped tightly around me. There was a tremor working its way through her whole body, indicating she was still afraid, but her next words let me know it wasn't the storm that had her shaken.

"Is it because you know what Sawyer did? Are you disgusted that I let him get away with manipulating me for so long? Are you appalled by how weak I was once you left?" I still had a hold of her shoulder, so I pushed her back, put my other hand under her chin, and forced her to look up at me. She blinked and quietly admitted, "Because I am. For a long time, I was so worried about getting away from him that I didn't have the time or energy to worry about my own complacency, but now I feel it eating away at my insides. I should've done something... anything... other than just take it. I should've fought for myself harder since no one else would. I realize now that was never your job, Huck."

I grunted and used my thumb to trace along the line of her jaw. "It wasn't my job, but I volunteered to do it anyway. Maybe it's my fault for doing such a good job that you had no defenses of your own when I left. I should've done a better job teaching you how to handle Sawyer. He played us both, but neither of us needs to be part of his game anymore. Nothing about you is bad, Ollie. He didn't ruin you. All he did was make you smarter and stronger. You got away from him, and so did I. We won. Even if he never stops trying to interfere in our lives, we still managed to get out from under his thumb, and that lack of control will drive him crazy. Take the small victories wherever you can find them because you never know what kind of loss you'll be looking at next." I hoped I was getting through to her, but it was hard to tell. "And I want you to know, I'm sorry to hear about your mom. I know losing her was hard and you went through it all alone."

Her dark eyes were unusually unreadable and gave nothing away. Unable to resist her parted lips and the wounded expression that was simply screaming for comfort, I bent down and angled my head so I could drop a soft kiss on her mouth. She sucked in a breath at the barely there contact, but immediately kissed me back.

I still didn't think sex or anything similar was the best option considering her current state of mind, but it was near impossible to pull back when her tongue darted out to tangle with mine. Her actions went to my head too fast for my willpower and common sense to intervene with my good intentions. Plus, being chivalrous wasn't really my thing, so I was woefully out of practice.

Alone, neither one of us had been able to slay the dragon that kept burning us both. Maybe the key was staying together and fighting as one, so we were twice as powerful. When we were kids and attached at the hip, Sawyer never had the upper hand in our relationship. It was entirely possible we had to go back to the beginning before we could break free of the past. We could set the scales back to being balanced without his influence adding weight to either side.

I lifted my head and looked down at her, silently making promises with my eyes that I hoped to God I could keep. She gave me a lopsided grin, and I knew in that instant that I would move mountains and catch stars if she asked me to.

It was on the tip of my tongue to remind her we needed to get out of our wet clothes, but the words never formed because, again, her lips landed on my stomach. Only this time, they didn't stay still. She kissed a line down my stomach and stopped to dip the tip of her tongue into the divot of my belly button. Her arms around my waist tightened and pulled me closer as she adjusted her hold so she could catch the elastic waistband of my pants with her fingers. She might've run out of the house without bothering to put on a bra, but I'd left without pausing to put on a pair of boxers. As she determinedly brought the top of my pants down around my steadily growing erection, we were both suddenly almost naked in the small room.

I made a noise of warning because she was about to go past the point of no return, and I was still doing my best to be the responsible one in this storm.

She ignored me, lips moving lower and lower. By the time she reached the end of my happy trail, my cock was rigidly erect and pointing upward like a beacon. She had my pants down around my ankles, and her mouth wrapped around the width of my dick before I could formulate a real reason to stop her.

Her movements were far from smooth and adorably uncoordinated, but I was pretty sure I'd never enjoyed anyone giving me head as much. The inside of her mouth was warm and wet, and the way her hand slightly shook when it wrapped around the wide base was innocently charming. I felt like I was going to blow down the back of her throat before I could memorize her expression and all the questions she had in her eyes. I worked a hand under her heavy fall of wet hair and gripped the back of her neck in one hand. She was trying to take too much and move too fast for someone who had so clearly never done this before, so instead of pressing her further and trying to go deeper, I used my hold to slow her down and keep her movements shallow.

I grunted when she flicked the tip of her tongue along the sensitive slit running across the front of my cock. She might be new at this, but her instincts were spot on. That tiny little lick had my eyes roll back in my head and my knees lock so I didn't sway in delight. She bobbed up and down, finding a fast rhythm that worked for her, and quickly figured out that whatever she couldn't swallow, she could instead cover and squeeze with her hand once the surface was slick.

I felt like she was trying to undo all the damage that had been done, and I would have to let her because I was helpless against her tentative touches. I growled as she suddenly sucked hard enough to pull her cheeks in as she swirled her tongue in an artful circle. I could feel pleasure pulsing hard at the base of my spine and knew she was about to get a mouthful of cum if she didn't pull back.

"Ollie." Her name came out on a breathless gasp because she switched her attention to the heavy vein that ran along the underside of my cock. It felt like she was licking along with my heartbeat as she chased the pulse all the way to the base. I felt her fingers start to slide along the inside of my thigh and nearly lost it then and there. I clamped down on her neck harder than intended, and forced her to pull off the throbbing flesh she was licking like a lollipop. "We have to stop."

Didn't we?

It wasn't the time or place for where this was going, right?

Her friend might show up for work any minute, and I was still worried about how easily she collapsed earlier. Not to mention how torn up her soul had to feel after sharing all that insight with the old man earlier.

Instead of quietly agreeing like I expected her to, she suddenly pushed me back with a hand on my stomach and got to her feet in front of me. She clasped my face between her hands and gave me a hard kiss. She stepped around me as I was still trying to get my bearings. As she walked across the room to an antique vanity, she stripped out of her wet jeans, and I realized she was as naked under her clothes as I was. I should've bent down and yanked my track pants back up, but I was too busy watching her as she leaned over to rummage through one of the drawers. I had no idea what she was doing, but

I liked looking at her rounded backside as she searched for something.

She'd grown up well, and I suddenly understood why I never really had a type and why all women had their own appeal to me.

She was the only one I preferred.

She was the only one I picked for myself to keep and to sacrifice myself for.

She was the only one I'd tried to keep with me when I'd always been able to walk away from everyone else.

No one else was Ollie, so they just filled in the blanks she left in my life when we said goodbye.

"Ah-ha. I knew Mercer had these stashed somewhere." She turned and held up a familiar square foil packet. A condom. She'd been looking for a condom, which meant she was going to do anything other than stop.

"Ollie." I kept my warning tone as I pushed my hands through my hair. "Do you know what you're doing right now?" She had been an emotional mess not too long ago; now, she was playing with fire.

She cocked her head to the side and pointed to the pants hung up on my sneakers. "Take those off and sit down."

Stunned slightly stupid, I followed her command. After I kicked my sneakers off and ditched the pants, she moved forward, eyes intent on mine.

"Even if it's only once, I want to do this with someone I care about. I want to be with someone I know cares about me. Let me have this, Huck." She stepped between my legs and held out the condom until I reluctantly took it from her. "You said we don't know what losses are coming, so we should celebrate the wins when we have them. Let me win just this one time, please?"

How could I deny her when she asked me like that? Not that I really wanted to say no in the first place.

I wanted her.

I could admit it and no longer feel conflicted about it.

There were a million-and-one things we still needed to get straight between us, but for the moment, I could focus on making her feel good if that was what she wanted from me.

It only took a second to get the protection situated. After all, unlike her, I had more than enough practice at this. Maybe too much, when I looked back on it, but there was no redo button for the past, so we had to live with all of the faults as well as the things we were most proud of.

I caught Ollie around the waist and tugged her forward. She caught on quick and settled herself on my lap as she straddled my legs. Her thighs were smooth against mine, her skin still slightly cool from being wet for so long. She curled her arms around my neck and pressed her breasts against my chest. I could feel her nipples lift against my skin as I slid my palm down the length of her spine.

I latched my mouth over hers and helped shift so that she was hovering right over the top of my very erect cock. I could feel goosebumps lift on her skin as the kiss deepened, and her body began to move as if she couldn't help but try and find the hardness to grind against. Her breaths were fast and raspy, and her fingers dug into my shoulder hard enough to leave a mark.

None of this was the kind of build-up I usually preferred to get myself or someone else in the mood, but the basics of it, the fact that it was me and her, was more of a turn-on than any bout of prolonged foreplay I'd experienced. Having her skin on mine was enough to make me feel like I was going to lose control. The touch of her mouth against mine as I inhaled her and breathed out all the bad memories we shared made me harder than I'd ever been.

"I want you, Huck." The words were whispered, but I swore she shouted them because they were the only sounds I could hear.

"You have me, Ollie." Even without the sex and the surprise of her showing up unannounced. She'd always had me. Even when I'd convinced myself otherwise.

Since she was inexperienced and more hesitant than I would've guessed, I had to help her get into position and guide myself inside of her.

The first press of my sensitive tip inside her scorching heat pulled a deep moan of pleasure from the center of my chest. She gasped in return and started to roll her hips back and forth. The back of my knuckles dragged through wet folds and through silky moisture as I held onto my cock until she sank all the way down and I bottomed out inside of her. Immediately, all of her inner muscles clenched and squeezed the thick length planted inside of her.

I put a hand behind me on the damp edge of the mattress and bent back a little bit so I could look at the point where we were joined. She had freckles everywhere. Even down there. It was cute as hell, and just another reason she made me forget I was supposed to be a good guy in her eyes.

She started to move without any guidance from me.

She held onto my shoulders for balance and tossed her head back as she started to ride up and down on my cock like she'd done it a thousand times. Her body gripped mine like it would never let it go, and my cock was all too happy to throb and pulse inside her snug heat. I watched as she rose and fell on the rigid flesh between us, loving the way she sucked me in and covered me in silky wetness with every movement.

I kept one hand on her hip and moved the other to stroke across the crest of her breast. I palmed the full globe and rolled my thumb over the swollen peak of her nipple. She made a strangled noise in response, and I felt her lips land on the side of my neck. The nip of her teeth soon followed as her movements picked up speed and got slightly more frantic.

It felt beyond good being inside of her, but it also felt good to simply be close to her. To touch her. To taste her. Being connected to her physically was one pleasure. But being connected to her in the way we used to be, where it felt like no one knew me better or cared about me more, that was the hole I'd been trying to fill since I'd left her. That was the void that only she could erase.

"I feel funny." She spoke into my skin, her words drifting across my pulse. "What's happening to me?"

I was so caught up in trying to make sure I didn't blow before she did, it took me a minute to realize what she meant. I could feel her inner muscles flexing and fluttering around my dick. I could also feel a rush of wetness that was starting to flow around me. Everything intensified when I played with her nipple a little rougher than I had before.

She wasn't a virgin, but that didn't mean she had any kind of experience in what sex was supposed to be. I wasn't her first, but I might as well have been.

"You're gonna come."

She lifted her head and looked at me like she was in shock.

Her mouth made a cute little 'o' of surprise, and a second later, she let out a low moan, and I felt her body release all around mine.

Her shock was sweet, and her unfiltered expression and response were enough to pull me over the edge right after her. Overall, not my best performance, everything was too fast and too sloppy, but it might go down in history as the most important sex I'd ever had.

"I wasn't expecting that." I liked it when she was finally honest with me about everything.

"The sex or the orgasm?" Both were a bit of a surprise. We'd been friends and enemies. I never imagined we'd eventually become lovers.

"All of it, and you. It's an endless surprise." Her voice was soft and had a dreamy quality.

When we were young, the world was too small, too tight, and too confining.

When we got a bit older, it seemed too big, too vast, too scary.

GOLDILOCKS

Now, when we were together, everything felt like it was exactly the way it was supposed to be. It was a perfect fit. Not too big or too small. Not too hot or cold. Not too hard or too soft. Everything finally felt like it was just right.

CHAPTER 17

Ollie

I was still slightly dazed and a little loopy from the aftermath of all the pleasure and satisfaction that was still swirling through my blood. There was no room inside my body or my brain for the fear that usually immobilized me during a storm. Not when I was consumed by what it was like to be with Huck in an entirely new way.

While friends had previously been my favorite role to play, there was no denying that lovers had benefits I wasn't familiar with before our steamy encounter. I honestly didn't know sex could feel so good. I didn't know it was powerful enough to sweep away all other emotions. I didn't know it was going to let me see a different side of Huck and myself. We'd always been innocently honest with each other as kids, but there was something even more truthful and open about being naked and joined together. It felt like it would be impossible to hide anything from him anymore, and I hoped after today, it would be easier to read him. Staring into his gold-tinted eyes as his body moved with mine, it was the first time in forever that I felt like I was seeing the real him, the Huck without all the barriers he'd built over the years to protect himself.

He was still very different than the little boy who'd been my everything, but I was starting to get used to the colder, harder version of him. And I realized I wanted him to know the real me. I was no longer the wide-eyed girl who blindly followed him. I was only partially the shell-shocked teenager making snap judgments out of guilt. Now, I was more of a young woman who was admittedly scared, but determined to take control of my own life. I just didn't know how to do that. I was confused and lost, but instead of needing him to guide me like he had when we were younger, I wanted to be able to walk out of the fog that shrouded our past together—side by side. I wanted to be able to stand on my own next to him.

I wanted to dance in the rain, not run from it.

I was scrambling into my now-dry clothes, trying not to stare at Huck's bare backside, and he did the same. Then, I heard the backdoor rattle open. I hurried into the rest of my clothes and yanked my damp hair into a messy ponytail when Mercer poked her head into the room. Her eyes got big and curious when they skimmed over me and landed on Huck, who was just tugging his shirt down over his ripped abs.

"We got caught in the storm on the way back to the house. I dragged him here to wait it out. Huck, this is my boss, Mercer. Mercer, my roommate, Huck Snyder." The introductions were awkward because Mercer's look was downright gleeful when she turned it on me. I had no doubt she was filling in the blanks as to why we were both disheveled and fixing our clothes when she came in.

"No problem. I know you can't stand it when it storms. I'm glad you were close by and could take shelter. It's nice to meet you, Huck. I've heard a lot about you lately." She stuck out her hand, bracelets jangling merrily as Huck gave it a polite shake. She gave me an obvious and over-the-top look of approval over his shoulder.

She was literally just seconds away from flashing a cheesy thumbs-up sign, so I cleared my throat loudly to distract her before she could embarrass me further.

"Mercer took me in when I first came to town and helped me find my footing. She's the first real friend, aside from you, I've ever had. I don't know where I would be without her." I frowned at her. "At least when I can get a hold of her. That's been harder to do these days."

Huck grinned, which dissolved the tension that followed my sharp words. "It's good to find a friend like that. I've been lucky to find a few of my own over the years. They helped me keep it together when I wasn't sure what I was doing with my life anymore."

Mercer lifted an eyebrow knowingly and flipped her long, colorful hair over her shoulder. "Oh, I know all about you and your group of friends. I think everyone in this town does."

Huck cocked his head to the side and gave me a look out of the corner of his eye. It was clear he had no clue just how popular he and his crew were on the Internet but was willing to play along. "We're just a group of guys who had it a little tougher than others. We happened to find each other when we needed each other the most. We all think we're pretty lucky. Once upon a time, Ollie and I actually used to be closer than I am with the guys. We were best friends."

Mercer hummed a little and dipped her chin in a bit of a nod. "I heard you guys were tight. It looks like you're getting back to that. I have to say, I'm glad to see it. Ollie needs more than me to keep an eye on her. She's the type that seems to attract trouble whether she wants it or not."

Huck gave me a look that silently agreed with everything Mercer said. "That hasn't changed since we were kids. I got sidetracked this morning and missed my first class. I have a test in my next one, so I have to go change and get to school."

"Oh, it's still raining out. You must've been distracted and not noticed the storm is still going strong." She smirked at me, and I rolled my eyes so hard I was surprised I couldn't see the back of my skull. Mercer hooked a thumb over her shoulder in the direction of the back door. "I have an umbrella if you want to use that. Or you might wanna call for a ride. I don't have a car or I'd offer to take you."

Huck shook his head. "I'm fine. I'll run for it. Like I said, I'm headed home to change anyway. It doesn't matter if I get wet." He turned his attention to me. "Are you going to be okay?"

I nodded. "I'm going to hang out here until the storm passes."

Plus, I needed a minute or two to get my thoughts back in line. I'd gone from running away from him to having sex with him quick enough to give anyone whiplash. And it seemed Huck hadn't forgotten why he'd had to chase me in the first place.

"Don't disappear again." His tone was filled with warning.

"I won't. I swear." I tried to sound earnest, but Huck's look indicated that he couldn't decide if he was going to believe me or not. I couldn't blame him. It wasn't like any of my choices lately had made much sense.

Regardless, Huck gave me a final warning look and headed out the door. Once he was gone, Mercer turned and clapped her hands on my shoulders, giving me a hard shake.

"You really did it. You slept with him, and now he won't kick you out of the house. I didn't think you had it in you, Ollie." She smiled at me as she wiggled my body back and forth. "I think that very handsome boy might bring out the best in you."

I shifted free of her grasp and frowned at her. "I didn't sleep with him so he wouldn't kick me out of his house." I found the idea kind of appalling now that I'd actually had sex with him for no other reason than I wanted to. Silently, I was chastising myself for even considering it when last Mercer and I spoke.

I didn't want the moment turned into something that was tainted with cheap manipulation and suspect motivations. I wanted the memory to remain pure and untouched in my mind forever.

Mercer lifted her eyebrows. "Then, why did you? You aren't the type to jump into bed with someone on a whim."

I sighed and shoved my hands through my hair. The damp curls stuck to my fingers, which made the gesture look clumsy and uncoordinated. Which was pretty much how I was feeling at the moment.

"I slept with him because I really wanted to. He makes me feel good. He makes me feel like I matter. He's the only one who made me feel like I was enough on my own. It's hard to think straight around him." And he came after me, not once, but twice today when I tried to run away. I regretted more than anything that I hadn't done the same for him back in the day. I finally understood what it was like to have someone care enough to come after you when you were headed in the wrong direction. "He makes me feel safe."

And at the end of the day, that was the reason why I sought him out again and again.

Mercer clicked her tongue. "You might not be using him, but are you sure he doesn't see you as an easy target? Are you positive he isn't using you?"

I wasn't sure how to answer that. My instincts said Huck had no reason to use me or mess with me. In fact, it would've been super easy for him to let me go when I tried to leave this morning. But he had sharp edges and hidden agendas now that hadn't been part of who he was back when I knew him best, so there was always the possibility he was playing me. Even if that was the case, I'd rather lose to him than win with anyone else.

Instead of answering, I deflected the question back to her. "So, you've been MIA again. Did you get things sorted with your new guy? Did you talk to him about the issues you were having?" Her love life might be messy, but it was bound to be less complicated than mine. "You met Huck. How about I get a chance to meet your mystery man? You said he wanted to tag along last time we hung out." I lifted my eyebrows at her. "I promise not to embarrass you the way you embarrassed me just now."

She snorted and stepped out of the backroom, flipping on the lights in the rest of the store as she went. "I wanted to see how Huck would react when he was on the spot. That boy is ice cold, though. I can't imagine anything that would rattle him."

He'd been pretty shaken up when he heard just how bad things had gotten with Sawyer, but I didn't tell her that because I realized she was trying to flip the conversation back to focus on me. She obviously didn't want to talk about whatever was going on with her new man. It wasn't like her to be so secretive.

Her evasion made me worry even more about how she was really doing.

I shot a hand out and caught her arm. This time when her bracelets jangled, they sounded less cheery and more ominous. She pulled free and frowned at me. "Think you need to be worrying about what you're going to do and not worry so much about what I'm doing. After all, this is far from my first relationship, and we both know you have absolutely no clue what it is you're doing with Huck."

I couldn't hold back a startled gasp. Mercer never spoke like that to anyone, but especially not to me. She always handled me like I was something fragile. I put a hand to my chest and blinked, not only because her words and tone stung, but also because a loud bang of thunder echoed through the small building. With Huck gone, and with her being so defensive, all the fizzy, fun feelings began to dissipate, and my lingering fear of storms was starting to creep back under my skin.

I held up my hands in a gesture of surrender. "All right, I get it. I won't ask about the guy or your relationship anymore. Just know that I'm here if you decide you want to talk to me about why you've been acting so weird lately. You've been there for me, no matter what. It's the least I can do in return. I just want to be the kind of friend to you that you've been to me."

I yelped and did an embarrassing little hop-skip thing as another crack of thunder rattled the walls and windows.

Mercer sighed and gave me a look that I couldn't really read. I hated that there seemed to be this gap building between us that I couldn't figure out how to cross. "No one's going to come in with the weather being like this. How about I keep the closed sign out, and we hide out in the back and watch Netflix? I'll order delivery, and you can play hooky from school in style. It's been a while since it was just you and me on a rainy day."

It'd been a while because we both had boys on the brain, but for very different reasons. I thought I would never know what it was like to have my own life without Huck's help. Mercer seemed to have sacrificed her happy-go-lucky lifestyle for the new man in her life. Come to think of it, I couldn't recall the last time I'd seen her with one of her signature smiles that lit up the whole room.

While I would rather have been alone to weed through all my rambling thoughts, I forced a smile and nodded. "Sure. That sounds fun. You always make rainy days better."

Or, at least she had. Today she looked like she was going to her own execution rather than sitting down to binge something with me.

I guess it wasn't only me and Huck who had a change of heart recently.

CHAPTER 18

Huck

"Do you really think someone was in the house last night?"

Harlen looked pissed as he asked the question. Vernon looked concerned. Both ambushed me as soon as I walked in the front door, soaking wet and still reeling from everything that had gone down between me and Ollie over the last handful of hours. From waking up alone, to chasing after her in the rain, to realizing I wasn't going to be able to let her go again; it was a lot to absorb. It had taken me a very long time to get to a point where I finally felt like my life wasn't in a constant state of flux, but now I was standing right back on the edge of a cliff of uncertainty. Logic told me I needed to back away as quickly as possible, but my heart wasn't having any of it. My heart wanted me to jump.

I rubbed a towel over my head to try and dry my hair. I'd needed a shower to chase away the chill of not only jogging home in the rain, but also the one that made the only place that ever felt like home feel tainted. It felt like my sanctuary had been corrupted and violated. It felt like all the shadows had once again found their way back into my world.

"I don't know if someone was in the house last night, but if *we* didn't fix those stairs, and Mr. Peters didn't touch them, I think it's safe to say someone was in here tinkering around with things that would make it easier to come and go without being noticed."

Harlen let out a growl that rumbled from low within his muscular chest. "Fuck that. Do you think your brother hired someone to track Ollie down?"

Vernon scowled and ran a hand over his white hair. "But that doesn't make any sense. Why would he wait until Ollie found you to fuck with her? If he really wanted to mess with her or scare her into going back home, wouldn't he have done that when she first got here? She was all alone then. This guy sounds like a certified psychopath, but he doesn't sound stupid. In fact, he seems far from it."

I finished getting dressed and shifted my worried gaze between the two of them.

"When I tell you that Sawyer is obsessed with Ollie, I don't think you understand just how perverse and twisted he is."

I hadn't even known the level of his depravity until I overheard her pleading with our landlord earlier. I wanted to say that nothing about my half brother could surprise me anymore, but I was wrong. He hadn't just gone off the deep end; he was drowning in a sea of blackness and sinking underneath waves of unchecked mental illness. I was horrified I never realized what he was doing to Ollie's mother. I'd always called him evil and told myself he was a monster, but it was more than that. It was clear his wiring wasn't right, and no one in his life had tried to get him any help. He was sick, but the people who surrounded him enabled him, sheltered him, coddled him; they were the ones who had a special place in hell waiting for them.

"I think Sawyer was okay watching from a distance when she was on her own. He probably thought she would fail. I'm sure he assumed I would turn my back on her because it was no secret how hurt I was when she turned on me. Once she was under the same roof as me, I bet he lost what little is left of his mind. There's no way he could handle the two of us rekindling any kind of relationship. If he had someone watching her before and feeding him information, he would need to know for certain what was going on between me and her. He'd have to see it himself." Nothing else would suffice. "Ollie said he was watching her before as well."

Harlen shook his head. "We would've noticed a dude in a wheelchair hanging around. This is a small town and a tiny campus, all things considered. Ollie, especially, would be on alert for anyone who reminded her of Sawyer. She's scared, so she is extra cautious. She's jumpy as a cat, and I can't believe she doesn't have a neck sprain from the way she's constantly scoping out her surroundings."

I grunted as I shoved my hands through my hair. I looked out the window to see if it had stopped raining. I was planning on walking to class, but I didn't want to spend another hour wet and miserable. The storm had died down some, but it was still drizzling enough that I was going to call for a ride. The current conditions meant Ollie was more than likely going to stay put with her friend for the rest of the afternoon. I was relieved. I wouldn't have left the quirky little store if I thought she was really going to run again, but I was glad to have a bit of assurance that the weather would keep her grounded.

"That's why I'm wondering if I've been worried about the wrong situation all along." What if Sawyer wasn't as hurt as he wanted everyone to believe? What if he faked his injury just to get rid of me and keep Ollie on a leash? I tilted my head and gave Vernon a serious look. "How hard would it be to hack into a hospital and access medical records from around the time of our car accident?"

His unusual eyes widened as he rocked back on the bed, flopping backward, so he was looking up at the ceiling. "Not the hardest hack, but not the easiest either. You don't really think that guy faked it this whole time, do you?" He sounded bewildered and slightly scared.

He sounded bewildered, but Harlen and I shared a knowing look. We both knew all about the long con. One surefire way to fool all your enemies was to make them believe you were no longer a threat. Appearing injured and harmless was the easiest way to lure prey into your trap. It was entirely possible Sawyer had tricked everyone and decided it would be best to play at being partially immobile in order to get all the pieces of his diabolical plan to fall into place. Any kind of major injury would keep Ollie by his side out of guilt. It would make my father and his mother even more willing to give him whatever he wanted. He perfectly orchestrated the situation to keep Ollie tied to him and isolated from the get-go, but once Ollie found her footing and ran away, Sawyer may have realized he could no longer pretend to be weak and incapable. Not if he wanted to force her home. Once he found out I'd let her back in my life, he would have no choice but to act because of his bizarre fixation with her and his intense hatred of me. He would have to make a move, both figuratively and literally.

"I don't know if he's been faking this whole time. Maybe he was initially unable to walk and regained some feeling in his legs after I was gone. Who knows with him? He's impossible to figure out. But if we do a deep dive on all his medical records, we'll find out for sure." Better to fight against the enemy you knew than the one you didn't.

"Would your old man go along with a con like that? What could he possibly get out of it? I know he was a shit parent overall, but he didn't really go all-in on disowning you until after the accident. He did offer a bit of a buffer while you were living with that nutcase." Harlen dragged a hand down his face as if this conversation was exhausting him. None of us liked to take a stroll down memory lane. The path was not an easy one to walk, and only these two and Fisher, and I guess Ollie, knew how dark it could get on the journey backward.

I grabbed my phone and tapped out a message to Ollie, telling her to text me when she left the store and letting her know I was going to class, but Harlen and Vernon were home for the rest of the afternoon. I didn't want her alone in this house until we had a solid handle on how the intruder had gotten in and we boosted our security. Harlen was changing locks and adding motion sensor lights, and Vernon was getting security cameras and an alarm system installed. Mr. Peters gave his approval while I was at his place earlier, and he even agreed to foot a huge chunk of the bill for the upgrades. I didn't care if our beloved Victorian had to become a fortress. We would do what had to be done to protect our home—and everyone in it.

Ollie messaged back that she was spending the rest of the day at the store with her colorful friend. The eccentric shop owner seemed to really care about Ollie, so I wasn't too concerned about her being at the store without someone else looking out for her. It was actually better she was away from the house while the boys and I brainstormed our next move. I didn't want to freak her out with unverified suspicions. Not after she'd already tried to run. Her misguided attempt at protecting me and my friends was touching but foolish. I'd learned it was better to go into battle with soldiers who had your back no matter what than it was trying to win a war all on your own. She'd learn that in time, too.

I slung my bag over my shoulder and ordered a ride to the campus.

"I don't think my dad is aware of anything that doesn't directly relate to making money and protecting his reputation. If Sawyer wanted to fake an injury, his mother would move heaven and Earth to help him keep up the pretense. Especially if it benefited her in the long run. With me out of the way and written out of the will, everything my father has goes to her and Sawyer. When

I say my dad is rich, I mean the kind of rich that can buy private islands and the governments of corrupt countries. He could fund his own army and still have money left over. Keeping her only child in a wheelchair to keep up a beneficial charade would be nothing to her if it keeps me out of the picture for good. She hated that my dad took me in after he paid off my mom. I was a constant reminder of just how fake and worthless her marriage was. It made her livid that my dad defied her by bringing me into her home and ordering her to treat me like I was part of the family. She could easily buy off doctors and physical therapists, if need be. Neither mother nor son has much of a conscience."

Harlen let out a low whistle and shook his head. "When you said things were going to go sideways when Ollie moved in, you really meant it. This is some crazy, soap telenovela shit we're talking about, Huck. None of this sounds like real life."

I snorted and started for the door. "The three of us are very aware that sometimes the truth is stranger than fiction. We wouldn't have found each other if we lived easy lives."

Vernon was a runaway genius. Harlen was an abused kid who ended up as the only witness to the horrific murder of his mother by his father. He and Fisher found each other at the same foster home, from which they both eventually ran away. I was the bastard son of a billionaire who was unwanted and unloved. I barely survived that military academy I was forced to attend, and spent the years up to graduation enduring some of the harshest punishments known to man. All of our childhoods could be a made-for-tv movie.

"I guess that's true." Harlen muttered the words as Vernon suddenly sat up on the bed.

"Do you think we're all in danger, or is he just going to come after Ollie?" His too-pretty face looked worried, so Harlen reached out to ruffle his pale hair comfortingly. Vernon dropped his head onto the beefy football player's shoulder, and I watched as Harlen's big body stiffened.

It was my turn to shake my head. I hid a grin as I stepped through the door. "All he wants is Ollie. She's the one thing he could never really have. He crashed his car and nearly killed all three of us the last time he felt like he was losing his hold on her. So there's literally no line he won't cross to get what he wants."

And he very well might have resigned himself to being in a wheelchair he didn't need just to manipulate her guilty conscience and to keep her under his control.

One thing was certain about this fucked-up situation: Sawyer was the last person in the world I was ever going to underestimate.

CHAPTER 19

Ollie

They say practice makes perfect.

I was determined to be as good as Huck in bed. I didn't have his wealth of experience, so of course there was bound to be a learning curve. But I was over feeling like a bumbling novice while he came across as a slick and seasoned professional. I'd been following his lead and learning from him since I was young. It was only natural that I fell into the same habit now that I was older.

It might be weird for anyone else, but Huck took it in stride when I asked him to teach me how to blow his mind, as well as other parts of him. His only condition was that whatever I learned, I wasn't allowed to use that knowledge on anyone else. All his tips and tricks of the trade had to stay between the two of us. At first, I thought he was joking, but his gaze told me he was serious. He hadn't said if he was sleeping with anyone else while we were hooking up on the regular these days, but it was clear he didn't like the idea of me sleeping with someone who wasn't him. I was too chicken to ask him what exactly he considered our relationship to be now that he had welcomed me into his bed. I was pretty sure the fact he came after me and caught me the minute I tried to run meant he might want to keep me.

The last couple of days, I'd barely been in the attic room. I was still creeped out by the shadows on the wall when it got dark, and it felt too isolated from the rest of the house. Plus, the slanted ceiling was too low for Huck. He hit his head more than once trying to navigate the odd room when he decided to crawl into bed with me after his shift at the bar. The next morning, he woke up with a knot on his head and was fighting a headache. He grumpily told me to just sleep in his bed and wait for him in his room. At first, I didn't want to overstep, so I told him to call me when he got home and I would come down. But I found it impossible to sleep or study when I was alone upstairs, and I camped out in the living room instead. I was asleep on the couch when Huck came home, and I heard him grumbling that he knew how uncomfortable the old couch was when he picked me up and carried me into his room. When I looked at him after he laid me down on his admittedly much cozier mattress, he quietly told me he was worried about me and would feel better while he was gone if I took up his offer to treat his room as my own. He also mentioned it might be a bit awkward for Vernon and Harlen to have me take up the entire living room since neither had lived with a girl before.

I knew Vernon didn't care, but he was probably right about Harlen. I'd settled into an uneasy kind of truce with the stoic football player, but it was obvious he still didn't trust me, even more so now that Huck had sort of claimed me as his own.

It was inconsiderate to treat the common spaces as my own just because I was scared all the time, so I agreed to start spending time in his room when I was home and he was at work. I thought it would be awkward, but it was kind of like when we had sleepovers as kids, or when I waited for him to get home from school when we were teenagers. Only now, we did a lot more than innocently sleep side-by-side.

Tonight I'd learned that I needed to get a handle on my sexual prowess in the bathroom as well as the bedroom. Huck came home later than usual, looking tired and smelling like stale beer, cigarette smoke, and something a lot fouler. He mentioned that there was a bachelorette party that got out of hand, and he'd had to stay and clean up the kind of mess he didn't wish on his worst enemy. He wanted to take a shower before falling into bed, so I offered to get up and scrub his very broad, very tattooed back.

Of course, getting to rub my soapy hands all over a wet, slippery Huck in an uninhibited way meant things went from clean to dirty pretty quickly. Once all the soap bubbles washed away, I kissed my way down his delectable body and finally let myself explore those silver rings pierced through his nipples. The little noises he made and the way he tensed and tightened his hold on me let me know when I kissed and licked a particularly sensitive spot, so the journey to what was waiting eagerly between his legs took a bit longer than usual.

By the time I wrapped my lips around his rigid cock, the water had turned cold, and I was shivering more from the temperature than from being turned on. I learned pretty quickly that kneeling in the shower with water trickling into my face was a lot less comfortable than getting on my knees in the bedroom. I wanted to power through and get him off because, without fail, he made sure I lost my mind with pleasure every single time he touched me.

Apparently, I was too cold to focus and forgot the first rule of going down on him: no teeth. I shivered so hard that I lost my rhythm and raked the edge of my teeth along the sensitive rim that flared around the head of his cock.

Huck yelped in surprise and put his hand on top of my head to still my up and down motion. A moment later, he had the water cranked off and was hauling me out of the shower. He hustled me into his big bed, wrapping the fluffy comforter around me without even drying me off first.

He chuckled when I looked up at him with apologetic eyes and patted the top of my wet head, using his fingers to smooth down my soaked hair. The curls were going to be a mess tomorrow, but I couldn't muster the energy to care.

"The first rule I should've taught you: we both have to like what we're doing when we hook up. If only one of us is into it, what's the point? If you're miserable and just going through the motions because you want me to feel some kind of way, it's just going to make me upset. I don't want to see you suffer. Especially when you have my dick in your mouth. Do you get where I'm coming from?"

I saw him shiver and held open my arms so he could climb into the cocoon I made with the comforter. Once I had my arms around his neck, he fell to the side so that we were lying diagonally on the mattress.

"You don't seem to get distracted by anything when we're together. I feel like your entire focus is on me, and the rest of the world falls away whenever you touch me. I want to be the same for you. A little cold water shouldn't ruin the moment." I pouted a little, and he immediately put his mouth over my protruding bottom lip.

"There are a million moments. Good moments. Bad moments. It's okay if one or two get ruined. Another one will come along to make up for it, okay?" He rubbed his thumb along my bottom lip and grinned at me. "You have to stop thinking I'm always going to get everything right. I'm not a kid anymore, and the mistakes I make now have consequences. I'm more careful than I was back then, but I am far from perfect. Remember how mean I was to you when you first showed up?" I nodded slightly. "I have a lot to make up for. That's part of the reason it seems like I can't see anything else when I put my hands on you. I don't want there to be any doubt about where you belong, Ollie." His eyebrows twitched upward, and a smirk drifted across his mouth. "With me."

My heart skipped a beat as I lifted a hand to trace the possessive expression on his handsome face.

"I can honestly say I don't have any good moments without you, Huck." From the minute he left, life had been bleak and dreary. It was only now I was starting to see the colors and light in things again. It could be overwhelming, and I was so worried about disappointing him.

One of his arms struggled free from the comforter and reached for the nightstand. He grasped a familiar square packet and ripped it open with his teeth.

I shifted in his hold, throwing a leg over his hip, and wiggled closer to his warm body. My chest pressed against his, nipples hardening at the contact. I felt his hands move quickly and efficiently between us. He was still hard, and every time he moved, all my sensitive places brushed against either his hands or his erection. All it would take was for him to lean forward just a little bit, and the tip of his cock would be rubbing against my soft center.

Once he was situated, he ran his palm over my hip. His fingers skated over my skin until they hooked behind my elevated thigh and lifted it up even higher on his waist. He braced his other arm underneath my head, wrapping me up, so I was surrounded by his heat and his intoxicating scent.

Huck rocked forward just slightly, dragging the tip of his cock along my slick opening. I felt my body quiver in response. It didn't take much for him to turn me on, and as soon as he purposely used his hardness to bump against my clit in folds that were getting damp and hot, pleasure shot down my spine and sizzled along all my nerves.

I dug my nails into his shoulders as my hips started to undulate against him. My body had a mind of its own when we were together like this. My head always warned me not to read too much into it. My heart screamed that it had finally started to heal. But my body became a mindless, writhing mess that just wanted to feel everything and fall apart under Huck's talented hands.

He slid his palm up and down the back of my leg, which made me giggle because it tickled. However, the more he rubbed his stiffness against my fluttering opening, making sure to graze my stiff clit with each pass, the less I felt like laughing. It was hard to breathe as desire started to bubble uncontrollably throughout my limbs. I tightened my hold on him, moving my head to the side when I felt his lips land on the side of my neck. One thing I'd quickly picked up was that teeth on a cock weren't fun, but when they dug into the tender spots on the rest of the body, they were more than welcome. Huck liked to use his all over my body. So far, I knew I would lose my mind when he nibbled on my neck, and when he raked them over my nipples. I knew I nearly came out of my skin when he used them to carefully nip at my clit. He was better with the biting than I was, but I was bound and determined to get better.

I gasped his name when he started to slide inside of me. My body had just started to soften and loosen up at his gentle teasing, so it was a tight fit. I stiffened in response and dug my fingers deeper into his skin. As he worked his way in, the stretch and intrusion was a new sensation, one that made my breath catch and my back bow.

Huck made a deep, soothing sound and kept rubbing his hand up and down my leg, pausing to squeeze a handful of my ass as I rolled my hips instinctively against him. My body clenched down on him as his cock pressed deeper and deeper. Eventually, he was seated all the way inside. We were so close that there wasn't room for anything but sex and satisfaction between us.

He groaned as I wiggled in anticipation against him. Hips shifting eagerly to find some kind of relief. I felt full. Of him. Of Pleasure. Of desire. Of want and need. Of something that was probably love, but I was too far gone to give that thought the attention it needed.

"Huck." I moaned his name as he started to move with intent. He was no longer playing around or teasing me to get a reaction.

He grunted into the curve of my shoulder, and I felt his tongue flick against the spot where my pulse was pounding. I was slick and slippery where he moved in and out of my body. We were still wrapped up like a burrito in the comforter, so he didn't have a full range of motion and couldn't get as deep as he normally did when he pounded into me. The short, fast strokes were still intense and enough to have me move against him wantonly so I could feel as much of him as possible.

His hand sneakily ventured toward the crevasse that divided my backside. I went still at the foreign caress and felt Huck's answering chuckle all throughout my body. A moment later, that same hand found its way between my legs, and his knuckle brushed against my clit as he continued to move within me.

The light touch was playful and sweet, but it sent my head spinning. It only took a couple more strokes and the press of his thumb as he rubbed tight little circles over the sensitive nub to send me over the edge. My orgasm was quick and intense. It made my entire body go languid and loose, so I barely moved when Huck maneuvered me onto my back and started to thrust in earnest, chasing after his own completion.

It didn't take long until he was panting and pressing hard against me, his body going tight as he pulsed through his orgasm.

We lay still and quiet for a long moment until Huck's phone rang from the nightstand. It was stupidly late, so he immediately frowned and reached for it. He untangled himself from the blanket and got up to go toward the bathroom. I assumed he was going to clean up until he came back with a towel that he dropped on my head as he switched his call over to the speaker.

"What do you mean, you stopped by the house the other day?" Huck's low voice sounded tense and surprised as another rumbly male voice came over the line.

"I need my Social Security card for a thing at work. I can't find it here anywhere, so I drove to the house and was going to look for it in my old room. You never told me you rented it out. Also, I can't believe you still haven't had time to fix those squeaky stairs. I banged a few loose nails in while I was there because the noise still drives me crazy."

I sat up with a start and blinked at Huck in shock.

"Fisher, are you telling me you came in and didn't leave a note or any damn thing while you were here? Did you really not stick around to see any of us, but took the time to fix our squeaky stairs?" Huck sounded pissed and looked angry as he rubbed his own towel over his head.

"I did leave a note. I put it on the kitchen counter. I couldn't stick around and wait. I was surprised the house was empty, honestly. I had work stuff later, so it was really a quick trip. I'm going to come and see you guys on my next long weekend, I promise. And don't get pissy with me. You moved a chick into the house and didn't tell me. I couldn't even go into my old room and look for my stuff. I didn't want to invade someone's privacy."

"You son of a bitch." Huck barked out the words and scowled as our eyes met. "You have no idea what kind of mess those stairs caused in this house the last week or so."

"I was doing you a favor. You should say thank you, you rude asshole." The other voice scoffed, and I could see that he and Huck were close by how they insulted each other back and forth.

"I'm about to murder you, not thank you." Huck sighed heavily and sat down on the edge of the mattress. "It's late. I know you waited to call when you knew I would be home from the bar and that you have to work in the morning. I'll find your card for you. And I'll fill you in on the roommate and what's been going on when you make time to see your friends. It's honestly too much to get into over the phone."

There was a long pause on the other end of the line. "Are you guys okay? Do you need me to come back to town?"

I bit back a little gasp at the offer. These guys really were ride or die for each other. Their bonds were unbreakable. I didn't know much about Fisher, other than he was the oldest of the four of them and that he was working at some kind of development company several hours away in Chicago. The way Huck talked about him, I knew he looked up to his friend, and hearing Fisher offer to drop everything if the boys needed him, I understood why.

"No. It's better if you don't come by the house for a bit. There's some crazy shit going on that has ties to my past and involves the girl living in your old room. Like I said, I'll fill you in when I see you."

I sensed Fisher wasn't satisfied with that answer, but he let Huck end the call with minimal argument.

Huck tossed his towel on the floor and ruffled his dark hair with obvious aggravation. "Well, fuck. It never even occurred to me that Fisher could be the one who came in when we were gone."

He looked at me with a frown as I squeezed my unruly curls with the towel and asked, "I guess it's a good thing there wasn't a stranger lurking around when we weren't here. But I didn't see a note anywhere, did you?"

Huck shook his head and stretched his arms over his head as he yawned. "I didn't. And my guess is that Vernon and Harlen would've said something if one of them picked it up. It's all so damn weird. I asked Vernon to see if he could track down some personal info on Sawyer so we can have a clearer picture of what exactly it is we're dealing with, but he's run into a few roadblocks. It ended up being a more difficult task than we originally thought."

Huck yawned again, and I hopped off the bed, still covered by the comforter.

"Let me change the wet sheets. You need to go to bed. We aren't going to solve all our problems right now anyway." It seemed like every time we had a handle on what might be going on, the situation veered in a direction no one could predict.

I yelped when Huck caught the edge of the blanket and pulled me back to the bed, rolling me until I was underneath him. He dropped his forehead until it was touching mine, and I could see he was struggling to keep his golden eyes open.

"I don't mind that the bed is damp. It's just a little bit bigger wet spot than normal." He chuckled at his own joke and flipped us over so that I was sprawled across him. "For the record, that was a really good moment, followed by a really weird one. We're going to collect all kinds of moments together, Ollie. I promise."

I wanted to make sure he was comfortable and that I wasn't crushing him, but he fell asleep before I could get the words out.

I wrestled a hand free of the soft confinement of the comforter and lightly ran my fingers across the furrow that was still marring his brow. I hated that he had worries so big they followed him into his dreams.

Sighing heavily, I settled down on top of him and tried to believe we would have more good moments than bad, but with our combined luck, that seemed highly unlikely. He told me I had to stop thinking he would always get everything right, but I needed to get out of the habit of thinking everything I did was wrong. Those thoughts were a holdover from dealing with Sawyer throughout my entire childhood. All I wanted was to get to a place where things felt simple, not like a fight for survival every minute of every single day.

It took me a lot longer to fall asleep than it normally did when I was cuddled up next to him. No matter how right it felt to be pressed up against him surrounded by his warmth and security, there was always still that dark presence lingering outside of my consciousness, just waiting for a chance to sneak back in and take over.

CHAPTER 20

Huck

I grunted and tried to stay on my feet as Vernon plowed into me. He was a lot lighter than I was, so the fact he almost took me down to the ground with the impact was a testament to how fast he was moving.

I caught his slender arms in my hands and pulled him upright as he flailed about. His eyes were huge in his pretty face, and he looked pale under his naturally bronze skin.

"What are you doing on this side of campus?" The Computer Science building was a solid fifteen-minute walk across the campus, so I rarely saw Vernon when we were at school. "Did you forget your phone or something?"

It was weird that he sought me out in person instead of just shooting me a text message. But maybe he was trying to make amends.

After filling him and Harlen in on Fisher's ill-timed visit, and the fact that he was the one behind the fixed stairs, Vernon sheepishly admitted that there was something on the counter a few weeks ago, but he spilled something all over it before he looked at what it was. He tossed the note in the trash, figuring it was from one of the roommates and wasn't anything super important. Just like me, it never occurred to him that Fisher might be the one wandering around the house unannounced.

Vernon shook his head violently, which sent his white hair flying in a million directions. He sucked in a breath and looked up at me with huge eyes. "I finally found someone who could get into your brother's files and we figured out why everything was so hush-hush and encrypted. His medical records after the accident were just the tip of the iceberg."

I immediately went cold all over. Using the grip I already had on his arm, I dragged Vernon away from the entrance of the building and found a quiet spot away from foot traffic and other milling students.

"What did you find out?"

Vernon shifted his weight and wrenched his arm free. He scowled at me as he rubbed the spot where I'd clamped my hand. It was already red and angry. He was probably going to have a bruise tomorrow. I forgot how delicate he could be on the outside because inside, he was pure iron and steel.

"Sorry. I didn't mean to hurt you. I've just been on edge since we decided to dig into Sawyer's past. It feels like we're summoning a demon."

Vernon pouted, but I knew he couldn't stay mad at me for too long. "Everyone is anxious, so I get it. That's why I rushed over when I got the news." He lifted a hand and pushed his hair out of his wild eyes. "I'm not sure if it's good or bad news, but Sawyer Richman really couldn't walk after the accident. He has a T-10 fracture for real. His mother did try and keep his condition quiet like you guessed, and it looks like she had him participate in a whole bunch of experimental therapies. Until recently, they were exploring some really outrageous treatment options to try and help him gain mobility. It seems like she was the one trying to keeping the severity of his condition quiet, like you thought. But not for the reasons you thought."

I made a strangled noise low in my throat and crossed my arms over my chest as I considered what this news meant for my theory that my half brother was the one personally terrorizing Ollie. "She probably told my old man that Sawyer would be able to walk again. She more than likely didn't want to take any chances that my father would write him out of the will. She's obsessed with perfection, and probably believes my father would see Sawyer as irreparably damaged and unworthy of his inheritance if he couldn't walk again. Savage doesn't even start to cover it when it comes to those people."

Vernon waved a hand in the air between us and spoke quickly, in a low tone. "Well, it seems like Sawyer went along with all her weird treatments willingly, right up until Ollie vanished. As soon as she disappeared, all his normal medical records stopped." Vernon blinked and gave me an intense look. "But, that's exactly when his criminal records start. The reason I couldn't find anything was because everything that happened with him after Ollie ran away was locked behind sealed legal documents and court cases."

I rocked back on my heels as if a strong gust of wind had hit me. I was stunned. Sawyer was crazy, but I never thought he would break the law and get caught. There was no way his mother would let him suffer those kinds of consequences. People of their stature were supposed to be above the law.

"Sawyer got arrested?" It seemed so unbelievable. I couldn't get my head around it.

Vernon reached out, and now he was the one holding onto my arm so hard that I might bruise. "He didn't just get arrested, Huck. He got committed."

"What?" I mean, I said he was crazy all the time, but I never thought anyone else would take his mental condition seriously.

"After Ollie left, he turned his attention to some guy she knew at her previous college. Apparently, she casually hooked up with him and that's how she found out your brother was spying on her. He had video footage of Ollie and this guy together, and apparently, he went nuts once she was gone and tried to threaten this kid with the footage. He blamed the kid for driving Ollie away. He did not like anyone else touching her, and it obviously severed the small tie he had left to reality."

I interjected, "She left because her mom passed away and left her some money. She was finally free because Sawyer and his mom couldn't hold her mom's health over her head any longer. That guy didn't mean anything to her."

I wasn't sure why I was so defensive about it, but I knew I didn't like the idea of some other guy being the reason she finally broke free of my brother's control.

Vernon shrugged and went on, "Unlike everyone enabling Sawyer, this dude did not let Sawyer's obsessive behavior slide. He also comes from a well-off family and was not about to let your brother steamroll him or mess with his future by leaking a sex tape. He filed a restraining order. He pressed charges for stalking. He pushed back at every turn, and it looks like Sawyer snapped. They even got into a physical altercation at one point. But that might be what made Sawyer realize he couldn't win in a fight against someone who wasn't under his thumb. He tried to hire someone to kill the guy. Luckily, his behavior was so concerning, the cops who were handling all the complaints against Sawyer knew something like that might happen. It was obvious your brother was unhinged. Also, because the other guy came from money, they couldn't look the other way. His parents were just as influential as Sawyer's mom and your dad. They set a trap, and your brother fell right into it. The hitman he found to kill the guy was an undercover cop. They were going to arrest him, at the very least, on conspiracy to commit murder. It looks like his mom stepped in and tried to bribe the law enforcement officers involved in the case, so she ended up in some hot water too. Sawyer tried to commit suicide before they could take him into custody. For the most part, all of this is buried in redacted court documents, but the trail is bananas when you start to follow it."

"What the fuck?" The exclamation burst out way louder than I intended. Several students walking by stopped to give me and Vernon questioning looks. "No way he tried to kill himself. He wouldn't see Ollie again if he succeeded, and that's the only thing he's ever cared about."

"He took a full bottle of pills and chased it with stupidly expensive cognac." Vernon shook his head again and shifted his backpack straps on his shoulders. "Instead of putting him through a full jury trial where he would plead temporary insanity and likely win, the prosecutor in charge of the case agreed to send Sawyer to a state psychiatric facility for long-term treatment. He's on a permanent suicide watch and has to undergo intensive therapy sessions. He won't get out for at least a decade. It's impossible that he followed Ollie here and highly unlikely he paid for someone to bring her back."

I dragged a hand over my face and exhaled slowly. "I can't believe this. How is it possible he went from the boogeyman to being harmless in the blink of an eye?" And how come I hadn't heard a word about what was going on back at home? It wasn't like I checked in on anyone from my past, but it seemed like something as huge as this should be on my radar. "I can't tell if this is good news or bad news, if I'm honest."

And what about Ollie?

Was she just so traumatized from the past that it was all in her head that someone was after her? Had she simply been afraid of Sawyer for so long that she didn't know he was no longer a shadow lurking over her every move?

I was confused and pissed off by this new information. I hated the feeling of certainty slipping away as the unknown once again overtook everything.

Vernon sounded sympathetic as he told me, "I dunno either. I think you tell Ollie what's going on and let her figure out how she feels first, and then we just follow her lead. If she's relieved he's locked away and it can't be him, then we follow suit. If she seems even more freaked out and is still worried about someone trying to make her go back, we go from there. The priority is making sure she knows she's safe no matter what."

I lifted a finger to my lips and made a shushing sound as a familiar head of curly blond hair separated from the other students and made its way in our direction.

Ollie gave a little finger wave that Vernon returned. Low, under his breath, he muttered, "We're keeping her. She's one of us now. We can't let anyone hurt her anymore, even if the culprit is Ollie herself."

I nodded in agreement and reached out an arm to pull her close when she was within touching distance. She fit against my side like she was custom-made to be there.

"You're so far away from the technology building, Vernon. What's going on? Are you okay?" Her dark eyes were full of curiosity. She made a startled sound when Vernon suddenly lunged toward her and wrapped her up in a hug so that she was trapped between him and me.

"Everything is going to be fine. I promise." Vernon let her go and flipped his hair out of his eyes with a sassy toss of his head. "You fill Ollie in. I'm going to find Harlen and give him a rundown. I haven't been over to the athletic department in a long time. I should be better about checking up on him and making sure his teammates are treating him well."

Ollie watched him slip away with a bemused expression on her face, then turned to look at me with a million questions in her eyes.

"Let's talk when we get back to the house." It wouldn't change anything if I unloaded everything on her right now. She still had classes to get through this afternoon. Her world was about to go topsy-turvy. It was better she heard about all the changes when she was somewhere safe and could process them. I still felt a little like I'd been sucker-punched, so it would serve no purpose for both of us to feel that way.

She leaned more heavily into my side and lifted a hand to hold my jaw. She turned my face so we were looking at each other. One day I was going to figure out all the secrets she kept hidden in those dark eyes.

"I'm going to ask you something, and I want you to tell me if I sound irrational." She frowned a little bit as she rubbed her thumb over the curve of my bottom lip.

"All right. If you sound crazy, I will let you know." It would be hard for her to come close to that, considering what I'd just heard.

Ollie cleared her throat, and the hand she had wrapped around my waist clutched at the fabric of my t-shirt. I could tell she was trying to make light of whatever was weighing on her mind, but it really was bothering her.

"I haven't heard from Mercer in a couple of days. It's nothing new. She's been acting weird since she started seeing this guy, and she's the type to fall in love fast and hard. But she won't let me meet him. She gets super touchy whenever I bring up how weird their relationship seems. She's so defensive where he's concerned. At first, I just figured she really liked him and was being extra protective, but now," she frowned, and her fingers tightened their hold on my face. "I'm wondering if she might be caught up in something that has to do with me. What if the guy she's seeing has ties to Sawyer? What if Sawyer paid someone to get close to Mercer so he could keep tabs on me? I didn't want to worry her with that speculation, but the longer the relationship goes on, and the stranger her behavior becomes, the more worried I get." She gave me a doe-eyed look that made me want to move mountains for her. "You know, now that I think about it, I don't even know his name. She's never mentioned and I was too caught up in my own stuff to ask. I want to find out who she's seeing. Since she won't give me any information, I'll have to resort to being sneaky. But after having Sawyer creep through my whole life, I think I sound nuts. I don't want to be like him."

I sighed and bent to drop a kiss on her forehead. Easy affection was something I'd only ever been able to share with her. It came back to me the minute I held her in my arms once again. It was like all the time I'd tried to forget her was forgotten. My body and my heart knew where she belonged.

"No. You sound like a concerned friend. Not an obsessed lunatic." I shifted so I could kiss the tip of her nose, lifting my head when I heard sounds of surprise from a group of girls walking past us. It looked like word that I was seeing someone was bound to make it around campus sooner rather than later. "What are you planning to do?"

"I don't actually have a plan. But, she always leaves her phone laying around, and it doesn't have a password or lock screen. I thought about taking a peek at when and where their next date is and show up unexpectedly. Or look for photos of them or details about him so that maybe Vernon could help me dig up more digital details. I have a bad feeling about the relationship, and it only intensifies the longer Mercer is involved with him and the longer she keeps him a secret."

I grunted in response and grabbed her hand to tug her after me as I headed toward her next class. Ollie was the only girl I'd ever walked to class. "Crashing her date is a bit extreme, but as long as it's a public place with a lot of people, and you don't go alone, I think you'd be okay. You have to resign yourself to the fact that Mercer might get very angry with you. You might be risking not only your job, but your friendship, and I know she means a lot to you."

"I can't be friends with her if something terrible happens to her. There are a lot of red flags about her behavior lately. I can't ignore them."

I squeezed her hand reassuringly. She might reevaluate her concern once she had the whole picture of what happened with my half brother. "Let me know what you need from me or the boys. We're here for you. No matter what."

Vernon was right. We had to keep her safe, even from herself. After everything she'd been through, she might be her own worst enemy.

Briefly, I was really jealous of the guy she lured in to test Sawyer. Not only because he'd been her first, but because he was the one who finally made my half brother pay for his actions. In a perfect world, I would be the one who sent Sawyer far, far away from both of us. I should've been the one who helped her become unreachable.

But when had my world ever been perfect?

Instead, I'd learned to thrive within imperfection. To embrace it. To adapt to it. And now, as broken and damaged as Ollie was, like our battered, ever-changing relationship, I'd learned to love it. Our imperfection was a perfect fit.

The pursuit of his idea of perfection had driven my brother mad.

CHAPTER 21

Ollie

"**Y**ou look ridiculous. At least take the sunglasses off. It's nighttime and we're inside, for God's sake."

I turned my head and made a face at Vernon. Not that he could see it clearly since I had one of Huck's baseball hats pulled down low on my forehead, and my eyes were covered with dark, mirrored sunglasses. I had on Huck's leather jacket, which was way too big for me, and all of my curly hair was braided and tucked down the collar. It wasn't a CIA-level disguise by any means, but it was good enough that when Mercer walked to the table in the dimly lit Italian restaurant where she was supposed to meet her date, she didn't even spare me a glance.

Vernon still stood out like a sore thumb, but the only way Huck would let me out of the house to follow through on my crazy plan was if I agreed to take him with me. Huck didn't want me to go at all. He'd been called into work to cover a shift and wanted me to wait until he was free, but I was worried about waiting any longer. Mercer just happened to mention this date in passing while we switched shifts at the shop, so I didn't even have to invade her privacy and look at her phone to figure out what she was up to. I jumped at the chance to stake out her date and figure out what was going on with her secretive lover, even if I might cross several friendship boundaries.

I took off the sunglasses and wrinkled my nose at the pretty, young boy sitting across the table. He wasn't thrilled to be here, but he'd come after I begged and Huck threatened. I could tell he was uneasy, but I had a feeling it didn't have much to do with this crazy scheme of mine.

Vernon sighed, and the front part of his white hair fluttered over his forehead. "I still don't really understand why you're so suspicious. So what if she doesn't want to talk about the guy she's seeing and doesn't want to introduce you? Maybe he's just a private person. Maybe he's married, and she doesn't want to tell you. I think you're jumping to conclusions because of your own history with toxic relationships. Not everyone attracts trouble the way you do."

He smirked at me as he reached for a breadstick in the middle of the table. The basket was practically overflowing because our waiter took one look at Vernon and fell in love. He was extra attentive, even though Vernon seemed oblivious to his interest.

I tugged the bill of the hat down lower on my face as I watched each and every man who passed by the table with suspicious eyes. So far, Mercer had been at the table alone for several minutes. She kept looking down at her phone, but she didn't act like waiting for her date was anything new.

"My history with toxic relationships is exactly why I'm worried. What if the guy has ties to Sawyer? It wouldn't be the first time he manipulated his way into my life through someone I was close to."

Vernon suddenly hacked and then started to clear his throat like he was choking. Almost immediately, the smitten waiter was tableside handing over a glass of water and asking if everything was okay. Vernon waved him off and gulped the water as I hid behind the menu just in case the commotion drew Mercer's attention in our direction.

I peeked around the edge of the menu as Vernon hissed, "I can't believe Huck hasn't told you everything."

I blinked in surprise at the irritation in his voice and slowly lowered the menu so I could meet his angry gaze.

"Huck hasn't told me everything about what?"

Vernon averted his gaze and shook his head slightly. "Never mind. But I seriously doubt this guy is dating your friend because Sawyer ordered it. Whatever Huck is keeping to himself is just because he has your best interest in mind, and he wants you to remain as vigilant as you've always been."

I was under the impression that Huck and I had moved past the point of making decisions for one another. We were supposed to share everything and stay on the same page so we didn't end up back where we'd been when all we did was misunderstand each other. It was possible to do the wrong thing for the right reasons, which didn't mean someone wasn't going to get hurt anyway.

I didn't need Huck hiding things from me for my own good.

I didn't have time to delve too deeply into these thoughts, because just as the bouncy waiter stepped to the table, a tall, dark-haired man walked behind him and headed purposely toward Mercer's table. I instantly recognized him.

I felt my jaw practically unhinge, and my breath froze in my lungs. I blinked a couple times, even rubbed my eyes to make sure I wasn't hallucinating. If only I'd asked his name, if I pushed Mercer harder for more information, I wouldn't have been so blindsided right now.

I thought I was prepared. I thought I'd braced myself. I told myself Mercer's change in behavior and the secrecy *had* to have something to do with my past, and I was right.

But I never in a million years would've guessed that the man my best friend was seeing was the same one I'd befriended my freshman year of college. The one I took home and dangled on the end of a string like a puppet just to see how far my nemesis would go.

Jack Darling was supposed to be a one-night stand and nothing more than a means to an end. He definitely wasn't supposed to be here in my new life. He wasn't as scary as Sawyer, but just about as welcome.

For the life of me, I couldn't figure out why Jack was *here* and on a date with my new best friend.

Vernon reached across the table and silently tapped my chin so I would close my mouth. I blinked at him and put both my hands on the top of the table, torn between running across the restaurant and pulling Mercer away from that man, or running out the front door. That was how I usually handled baggage from my past. It was always a mess I hated to clean up.

"I take it you know him?" Vernon's pierced eyebrow lifted and a frown pulled at his mouth. He typed something on his phone, and I knew without asking that he was letting Huck know I was on the verge of a freakout and that I definitely recognized the guy with Mercer.

"Just a little. He was my friend from school and a little more." I gulped and clenched my shaking hands into fists. "We flirted a bit and hooked up once, but it wasn't anything serious. I knew going in that Sawyer wasn't going to let another guy get close to me. I was pretty sure I was never going to see him again after he found out Sawyer had secretly recorded us when we were together. He didn't take Sawyer's threats well. Him being here can't be a simple coincidence." Especially if he was treating Mercer like garbage and purposely trying to isolate her from me.

Vernon put one of his hands over mine and gave a gentle squeeze to remind me that we were in public.

"What do you want to do? Confront him? Continue to follow them? We never talked about the endgame."

"I... I don't know. I want to know why he's here. I don't want to hurt or embarrass Mercer. She's one of the few people who has unconditionally had my back with no questions asked. I was so worried about Sawyer, it never occurred to me there were other people out there who might have something against me." I did drag this guy into a sticky situation, and he was yet another rich kid whose status and image apparently mattered more than basic human decency.

Vernon watched the couple over his shoulder as I kept my head down and tried to work out what I should do next. I should've listened to Huck's warning about this plan, possibly costing me more than I was willing to lose.

"Ohh…" Vernon tapped my hand frantically to get my attention. "Your girl is getting up and going to the bathroom. That only gives you a minute or two if you want to talk to that guy alone, but I can go and try and distract her for a little longer." His unusual eyes watched mine carefully. "Or we can slip out now, and you can figure out how you want to approach her later. Either way, this is our only window to do something unnoticed."

I nodded and pulled in a deep breath. "I'm going to talk to him."

I waited until Mercer's colorful hair was totally out of sight before I got up and walked toward the table.

I heard Vernon mutter, "Good luck."

He also got up and hurried in the direction of my friend. I could hear an invisible clock ticking in my mind as I took the empty seat across from the young man I never expected to see again.

I used a finger to push up the bill of my hat, but Jack didn't seem at all surprised to see me. Instead, his expression was bland, almost bored, as he gave me a flat look over the rim of his wine glass.

"What are you doing here? Why are you dating my best friend? Why would you follow me here?"

The questions came out rapid-fire, one after the other. I was doing my best to keep my voice level, but I really wanted to scream at him at the top of my lungs. I hated how detached and unbothered he seemed. Wealthy people really were unaffected by most things. They knew they were basically untouchable, and it was so annoying.

He calmly put down the wine glass and stared at me in a way that made me feel like I should already have the answers.

"Do you know that the night I spent with you ruined my life? That guy you lived with made things very difficult for me. He caused quite a bit of concern for my family as well." My former classmate leaned closer to me by putting an arm on the table and pushing forward. "He got me suspended from school. He cost me an internship I worked my ass off for. He showed that video of us to my actual girlfriend, and obviously, she dumped me. She had no idea I was seeing other girls on the side. She told my family how I was slumming with the help, and she left me. Her father was an investor in one of my father's upcoming development projects and he was livid with me when he lost the backing because of my wandering eye. I was nearly cut off and written out of the will... all because I thought it would be fun to take your virginity."

I made a strangled sound and lifted a hand to my throat. It sounded exactly like how Sawyer would act when he was wronged. I had no idea he'd taken revenge beyond threatening to release the footage if Jack didn't leave me alone when we were at school.

He lifted an eyebrow in my direction and smirked. The expression on his face made my blood run cold.

"After I picked myself up and had some time to smooth things over with my family, I realized everything that happened to me was your fault. You brought that lunatic into my life. You put me in his crosshairs. I realized it wasn't fair that I was the only one suffering. You should lose the things that matter to you as well. I might've been able to get past my anger toward you if you kept suffering and continued to live such a pitiful life, but after your mother died, you became a totally different person. I could see how happy you were once you got away, how relieved when that poor guy in the Victorian let you get close to him. You're too close to living a perfectly normal life these days, and I don't think that's fair after all the trouble you caused me. There's not much I could do to ruin you, Olivia. Richman already did that. But your friend, she's so sweet, so innocent, so unsuspecting. How do you think she would feel if I put her through the same thing you dragged me into? I've been keeping her at just the right distance that when I finally let her get close, she won't question anything. Who knows who might be watching? What if she becomes a target, a laughingstock, a pariah just because she befriended you? Does she have any idea how dangerous your friendship is?"

The thought of Mercer being on display like that made my stomach hurt.

"You're right. I was thoughtless and careless when I befriended you and brought you home. I didn't think about anything beyond using you to get what I wanted. But that doesn't mean someone innocent like Mercer should get hurt. She's a good person. Way better than me or you. She doesn't deserve to be part of any of this, and if you hurt her, I won't let it go."

Jack chuckled, but there was zero humor in the sound. "What else is left for you to do? I have nothing to lose, and the guy who set this in motion in the first place is no longer a threat. You don't scare me. And Mercer is well on her way to being in love with me. I have no doubt she will pick me over you no matter what you tell her about me and our history."

There was a lot in that statement to unpack, but one part stuck out more than the others.

"What do you mean, Sawyer's no longer a threat?" How was that possible? Sawyer had been a threat for as long as I could remember. That defined him. That was who he was in my mind... a threat... a danger. What did this angry stranger know that I didn't?

"That lunatic is locked up. He was already crazy, but he went feral when you disappeared. He tried to have me killed, and when that didn't work, he tried to kill himself instead. His mother schemed to hide him away because she could no longer cover up how unhinged he was. He isn't coming after me or coming to save you. He's rotting in a padded cell somewhere."

I felt like someone had suddenly dumped a bucket of cold water over my head.

Sawyer was locked away.

He wasn't following me.

He wasn't coming after me.

He wasn't manipulating me or forcing me to return to his home.

I was safe. And so was Huck.

It was all too much to get my head around. It was as if the world as I knew it had been shaken up and dumped out just waiting to be put back together. It was a place I didn't recognize anymore.

"She never needed anyone to save her. She can do that all on her own. You're just pissed she used you when she did it last time." My head jerked around as Huck's voice suddenly came from behind me. He grabbed my wrist and pulled me to my feet. "And if you think my brother fucked your life up for messing with her, you haven't seen anything yet. When I'm through with you, you'll wish for the days that used to get your panties in a twist. If you think anything in your life is hard now, I'm about to make it impossible. Leave. Don't think about messing with Ollie or Mercer ever again. I know rich guys like you don't like to follow orders, but this is your best option."

After dropping the less than subtle threat, Huck pulled me along behind him out of the restaurant, and I heard concerned murmurs coming from the other diners. I chanced a look over my shoulder, hoping Vernon managed to delay Mercer a bit longer, but no such luck.

She was standing in the middle of the melee, watching Huck drag me out of the restaurant. I had no clue how I was supposed to explain all of this to her or if we would still be friends afterward, but she needed to know that Jack was no good for her.

"Where did you come from?" I whisper-growled the question to Huck as he continued to pull me along behind him like he was the one who had the right to be furious.

Between Vernon's slip of the tongue and his general unease earlier, and my one-night stand's admission about Sawyer, I knew Huck must've known his half brother was no longer able to get his fingers into our business. He kept that from me for reasons only known to him, and I hated it.

"I got a text from Vernon saying you knew the guy Mercer was with. I knew it couldn't be Sawyer, so I got worried and dipped out of work. I actually have to go back, but I want to make sure you get home first and aren't running around playing James Bond anymore tonight. I knew this was a bad idea."

I tugged my arm free and stood in the crowded parking lot, glaring at him from under the low brim of his hat.

"How long have you known that Sawyer was institutionalized?"

Huck lifted his hands and shoved them through his messy, dark hair. "Not long. I asked Vernon to look into Sawyer's medical records because I thought maybe he'd been lying about being hurt all this time. It seemed weird he'd been so quiet since you escaped. He stumbled upon Sawyer's current whereabouts during the deep dive. I was going to tell you, but I wanted to get a better handle on what was going on back home before I did. I didn't want you to stop watching your back just because Sawyer is harmless these days. With or without him, the world is still a cruel, twisted place. It's better that you keep your eyes open and an ear to the ground. It's not like he's the only villain in our story."

I blew out an angry breath and started walking toward the street. The house wasn't really within walking distance of the restaurant, but I was frustrated and heated, so I could power walk some of my feelings down to a simmer while I figured out a way to get home. Right now, they were about to boil over.

"You should've told me things have changed. We're supposed to tell each other everything now—no more secrets. We're supposed to be teammates, not a player and the coach. I don't appreciate you making all the calls without clueing me in, Huck." I'd been there and done that with Sawyer, and there was no way I was going back there. Not even for him.

Huck pulled out his phone and looked at the time. He swore in frustration and took a couple quick steps after me.

"Ollie..."

I held up a hand and kept up my hurried pace. "I know you think you were looking out for me, but it feels like you aren't letting me make up my own mind about things. That's the exact reason I ran away from my last home in the first place. That's what I came to you to get away from, Huck." I gave him a serious look.

He caught my arm once again and spun me around so we were face to face. "I messed up. I'm sorry."

I could see his sincerity shining out of his honey-colored eyes and dripping from every word when he told me, "I'm overly cautious where our childhood is concerned. I acted without thinking about how you would feel about it. I didn't realize it was similar to how my brother always treated you. I'm used to doing what I think is best for you without asking for permission. I forget that you aren't a kid who needs me all the time nowadays."

I took a breath to calm myself down, and after a few silent moments, I reached up to hold his face between my hands.

"I do need you all the time. But I can think for myself. I can decide what's best for me without anyone else's help." I sighed and frowned as I told him what was bothering me even more than his highhandedness. "Right now, I need to think about how to get Mercer away from Jack. He has a reason to hate me, and I don't blame him for wanting revenge, but he can't hurt her in the process. Go back to work. The last thing you need is to get fired because you ran to my rescue." I looked back toward the restaurant and realized I'd left Vernon alone with the mess I'd just made. "I need to go and rescue Vernon. Mercer is pretty laid back, but who knows how she's going to react to that shitshow I just unleashed."

Huck caught my shoulders and turned me back. "Vernon can take care of himself. And he's better at reading a situation than anyone I've ever met. He's the best person to get a feel for what your friend is feeling and how receptive she'll be to the truth when you tell her. You should head home and figure out what you want to say to Mercer after everyone cools down. Remember, an apology is more about who's giving it and receiving it than the actual words. Let's talk about our plan for that rich prick later. He's not on Sawyer's level by any means, but he's still a problem."

I nodded and gave him a lopsided grin. "You can piss me off without much effort, Huck, but I'm glad you are always there when I need you."

All his heart knew how to do was take care of me, and because of that, I was willing to let some of his bossy, overprotectiveness slide.

With him, there was the perfect balance of good and bad traits. I was sure the same could be said about myself, and we were both prone to leaning a little heavy in either direction. We just had to make sure we pulled each other back when the bad started to outweigh the good.

CHAPTER 22

Huck

"So the guy was going to exploit Mercer the same way Sawyer exploited him because he blamed Ollie for everything that happened after they hooked up. I can't believe she has the misfortune of having two separate spoiled rich kids intent on making her life hell. What are the odds?"

Vernon shook his head and watched as I shut down the bar for the night. I was supposed to get off at midnight, but after taking off in the middle of my shift with no explanation, my manager insisted I stay late and close. I'd like to think I was irreplaceable, but the bar was close to campus and had cheap drinks. All they needed was a reasonably attractive person to pour drinks and flirt with the regulars. I was far from indispensable. It was an easy, well-paying gig, so I didn't really want to get fired, but that hadn't stopped me from letting Vernon in through the back door, even though he was underage, once the business was done for the night. It was unlikely anyone was coming in this late to check up on me. "How can she have such bad luck when it comes to men?"

He made a disgruntled sound when I tossed a wet bar rag at him and reminded him, "We're also some of the men in her life."

He snorted and threw the towel back at me. "Yeah, and we're just as fucked up as the others. The only difference is we don't blame her for our issues or take out our frustrations on her." He lifted his eyebrows at me and reminded me pointedly, "Her life would be a lot easier if she thought she could live without you. That's what started all of this back then... she picked you as her favorite and the world crashed down around both of you."

It was true. It was the first domino that sent the rest crashing down.

I was self-aware enough to know that burning hot jealousy played a part in why I was ready to rip this new guy into pieces.

When I was young, I always thought of her as mine. Not in a romantic sense, but in the sense that she was the other half of me. She completed me. She brought out the best in me. Now, that sense of ownership was different and much more intense. The thought of someone else touching her, of another man knowing how sweet she tasted, and how sexy she sounded when she let go made me want to grind my teeth to dust. It was a careful line I knew I needed to walk with caution, because the last thing I wanted or she needed was me to start taking after Sawyer. I was into her, but I knew that didn't give me the right to start taking over her life.

"Did you explain to Mercer what was going on?" I rested my hands on the bar in front of him and watched as he tapped his black painted nails on the scarred wooden surface.

He nodded, sending white strands of hair into his eyes. "I did. She was confused and surprised. It didn't help that the douchebag freely admitted that he knew Ollie in the past once confronted, and then insisted it was just a coincidence they were both here now. It was obvious he was lying and hiding things from her. He had more of an issue explaining why he purposely tracked Mercer down and why he was so insistent that things stayed pretty PG between them. She had a healthy suspicion of his story by the time I left. I think once she hears everything from Ollie, she'll realize she was being used and that guy is a straight-up liar. He knows how to manipulate women. Mercer was on the brink of being brainwashed." His fingers stopped tapping as he braced himself with a hand and leaned closer to me conspiratorially. "What are we going to do about him?"

I pushed off the edge of the bar and lifted my hand up over my head, stretching until I heard the tightness in my spine pop. "Run him out of town and make sure he knows if he comes anywhere near Ollie or anyone she cares about in the future, that will be the last bad decision he ever gets to make."

Vernon leaned back on the barstool and smacked his hand on the bar. "Sounds fun, just like the old days. Better not let Fisher know what we're up to. We're supposed to have reformed and turned into decent people looking toward our future. We're supposed to have outgrown our rough roots. He'd be disappointed if he knew we were still nothing more than the uncivilized street kids he first met."

I snorted. "It doesn't matter what we change on the outside; who we are on the inside will always come through. Doesn't matter if I'm in a thousand-dollar suit or a leather jacket and jeans; I'm always going to stand up for what's right. I'm not going to let anyone hurt the people I care about regardless of what it takes."

"Which is exactly why I want to be you when I grow up." He gave me a grin as I reached out to mess up his hair.

"You don't want to be me now or then. I have a pretty girl in my bed, and we both know that isn't who you want to cuddle up to at night, kiddo." With a chuckle, I turned to count the money drop for the night. "You're a genius. I shouldn't have to tell you that."

Vernon made a strangled sound and followed me out the back door. I shut the lights off and made sure everything was locked up tight behind me.

He swiftly changed the subject.

"So, what happens now? You and Ollie don't have to worry about your brother anymore, and the thing that goes bump in the night now has a face. Is she going to stay with us indefinitely? Is your relationship going to be the same now that neither one of you has anyone to fear?"

I didn't want Ollie to go anywhere. I liked having her under the same roof, but I couldn't make that decision for her.

All she wanted was to live a normal life and make choices for herself without worrying about how they might blow up in her face. If she wanted to stay, I would be overjoyed. If she decided to go, I'd support her, but I wouldn't love it.

It was strange how far I'd come where she was concerned. When she first showed up, it felt like my well-ordered life had vanished. Now, I was starting to think all the ways I'd grown and adapted over the years had been so I could be the man Ollie needed me to be when she came back into my life. She was still so much a part of who I was and who I wanted to be.

"I'm not sure what happens next. I've never *not* lived life looking over my shoulder because of Sawyer. The same goes for Ollie. We'll have to figure out what our new normal looks like. Sawyer's always been like a parasite attached to any relationship she and I have had. With him out of the picture, maybe whatever we have between us can finally breathe."

"You've totally forgiven her for not going with you when you were kids?" Vernon made it sound like the possibility was farfetched. I couldn't blame him. I'd spent years feeling wounded and angry because I felt that she betrayed and abandoned me. "Did you ever officially accept her apology?"

"I don't know that I fully forgive her, but I understand where she was coming from now more than I did then. I get her motivations. We were all so young and just doing the best we could in a situation that was so much bigger than all of us." I hated that she had to lose her mom to find a way out, but that didn't change the fact she sacrificed me for the little time they had left together.

Vernon clapped a hand on my shoulder as we walked the last block toward our house. "I liked Ollie from the minute she showed up looking like a lost puppy. But I love the way she makes you stop and really look at things. You're so used to seeing the worst the world has to offer, I wondered for a long time if you would ever be able to see the good hidden in the cracks. I've always wanted you to remember what it feels like to be happy, and I don't think that would ever have been possible without Ollie in your life."

Happy might still be a long way off, but I was inching closer to it each and every day.

We pushed into the dark house, and our steps made the vintage floor creak under our weight.

I muttered a hurried goodnight in Vernon's direction and watched as he disappeared toward Harlen's room. It didn't slip past me that he hadn't come back with a smartass retort after I mentioned that he didn't want to crawl into bed with a girl after a long day. The kid always had something to say, but when I pointed out what was obvious to me and anyone else who saw how he and Harlen interacted, he went dead silent.

It was telling.

It was a situation that was bound to get complicated down the road if something didn't change. They were toying with denial and desire, which was a deadly combination.

I tried to stay as quiet as possible when I entered my room. Ollie was a light sleeper and rarely slept through my nightly routine when I got home from a shift. Tonight she was still under the comforter as I stripped and headed into the bathroom to take a quick shower before I crashed. She really must be worn out and emotionally drained if she didn't stir in the slightest. It was honestly one of my favorite surprises in the world when she suddenly appeared behind me in the shower. It happened pretty regularly now that she spent most nights in my room.

But not tonight.

I rubbed a towel over my head and tiptoed to the bed so I didn't disturb her. I crawled under the covers, still slightly damp and totally naked because I wasn't about to rustle through my drawers to find a pair of boxers in the dark.

Ollie was lying with a hand under her cheek and a few stray curls rested over the front of her face. She looked so innocent, so peaceful.

I realized this was the first night she went to bed knowing with absolute conviction that she wouldn't wake up with Sawyer hovering over her. There was no way he was still watching her from a distance. It was probably the first good night's sleep she'd gotten since she was a kid.

I reached out a finger to move her hair out of her face and smiled into the darkness at the soft sound she made. She wiggled closer to me, instinctively seeking out comfort and body heat. I wrapped an arm around her and closed my eyes.

It'd been a long, long time since I had such a sense of contentment. Maybe I was a lot closer to happiness than I thought.

I, too, slept better that night than I had in a handful of years.

And I woke up feeling leaps and bounds better than I normally did. The covers were thrown aside, and Ollie had her head bent over my cock.

I didn't know if I was hard before she put her mouth on me or if she made me that way. Not that it mattered. The way she used her lips and tongue was bound to make my body react regardless of the situation.

I propped one arm up behind my head so I could watch her do her thing in the faint morning light. I let the other hand fall to the crown of her head so I could hold her wild hair out of my line of sight.

She lifted her long lashes to look up at me, and I noticed that her cheeks were flushed and her freckles stood out even more than normal. She was equally cute and sexy. She had a charm that was all her own, and it got to me deep and fast. She wasn't a girl every guy would understand or have the patience for, but I wasn't the kind of guy who was simple and easy either.

We were a matched set in a lot of ways.

I grunted when I felt her nails dig into the flesh on the inside of my thigh.

I bent a knee to give her more access and room to move while her head bobbed up and down in a slow and sensual rhythm. The wet sounds that filled the room and the low groans that escaped my lips every now and then were heady and had anticipation and want pooling thickly in my blood.

I growled her name partly in warning, but more in encouragement, when I felt her fingers creeping higher between my legs. One of the biggest turn-ons was watching her get more confident and comfortable with herself the longer we were together. She might not have technically been a virgin when we first hooked up, but she was definitely a novice. Now, she knew just how to handle me to get the reaction she wanted.

She touched, tasted, and teased better than anyone else I'd been with. Maybe it was because so much more than my body was engaged when we were together, but I had no issue telling her that she was the best I ever had.

She sucked hard enough on the stiff length in her mouth that her cheeks hollowed out. My hips lifted in response, and my hand tightened in her hair.

I gasped her name when her tongue flicked across the sensitive slit at the tip buried deep in the warmth of her mouth. Pleasure pulled tight at the base of my spine, and I felt my muscles tense as her fingertips lightly grazed the tight, tender spot nestled underneath the rigid flesh she pulled deeper and deeper into her mouth.

The graze of her nails across the drawn-up sac had me thrust with more force than I intended. Ollie made a startled sound and rolled her eyes in my direction.

I shifted my hand and whispered an apology, and she hummed lightly around my cock.

The dual stimulation of her tonguing my dick and her hand lightly fondling me between my legs meant I wasn't going to last much longer.

I grunted out a warning to let her know she was about to get a mouthful, but she simply pushed her head down farther and swallowed hard when the tip of my erection touched the back of her throat. Between the suction, the heat, and the caress on my single most sensitive body part, there was no holding back the eruption of pleasure that rushed out of me.

I told myself not to hold her head in place because it was rude, but I couldn't help myself. My hips kicked upward as I thrust helplessly against her face. It was a bit rougher than I usually was with her, but Ollie didn't complain. She picked up the rhythm without missing a beat and continued her sweet manipulation of my cock, taking everything I had to give her.

After I went limp and she let my softening member fall from her mouth, she brushed her very red and damp mouth across my abs, leaving a wet trail. One of her eyebrows quirked upward playfully, and she muttered, "Good morning."

I grabbed her face in my hands and rubbed my thumb over her swollen mouth.

It was a very good morning, and not just because I woke up with her mouth wrapped around my dick.

It was a good morning because I got to wake up next to her.

As serious as I'd ever been, I told her, "Let's be happy. Let's figure out how to be happy, Ollie. We deserve it."

She smiled softly and rested her chin on her hands, which were stacked together on my abs.

"That sounds nice."

It really did.

CHAPTER 23

Ollie

I was juggling a notebook, my backpack, a half-empty iced coffee, and my house keys when my cell phone started to ring from the depths of my purse that was slung across my chest. I scowled in frustration as I tried to figure out the quickest way to dig it out. I opted to ditch the coffee as I switched my keys for my phone in my free hand. Now that I knew Sawyer was no longer a threat and Mercer was no longer seeing the suspicious guy who had it in for me, I'd been super focused on school. It was the first time since I enrolled in college that I felt like an average student. There wasn't an invisible ax hanging over my head any longer. I couldn't use the excuse of simply trying to survive as to why I was such a poor student anymore. I could put effort into my classes and my education.

So far, there had only been a minimal improvement, but Vernon was teaching me how to study better. Now that I was practically living in Huck's pocket, it was a constant reminder that I had to take control of my own future because nothing was ever going to be handed to me. I was going to have to work hard for whatever I wanted to be. Huck never let anything slow him down, and he never fell back on excuses even though his life had been as hard, if not harder, than mine. I'd always looked up to him, but even more so now. Even though he'd come home from the bar a few nights ago with busted knuckles, a gnarly scratch across his cheek, and wouldn't give me a straight answer as to why he was so disheveled, he was still the person I trusted and respected the most in my very flawed world.

Vernon wouldn't give me an explanation when I asked him if he knew who Huck got into a fight with either, which made me even more curious about what he got up to when I wasn't around. I thought maybe it was a simple bar fight, and he just didn't want me to worry, but surprisingly, it was Harlen who dropped the biggest hint that Huck was still protecting me with everything he had.

I was bitching about the fact that I still hadn't heard from Mercer. She didn't seem like she was in any hurry to mend the fallen fences between the two of us. She even sent me a text telling me not to come to the shop for the foreseeable future. I was frustrated by the cold shoulder, and I complained that she better not still be seeing Jack when Harlen muttered that there was absolutely no way he was still in the picture. I demanded to know what he meant, but it only took a hard look from him for me to remember Huck's damaged hands and refusal to fill me in on his injuries. Even though he promised to keep me in the loop with all the decisions he was making for my benefit, he was still doing his best to keep blowback as far away from me as possible.

And the truth was, Mercer needed Jack out of her life entirely for her to move on and heal. I was silently relieved I didn't have to worry about when he might pop back up and make trouble. My history of terrible luck when it came to the men in my life, aside from Huck, held true. Who else but me would have a one-night stand turn into the type of revenge plot saved for only the best thrillers and suspense novels?

I did remind Huck that we were supposed to share things nowadays and gently asked how he would feel if I came home all banged up and refused to tell him about it. The look on his face when he pictured me coming home as bruised as he was spoke volumes. I was pretty sure I got my point across because he'd been even more attentive than usual. He mentioned that sometimes brute force was the only way to fight against the wealthy. Money might talk, but bare fists and unfiltered rage did an even better job of getting some messages across. Guys like Sawyer and Jack didn't know what to do when they faced a real fight, which is why they always fought dirty and went after those they thought were weaker than them.

I thought the call that nearly caused me to drop everything would be Huck asking if I wanted to meet up after class. I was surprised to see Mr. Peters's information on the screen instead. It wasn't unusual for the landlord to check-in, especially after my mad dash from his home after my breakdown. He really had taken on the role of a surrogate grandfather figure for me, much like he had for the boys I lived with. While it wasn't weird for the older man to reach out, it was a bit strange he was calling during the week when he knew I was in and out of class. He usually tried to touch base on the weekends when there was a better chance one of us at the house would be free.

I swiped at the screen to answer the call and awkwardly shuffled my notebook into my backpack with one hand. "Hi, Mr. Peters. How are you doing?"

I slung my backpack back over my shoulder and, with a scowl, sidestepped a guy on a longboard when he almost ran me over.

"Actually, I'm not feeling very well today, Ollie. I'm a bit under the weather. I hate to be a bother, but do you think you could come by the house with some over-the-counter cold medicine? I called my girls, but they're both tied up at work. I tried to call Huck as well, but he didn't pick up." He did sound raspy and like he had a bit of a cold.

I looked at the time on my phone. Huck would be in class for at least another forty-five minutes, so he probably turned his phone off. I was free for the rest of the afternoon. I had planned on meeting up with Vernon to go over a study schedule he set up for me, but that wasn't urgent. Not when the old man really did sound kind of rough and winded. I was concerned about him.

"Sure. Tell me what you want me to grab, and I'll bring it by right away. Are you sure you don't need me to take you to the doctor? You sound terrible." But he was stubborn, and I bet he was the kind who waited until he was on death's doorstep before seeking medical attention.

He wheezed out a generic name of a common cold medicine and assured me he would be fine. I told him I would be as quick as possible, and he mumbled, "Be safe."

It was a very odd exchange.

I frowned as I shot a message to Vernon and let him know I would have to reschedule our study session. Mr. Peters often told me to take care of myself and jokingly ordered me to keep Huck and the other boys in line. But this was the first time he told me to be safe on the short trip to his place.

I pondered the subtext as I wandered the aisles of the closest drugstore to campus. I'd lived so much of life being suspicious of everyone and second-guessing everything, it was second nature to think there was more to the old man's words than he intended. I didn't want to be the girl who jumped at her own shadow anymore, but old habits die hard. Sadly, I couldn't talk myself out of grabbing a canister of pepper spray when I checked out. I already had one, but I'd taken it off my keychain a few days ago in an attempt to claim some sense of normalcy. Huck scolded me and reminded me that Sawyer wasn't the only person I would ever encounter in my life who had bad intentions, but I was convinced I could handle what any normal bad guy might throw my way after everything I'd been through.

Maybe I was arrogant and should've listened to him. After all, Huck hadn't been wrong about much.

As soon as I got out of the Uber in front of Mr. Peters's house, I sent another text to Vernon. I told him if he didn't hear from me in the next ten minutes, something was wrong, and I was in trouble. I got a flurry of messages back demanding to know what was going on and why I sent such a cryptic text, but I was already at the front door and didn't answer. Of course, Vernon immediately called when I didn't respond, but I just let it go to voicemail as Mr. Peters pulled the door open.

He looked incredibly frail and very green around the gills. His hands were shaking as he pushed the storm door open, and he was blinking rapidly. He didn't just look ill; he looked like he was about to keel over at any minute. I reached out to catch him as he practically crumbled into my arms as soon as I stepped over the threshold into his normally immaculate home. Out of the corner of my eye, I noticed a couple of pictures of his kids and grandkids were askew on the wall. I also noticed the lampshade on his antique table was tilted, like someone bumped into it and didn't bother to right it.

My phone started ringing again, and I knew without looking at it that it would be Huck blowing it up. Before seeing the look of terror on my landlord's face, I would've been annoyed that the boys were overreacting. Now, I was glad they were so overprotective of me. I handed Mr. Peters my phone and tried to gently move him onto the old house's porch. He looked like he'd been through the wringer already, and I wanted him as far away as possible from whatever threat was inside. I didn't know what was going on, but I was sure the elderly man had no business being caught in the middle of it.

Even as weak and trembling as he was, Mr. Peters resisted my efforts to move him. Still clutching my phone in his quaking hand, he whispered, "I can't risk my grandkids," under his breath. I nodded and put a finger to my lips after motioning that he should stay put. I pointed to the phone and lifted my eyebrows, telling him he should keep the call connected so Huck could hear what was going on through the connection. I would bet every single thing I owned that he was already on his way to the old man's house and cursing me out with every breath he took. Between him and Vernon, not only did I expect one of them to ride to the rescue, but also for them to have called the police by now.

There was no reason for me to walk into the lion's den. It was stupid. It was dangerous. It was reckless.

But I was going in anyway.

I was done running from everything that might be bigger than me. I was tired of letting other people make me feel small and powerless. I was sick of not feeling like I was in control of my own destiny.

I was done being afraid all the time.

If I couldn't face my fears now when I knew I had backup on the way, when else would I be able to?

If I didn't go inside right now, I was giving up all the hard-won progress I'd made toward living a normal life.

"Okay. Let me put this medicine in the kitchen, then I'll take you to the doctor, Mr. Peters. You just sit here by the door. You look really pale. You should've called me sooner if you were feeling so poorly." I spoke loudly so whoever was inside could hear me and know I was coming in alone.

After dropping everything on the floor by the entryway that I had I hauled with me, I clutched the pepper spray in my hand and quietly tiptoed my way through the house. I knew it couldn't be Sawyer terrorizing my elderly landlord. And I didn't think my wayward one-night stand would be bold enough to lure me to the house after dealing with an angry Huck. Considering Mr. Peters indicated the way his harasser got him to call me to his place was by threatening his grandkids, there was only one other person I was absolutely sure could be that cruel and callous... the person who turned Sawyer into the monster he was. His mother.

Sure enough, as soon as I slipped into the normally tidy kitchen, I encountered the woman I hadn't seen since she made my teenage years a living hell. She looked just as polished and wealthy as ever. She was even sipping nonchalantly on a cup of coffee from where she leaned against the counter in my landlord's home. It would almost look like a scene from an HGTV show, except for a nasty handgun on the countertop in front of the elegantly dressed woman. That and the pure, unfiltered hatred shining in her crazy eyes.

How could someone have everything... except a heart? Or any sense of right and wrong.

I kept my hand with the pepper spray behind my back and met the angry woman's hostile gaze. I used to be scared to death of her because she was so willing to do *anything* to make her son happy. It was almost like the rest of us weren't human and had no value or reason to exist beyond our usefulness to him.

"You really came all the way here and threatened an old man and his grandkids, Mrs. Richman?"

One of her perfectly groomed eyebrows arched upward as she sneered at me over the rim of the coffee cup. "You're the one who should be locked up. We both know you were the one driving the night of the accident, not Huck. You tried to kill yourself, and almost took Sawyer and Huck with you. I'm convinced of it. You've always been weak and pathetic, Olivia. I'll never understand why my son was so obsessed with you. You were never worthy of his time or affection."

She reached out a finger and tapped the handle of the weapon in front of her. "Regardless, my Sawyer hasn't been the same since you left. Something inside of him is broken, and the only way to fix it is to bring you back to him. I knew you wouldn't come if I asked nicely, and I knew there was no way my husband's bastard would let anyone else get close to you, so I decided to bring you back myself. You're going to fix Sawyer, Olivia. You owe us after everything we did for you and your mother."

I balked and curled my fingers even tighter around the canister hidden behind my back. I was going back over my dead body.

"You're underestimating how well I can take care of myself. All I ever wanted was to get away from Sawyer. I'm okay on my own. I miss my mom, but I'm grateful every single day you can no longer use her against me."

I was fortunate I found Huck and that we had reconciled, but I knew now that I could go on without him if I had to. He was my safe space in this chaotic and ruthless world. It was a treasured, hallowed place for sure. But he didn't make up the entirety of my world the way I had for Sawyer.

Mrs. Richman shrieked and slammed her coffee mug down on the counter with enough force it broke. I flinched as she reached for the handgun, eyes going wide and wild as she continued to scream at me.

"You should've died that night! Everything is your fault! I lost my son because of you! I lost my husband because of you! Do you know how people have looked at me since Sawyer went away? As if something is wrong with him. Like I was a bad mother. The world will be a better place without you in it!"

Her tirade was interesting, yet not at all surprising. Huck's dad had finally had enough and cut this awful woman loose? That would make why she had finally gone fully over the edge a little more understandable. All she had ever cared about was how much she had and how much she could keep others from having.

I recoiled when she suddenly pointed the gun at me, but I could tell by the awkward way she held it, she was unfamiliar with the weapon.

"You can threaten my landlord, my friends, and Huck. None of that is going to make Sawyer well or earn you any points with Huck's dad. At the rate you're going, you're going to end up in prison. Without your husband's name behind you, you're finally going to have to see how the justice system works for those who can't negotiate or barter for their innocence. If you end up behind bars, how are you ever going to check on Sawyer? How are you going to take care of him once he's released from that facility? No one, and I mean no one, is going to be there for him besides you. Is that what you want? Have you really thought this through, Mrs. Richman?" Even if she did manage to drag me back to the mansion, Sawyer was in a facility where going to see him was a whole ordeal.

Her threats served no purpose. She was just looking for someone to blame for her shortcomings.

She looked at me and then at the gun in her hand. Her maniacal gaze sharpened, and the look on her face was enough to make my blood go ice cold. "Of course that's not what I want. What I want is for you to tell my son you love him. Promise you'll be with him forever. Make him feel like he's your favorite for once in your pathetic life. I want you to make him the way he was before you broke him by abandoning him. What I really want is for you to die the way you should have the night of the accident. You should be the one ready to take your own life, not my Sawyer. He's destined for greatness. You're destined for..." she sneered a little and waved the gun in the air. "For nothing more than that heathen I was forced to share my home and my husband with."

She wasn't wrong.

I was pretty sure I was destined to be with Huck as well.

"I was never even slightly tempted to kill myself. Not even when Sawyer made me question if I had a life worth living. That night I was driving and I lost control because of him. It wasn't even an accident. That's it." Not that she would believe a word I had to say about that night anyway. "I'm sorry it happened, but whatever you think you're going to do to me won't change anything. I'm not going anywhere, and Sawyer won't magically get better. All you're going to do is make more enemies. Do you really want to get on Huck's bad side now that you're no longer in his father's good graces? You have no idea how much smarter and how completely unforgiving he's become since you and his dad forced him out on his own. He won't hold back if you hurt me."

She paused briefly, and I could see she was digesting my words. Finally, something other than rage flickered in her eyes.

Fear.

I recognized it all too well.

"I'll kill the old man. I'll kill his whole family. I'll take every single person you care about away from you. All you have to do is sacrifice yourself to keep them safe. Sawyer's handsome and rich. You could do so much worse than him. All he needs to hear is that you love him, that you'll wait for him. Make him feel like he has something to live for. If he dies, it's all your fault. I knew I should've tossed your mother out when she ended up pregnant without having a steady man in her life. I knew she would bring trouble into my house when you were born. I knew she was no good. She couldn't even find a man willing to care for her and her child."

I made a face as she started to move closer to me. My fingers flexed on the pepper spray as I braced myself for whatever attack she might throw at me. I knew it was better to keep her talking because help was bound to be on the way by now.

Huck always told anyone who would listen that I was fully capable of saving myself, so it was time to prove him right.

"My mom deserved better than what she ended up with. I also wish you'd made her leave. I wish she'd never brought me into your house. Because of you and your son, I never even got to tell her a proper goodbye. I didn't get to mourn her loss." I was in such a hurry to get away from them, grief hadn't had time to catch up to me yet. "You used a sick woman as a weapon. There is nothing lower than that in my book."

As soon as the unhinged woman was close enough to touch, I whipped the hand holding the pepper spray from behind my back and let a massive dose loose. I buried my nose and mouth in the crook of my other arm as the kitchen filled with the sound of her angry screams and the noxious fumes. I heard the gun clatter to the tiled floor as I turned and bolted for the front door. I nearly ran over Mr. Peters, who was back inside the entryway and hastily shuffling toward the commotion. I grabbed his elbow and hustled him outside, coughing as the chemicals from the spray lingered on my clothes and in my hair.

"Call the police and tell them you have an intruder." I gagged a little and used his frail form to keep me upright as my knees got wobbly. I gasped for air as he patted me on the back.

"I'm not as quick as I used to be. I couldn't stop her when she pushed into the house after I answered the door. We tussled around a bit, and she got me good on the back of the head with the gun. She saw the pictures of my grandkids and told me she would go after them if I didn't figure out a way to get you here. I didn't want to, but I remembered you telling me how crazy these people were. I'm so sorry I pretended to be sick to get you here. I didn't want to risk my family. I thought I could buy some time and maybe get to my own weapon that's hidden inside the house, but you showed up sooner than

I expected. I called the police on your phone as soon I got outside. These old bones don't put up a fight like they used to."

I hacked hard enough I was worried I was going to be sick. It took a minute to catch my breath. When I could finally breathe, I assured the older man, "You told me to be safe. It was enough of a warning that I knew something was up. You shouldn't have to deal with the monsters from my past. The only reason you were a target is because of me. All you've ever done is help me, Mr. Peters. I owe you so much, and I'm so sorry you were hurt because of me."

Accountability. I would take all of it from here on out.

I was bent over in another coughing fit when a police car pulled up in front of the house, followed quickly by another car carrying not only Huck and Vernon but also Harlen. All three of them had rushed to the rescue. It made me want to cry.

The police officers hurried to check on Mr. Peters, who was trying to tell them there was a woman who was armed and dangerous inside his house. He rushed out an explanation for the wild events that sounded slightly crazy, even though I'd just lived through them. Meanwhile, I collapsed against Huck as he grabbed me and held me in a hug tight enough to crack my ribs, even though I was still slightly coughing.

"Are you okay?" His voice was harsh, and I could feel his hands tremble where he held me against him. "I can't believe you went into that house, alone, knowing how dangerous it might be. When you can breathe again, I'm going to throttle you."

I wheezed out a short laugh and rested my forehead against the base of his throat. I wrapped an arm around his waist and closed my eyes, finally feeling like all the scattered pieces of my life had fallen into place.

"I wasn't alone. I knew you would come after me. I knew I had to face whomever was inside. If I didn't, nothing we've been through up to this point would matter." I wasn't ready to tell him yet, but seeing Sawyer's mother, and hearing all her deranged ranting about the night of the accident, made something else crystal clear. To move forward, I had to finally face the past. I had to right the wrong that had haunted me since the night of the accident. I couldn't let anyone still think Huck was the one driving that night. I needed to go back and take a stand, regardless of what the consequences might be. I needed it on record that I was driving and that he'd been innocent all along. It wouldn't get back the years he'd been forced to go to that awful school, but it would clear his record so that the accident could never be used against him in the future. It might be too little, too late, but it was the best apology I could offer.

I had to clear his name, even if I knew he was going to do everything in his power to stop me.

Not only was I fully capable of saving myself, but I was finally in a place where I could do my best to save him when he needed it.

CHAPTER 24

Huck

"I'm not supposed to have any surprise visitors. How did you convince them to let you see me?"

I looked at my half brother and tried to keep my shock in check at how much he'd changed in the five years since I'd last seen him.

I called him a monster.

I thought of him as a demon.

He was always the big bad in mind—the embodiment of evil.

Now, he looked as physically ill as I knew he was mentally. He had lost so much weight that he almost appeared skeletal. His face was hollowed out and sunken in. His skin was papery thin and had a sickly hint of yellow. His eyes, which had always blazed with passion and obsession, were dull and flat, much like Ollie's looked when she first showed up on my doorstep looking for salvation.

It was hard to reconcile the person sitting across from me with the person who had effectively ruined all of our lives. He seemed harmless and utterly defeated. And neither of those things had anything to do with his wheelchair.

"You know better than anyone that money makes magical things happen. If there's enough of it in play, nothing is impossible."

Never in a million years did I think I would be willing to reach out to my estranged father to ask him to pull some strings and throw some money around for me. I was happy having nothing to do with the man, but knew the only way I could get in to see Sawyer was with his help.

My old man didn't seem at all surprised to hear from me now that both his wife and son were locked away. He thought I wanted to make amends and reclaim my position as his heir, but I was never going to forget how easily he disowned me or failed to protect me from his miserable wife.

I told him in no uncertain terms that all I wanted was to see Sawyer. I had no desire to play the prodigal son. I didn't need his help or his money for anything else in my life. I was pretty sure the hard stance shocked him. Annoyingly, he agreed to help me, but only if I acquiesced to one of his requests as well. He demanded that I change my last name from Snyder to Richman. I was now the only child he had whom he could be semi-proud of, even with the accident still on my juvenile record. I was the only one who hadn't been declared legally insane. He told me that even if I didn't want what was rightfully mine now, that might change down the road. He no longer wanted me to be seen as his bastard.

He promised he wouldn't publicly claim me as his son if I agreed, but for all intents and purposes, I was his legacy now. The house where I grew up and hated with every fiber of my being would be mine one day. I told him I didn't want it.

My last name was really the only thing my mother gave me. I never once thought about changing it. But speaking with Sawyer and protecting Ollie was more important than hanging on to something that never amounted to much anyway.

I made the deal with my old man, but I didn't tell Ollie about it. I knew she was going to have a fit I was keeping something that big from her. But this time, it couldn't be helped. I didn't want her to know I was going to see Sawyer. I didn't want her to know I was once again playing games with my stupidly rich father. I didn't want her to know I had so much as dipped a toe back into our old life.

She was hellbent on making amends and taking accountability for the past. I knew there was no way to stop her once she had her mind set on it. She'd already made plans to go back to our hometown so she could clear my name and confess to being the one behind the wheel the night of the accident.

I would lie, cheat, and steal to make sure she didn't have to do that for me. Legally, I wasn't sure there were any major repercussions she would face since the accident had been so long ago and I'd already done the penance for it. But I wouldn't put it past Sawyer's mother to sue her for damages and medical fees once she confessed, even from behind bars. I just wanted the whole situation put to bed and Ollie in the clear.

Which is why I was sitting across from Sawyer right now.

My brother made a face and shifted in his chair. "Aren't you getting ready to head to law school? Shouldn't bribing the authorities to get what you want be against your moral code or something? Didn't you always pretend to be better than that because you didn't want anyone to think you were like your money-hungry mother?"

I shrugged a shoulder and fought to keep my face still, even though I was taken aback that he knew anything about my life. It was unnerving to hear that he'd kept tabs on me all this time.

"I'm going to be the kind of lawyer who gets the job done no matter what." I tapped my fingers on the table, separating us. "I don't survive in that house with you and your mom without learning when the rules are meant to be broken. So, I guess I can thank you for making me the kind of guy who thrives in the world's vast amounts of imperfection. Because of you, I can lean into the darkness when necessary, but I know better than to get lost in it. I'm smart enough to move toward the light when I get in too deep. As you know, Ollie has been shining since forever. As long as I move toward her, I'll be fine."

He tried to drag Ollie into the shadows with him instead of letting her glow the way she was always meant to.

Sawyer flinched, but it was barely noticeable. "Why are you here, Huck?"

I tapped my fingers hard enough on the table that they started to hurt. Maybe it was foolish to think I could reason with a mad man, but I had to try.

"Fall break is coming up. When it does, Ollie is heading back to our hometown, and she is going to tell anyone who will listen that she was driving that night, not me. She was underage, and five years have gone by. I don't know that anyone will care, but you have to know that your mother will not let her slide once she openly admits her guilt. Your mom pointed a gun at Ollie. She demanded that she come and tell you that she loves you, that she wants to be with you. She blames Ollie for you being in here and in this condition. I'm hoping you have a shred of humanity left and realize the only person who put you away is *you*. Your obsession made you sick, and it made you do some pretty dangerous things. I can't prove it, but I know you grabbed the wheel and jerked it out of her control when Ollie was driving." Sawyer made a strangled sound, but his stark face showed no reaction. "Now, maybe you saw the deer and were just trying to help her since she was an inexperienced driver." I doubted that, but I needed to cover all the bases. "Whatever the reason, you were as much at fault for the accident as she was, especially because you forced her to drive that night. That was a choice you made. And at the end of the day, I'm the one who called her to come to get me. I was the one drinking and partying without a care in the world. I put her in as much danger as you did. She was just a kid trying to do the right thing. You punished her endlessly for nothing more than that."

He shifted weight, but his face still showed no signs of remorse or understanding.

I sighed and leaned forward. "You've put her through hell and back, Sawyer. She's been alone and miserable for years because of you. She doesn't trust anyone, and she lives her life like she's ready to run at any moment. You thought you could force her to stay by your side, but your actions drove her back into my arms. I was always her favorite. Nothing you did ever changed that. I lost her once. I won't lose her again." I gave him a very pointed look. "No matter what it takes, I'm keeping her, and I will protect her. You need to let her go. You need to set her free. It's the least you can do for her after how you tortured her, how you used her mother against her for so long."

Finally, his stony face twisted into a bitter smile. He looked deranged—like the Joker when he fully embraced his insanity.

It gave me the creeps, but I'd come too far to back down.

"I could never figure out why she could only see you." His wiry eyebrows dipped low on his forehead. "Back then, you were so loud and annoying. You were fat and always filthy. Even when you got older and started to get interested in other girls and made new friends, Ollie sought you out for everything. You were the only person she would talk about. She revolved around you like you were the sun. All I wanted her to do was look at me, just once, the way she looked at you. I tried to tell her over and over again that you didn't need her the way I did, that you would never want her the way I did. She wouldn't listen." My brother's expression was downright sinister. "I begged her not to go get you that night. I pleaded with her to let you fend for yourself. Nothing I said mattered. When you called, she was always going to come running. I knew as we got older that infatuation was going to turn into something more. She was in love with you long before she knew what love was. I hated it. I hated you. And she made me hate her. As cliché as it is, I really thought that if I couldn't have her, no one should. I had no idea that the end I had planned for all of us would be the beginning of me and her. It took this chair for Olivia Adams to finally see me. Once I was hurt, I was all she could see. It was perfect... while it lasted."

I stiffened in my seat and pulled my hand off the table so Sawyer wouldn't see the way it curled into a fist.

This asshole.

He really had tried to kill us that night.

I shouldn't be surprised, but I was. He really was sick and twisted. It wasn't just an overblown exaggeration from my youthful memories.

I counted to ten and blew out a breath. I tried to school my features into a bland expression, but I could feel angry heat crawling up my neck and I was sure my skin was flushed.

"You're wrong. It wasn't you that she saw, Sawyer. It was that damn chair. Her guilt made it impossible for her to look away. It doesn't matter that it was you. Ollie would've dropped everything to be at the beck and call of anyone in your position. She's a good girl with a huge guilt complex. You aren't special to her. All you succeeded in doing was making her pity you."

"I also got rid of you, Huck. That was even more than I could ask for." Sawyer tossed his head back and laughed. "You always belonged on the streets. You never should've been born into my family."

262

I gritted my back teeth together and exhaled so hard I was sure my nostrils flared like an angry bull. No one got under my skin the way this lunatic did. Even knowing he had issues that should've been addressed long ago, it was still hard to let his words roll off my back. It was like we were back to being kids fighting over every little thing, and I hated how inferior it made me feel.

"I agree. I never belonged in that family, and I honestly owe you big time for forcing me to figure out how to make it on my own. It didn't take long for me to find a family that suits me much better. The family I have now is unbreakable, and they'll go to the mat for Ollie even if something happens to me. You got rid of me for a short period, but I came back stronger and better than before. Back then, I was trying to play the hero to your villain. These days, I know the only way to beat a monster is to become one yourself." I leaned back in my seat and lifted my eyebrows in Sawyer's direction. He was watching me closely now, all hints of maniacal amusement wiped off his face.

"This facility isn't so bad. You have your own room. The staff is fairly competent. Even though this is a state institution, it's the best place you could've ended up. If you're on your best behavior and continue to be docile and obedient, there is a chance you'll get out before you're an old man. The same goes for your mother. Right now, there's a solid chance she'll just end up on house arrest since she's never been in any kind of legal trouble before other than rich people stuff like bribery. I can make both of those things go away, though. I can have you transferred to a facility that is over capacity and understaffed. I can make sure you get so lost in the system that there is no hope you'll ever see the light of day again. Instead of therapy and medication, you'll end up tied to a bed for twenty-three hours a day. You haven't seen punishment yet, Sawyer. I can make sure your mom serves time somewhere she won't have a chance of surviving, regardless of how light her sentence is. Keep in mind, I'm Dad's favorite now. I'm the only one he wants to carry on his name. Money can make anything happen, and I can be far more ruthless now with it than I ever was without it. Decide to do the right thing and admit that you were the one who caused the accident that night; take Ollie out of the equation all together and I'll leave you and your mom alone. Do something redeemable for once in your life. Forget about Ollie and put in the work to get your mind straightened out. Take this time to be accountable for all you've done and try to heal. If you do what you're supposed to do, there's no reason you can't have a normal life when you get out. Who you were doesn't have to be who you are forever."

A heavy silence descended between us as we watched each other like the enemies that we were born to be. I didn't think he was going to give in. He's been so hung up on his obsession for so long, asking him to stop fixating on Ollie was like asking him to give up a fundamental part of who he was as a person. There was a good chance Sawyer didn't know how to be any other way. He needed help long before he'd finally been forced to accept it.

Suddenly he heaved a deep sigh and threw his head back. I could see all the veins under his pale skin on the side of his neck, and even the bony protrusion of his Adam's apple was a bit freaky in its prominence.

"I don't suppose I could talk you into letting me see Olivia one last time?" He asked it in such a way that I knew he already knew my answer.

"Not a chance in hell. You're never getting anywhere near her again as long as I live."

He laughed again, but this time it sounded slightly less unhinged. "That's the right answer, as much as I hate to admit it." He leaned forward in his chair a bit, eyes the exact same color as mine suddenly blazing with emotion. "What about the guy she hooked up with when she went to college? You do know you aren't her first, right? She may have worshiped you like you were some kind of god, but she threw her first time away on a cheap imitation of me."

I grunted and pushed out of my chair. The air in the small room felt thick, and I was close to suffocating on all the tension I was trying to swallow down.

"That's your entire problem, Sawyer. Her first, or her fiftieth, you get no say in who she chooses to be with. Or who she decides to love. She's her own person, and the choices she makes are hers and hers alone. They don't belong to you or me. I can only do my very best to be the person she picks as her favorite time and time again. If she ever decides she wants someone else, I'll let her go." *But not without putting up one hell of a fight.* "As for that guy, he's been taken care of. Not because he was her first, but because he was stupid and thought he could threaten her on my watch."

Like I said, the only way to win against a monster was to become an even bigger, more vicious one. When it came to protecting Ollie, there was never going to be anyone or anything more dangerous than me.

I left the room without saying goodbye, knowing that it was the last time I would ever have a conversation with my half brother. He didn't agree or disagree to come clean about his part in the accident, so I was going to have to force his hand. I hoped I changed his mind. I really didn't want to follow through on my threats.

But I would.

The reality was, Sawyer and I ended up a lot more alike than I think either of us wanted to admit.

We loved the same girl. We were willing to do whatever it took to have her. We both had mothers who only saw us as a means to an end, even if his was slightly more maternal. We both viewed our father as little more than a walking ATM and sperm donor. The biggest difference between the two of us was I had learned I needed to work for what I wanted and knew enough not to take anything for granted. Sawyer was handed everything without question, and that easy entitlement poisoned him.

As I was climbing into my sporty rental car I'd picked up for the weekend, my phone rang. I wasn't surprised to see that the caller was Ollie.

I told her I was going out of town for the weekend to visit Fisher. I felt bad lying to her, but I didn't want to fight with her over Sawyer ever again. I wanted the Richmans out of her life once and for all. Just like when we were little, I planned to stand between her and whomever tried to hurt her.

"Hey. Miss me already?" I'd only left earlier that morning after I made sure she was satisfied and would feel me every time she moved for the next few days.

"You went to see Sawyer?" Her voice snapped over the line, and I could picture her cheeks flooded with angry pink, making her cute freckles stand out and her scar stark white in contrast. "What were you thinking, Huck?"

I chuckled as I climbed into the low-slung car. "Vernon ratted me out. I swear, that kid likes you better than he likes me these days."

I heard Ollie huff out an annoyed breath. "No. Fisher stopped by to see the guys, and imagine my surprise to finally get to meet him when he was supposed to be with you instead. You lied to me, you asshole."

Damnit. I was in such a hurry to beat her back home, it slipped my mind that I needed to call Fisher and let him know I needed him as an alibi.

I sighed and leaned forward to rest my forehead against the steering wheel. "I did. But I'm not sorry about it. I know you want to clear my name and take responsibility for the accident, but it wasn't all your fault. Both Sawyer and I had a hand in it, and we've all paid the price. You were enslaved for years. Sawyer is in that chair and this institution for the foreseeable future. I had to suffer through that military academy on my own. All of those things are far worse than anything the legal system would put us through. I want Sawyer to admit what he did so you can stop being a martyr. I knew you didn't want me to see him or my dad before you tried to get someone to listen to your confession, so I did what I had to do."

She went quiet for a long moment, and while I could tell she was good and pissed, I also knew my words got through to her.

"I'm so mad at you, Huck." Her voice was quiet, but there was a thin thread of tenderness throughout it. "You're supposed to let me save myself from now on. And occasionally, it would be nice if you pretended I was saving you."

"You can save yourself when I'm late and can't get to you in time." I let out a soft sound. "And of course you've saved me. If you hadn't shown up, I would've kept living my life, jumping from one goal and achievement to the next. My life was moving forward, but I was stuck firmly in the past. I thought I moved beyond all the hurt and anger I harbored, but it was still there, taking up all the space where happiness should be. Everything I accomplished was empty. I needed you to fill my life up." I smiled even though she couldn't see me, but I figured she would be able to hear it in my voice. "You know, without Goldilocks, the bears lived a pretty boring life alone in the woods. They had each other, but they needed her to shake things up so they had a story to tell." Ollie snort-laughed at my analogy, and if I was flexible enough, I would've patted myself on the back for lightening the mood.

Now that she seemed less like she wanted to strangle me, I told her, "Sawyer told me that you loved me before you knew what love was. I think the same was true for me. I loved you without knowing that's what I was doing or how to do it right. That's why it hurt so bad when you had to turn on me. Maybe what I was feeling wasn't betrayal like I always thought. Maybe it was a broken heart. That's why I could never let it go and why an apology never felt like enough."

She made a distressed sound and I worried that I was going to make her cry while I was too far away to comfort her. I would have to give Vernon a call and tell him to go hug her for me.

"Don't cry. I'll be home before you know it. I'm going to stick around a day or two to make sure Sawyer does the right thing. If he comes through, you have no reason to come back here. We can move forward from here on out. For what it's worth, I know I fully forgive you, Ollie. I really don't need you to claim responsibility in search of redemption. You got that when you gave me a second chance to be with you." Finally, the past would be put to rest, and the only thing that would remain from that night was the scar on her cheek. And even that could be removed if she wanted.

She made a hiccupping sound, and I could hear her pull herself together. "We'll talk more about you running off without me when you get home, Huck. Stay safe and hurry back."

"Will do."

I didn't tell her to wait for me.

I didn't ask her not to run away while I was gone and couldn't stop her.

I didn't tell her I would find her wherever she went.

I didn't ask her to forgive me this time because I wasn't sorry for doing what had to be done.

269

"I love you."

"I love you, too. I'm so glad I found you after I lost you."

It'd taken a long time for us to get together, for the stars to align, and for the scales of our fate to find the perfect balance. But finally, after a lot of ups and downs, back and forth, and a knock down fight between good and evil, things between us felt just right.

And I knew I was keeping this Goldilocks in the bed next to me from here on out. I was never going to give her a reason to search for a better fit.

EPILOGUE

"**A**re you sure you have everything?"

It was the fifth time I'd asked Huck the same question, but each and every time, he remained patient and replied that he had triple-checked his bags before he loaded them into the back of the shiny new SUV he'd bought himself as a graduation present. His new last name came with a trust fund, but Huck insisted he wasn't going to touch a dime of it. He bought the new car with money he saved from his job for a down payment, and he was now looking at a loan payment every month like any other recent college grad to cover the rest. He remained determined to make it on his own with no help from his dad or the last name he never wanted.

Even after Sawyer came clean and admitted to his part in the accident, his father remained unforgiving and unmoved. I asked Huck how he managed to convince Sawyer to do the right thing, and he told me he simply used his brother's tactics against him. He also alluded to Sawyer knowing that now my mom was gone, he had no hope to get me back in his life. He seemed surprised by the way it all turned out, and I couldn't blame him. The last thing I expected after the showdown with Mrs. Richman and Huck's uneasy reunion with his father and brother was for Sawyer to take accountability for his part in the accident. None of it changed the fact I was driving, but now, who would listen to me with both boys taking responsibility? All that mattered was that Huck's name was clear. I wasn't going to keep pushing since that's what I wanted, after all.

I couldn't believe how fast the summer flew by. I couldn't get my head around the fact that today was the last day Huck and I would be living under the same roof. He'd gotten accepted to his first choice of post-grad law school, which was located in the same city where Fisher worked. He already had a job lined up and planned on living with Fisher for at least the first semester. He'd been busy packing up his part of the Victorian and making plans to move; I went back to work for Mercer and took a few summer courses so I could seamlessly transfer over to the Computer Science department next semester.

Huck asked me to go with him when he first got accepted to law school. We talked about it at length, and I'd been seriously tempted to agree.

Ultimately, I knew if we had any hope of a real future together, we had to stop living in the dark fairytale that had always been the story of our lives. A long distance relationship should be child's play compared to what we'd already been through together. But that didn't make the thought of not being able to see him, touch him, taste him, talk to him, and lean on him whenever I wanted bearable.

We'd been almost inseparable since he returned from his visit with Sawyer, and just like I always longed for, my life finally settled into something normal. It terrified me to think of letting him go while we lived our own individual lives. That fear was ultimately what made me decide to stay behind. I didn't want to want him just because I was afraid of being without him. I wanted to want him because we were better when we were together, but still pretty great when we were apart.

I needed to prove to myself that I could function on my own. That just like him, I could thrive in an imperfect situation and make it one that was perfect for me... for us.

None of the pep talks I got from Mercer and Vernon on a near daily basis changed the fact that I was devastated to see him go and worried about how I would do without him. I cried about it at least once a week in secret. But I wasn't very good at hiding my feelings, because Huck even offered to stay behind and switch to a school with a lower-rated law program closer to town, which only made me feel worse. I was sad at the thought of there being distance between us when it had taken so long for us to get close, but I was determined to do the right thing by letting him go chase his dream. I was going to support him from afar while I figured out who and what I wanted to be now that I had the space and freedom to do so.

"The drive isn't too bad. I promise to come back and see you on the weekends I'm not working." Huck muttered the promise as he bent down to grab my face between his big hands. I was sitting on the edge of our bed. I'd decided to take over his room officially since he was leaving. I never actually moved my stuff down from the attic, but I hadn't spent a single night in the eerie room since Huck and I started hooking up.

With both Huck and Harlen moving to different cities, Vernon and I were soon going to be on our own in the big, sprawling house. I nearly wept tears of relief when the pretty computer savant told me he was sticking around for grad school. So, not only was he staying in my department and would remain my mentor, but he was also sticking around as my favorite roommate. I'd also been lucky enough to have Mercer forgive me. It took some time, and some serious persistence on my part, but eventually she started to cave. She was mad I followed her and embarrassed her. She was upset I didn't trust her enough to make good choices for herself. In fact, the night of the date I ruined, she was planning on breaking up with my former classmate because she was tired of his mind games. She knew something was up, and the reason she was being so evasive was because she was worried he might have something to do with my past. She was trying to protect me all along. Mercer was what a true friend should be, and I loved her even more than I already had once we got everything straightened out. I don't know that I would've been able to process Huck leaving, or the eventual grief over losing my mom that had finally caught up with me, without her. I think seeing me finally come to terms with what a huge loss my mom's death was went a long way toward softening Mercer's anger at me.

GOLDILOCKS

My relationship with my mother was always complicated, but every questionable thing I'd ever done had been to keep her with me for as long as possible. Letting go of the weight of the responsibility for her wellbeing was life changing. I felt like I could finally breathe and move without bumping into a new, impossible obstacle.

Vernon and I were trying to decide if we wanted new roommates to help split the cost of the rent, or if we wanted to try and cover the expenses by ourselves. Neither one of us was exactly trusting or liked strangers in our space, so it looked like I might have to find a second part-time job before the semester started. No matter how much I enjoyed working at the store, there was no way I made enough to cover all my expenses. If I were a better student, I could tutor like Vernon, but that wasn't likely to happen anytime soon.

Truthfully, Vernon seemed more depressed that Harlen was leaving than I was about Huck. He'd been mopey and distracted since the draft picks were announced.

Huck touched his forehead to mine as I rested my hands on either side of his narrow waist.

"I know it isn't like you're moving halfway across the country, but I'll still miss you." I sighed and closed my eyes as his warmth slowly seeped into me. "And I'll come to you, too. You don't always have to come to me. You'll be busy with school and work."

He tried to convince me I needed a car now that he would be so far away. He didn't want me stuck without transportation in case of an emergency. I resisted because I knew how much grad school was going to cost him and how expensive moving to a big city was going to be. He insisted he had enough to cover all the things, but I was stubborn. As always, Huck was tricky and just figured a work-around. He bought a used little economy car for Vernon, with explicit instructions to share it with me whenever I asked. Vernon played along to make Huck happy, but we both knew the car was mine, even if my name was nowhere on the paperwork.

He chuckled softly, and his breath drifted across my lips, forcing them to part slightly. "So will you."

I made a face and tightened my hold on his shirt. "Yeah, but you care more about your grades than I do. I'll tolerate being apart the best I can, but don't be surprised when I show up on your doorstep out of the blue. Just in case, you better tell Fisher you're giving me a key."

He laughed again and tilted his head so his lips could skim over the tip of my nose. The soft gesture made me sigh and shift my hold from fabric to skin. He was supposed to be on the road over an hour ago, but our goodbye was dragging on much longer than anticipated.

I dragged my hands up along his sides, letting my fingers drift over his ribcage.

What was I going to do now that I couldn't jump him anytime I wanted?

I was going to miss having him crawl into bed all hot and hungry in the wee hours of the morning. I was going to miss his impatient hands and ravenous mouth. I was going to miss his hard body and unrelenting passion.

But most of all, I was going to miss his heart.

The steady thump when I laid on his chest to fall asleep made me feel safe and secure.

It acted like a beacon, a bright light in the darkness that had always surrounded me. I could find him no matter where he was in the world because of its glow.

I knew the upcoming distance wouldn't do anything to dim its radiance, but I was really going to long for the days where I could put my palm on his chest and feel that the most beautiful and important part of him was right at my fingertips.

Huck let me tug his Balenciaga t-shirt off over his head. He shifted his hold on my face so that one of his hands curled around the back of my skull and the other rested across my throat so his thumb could tip my chin upward. His mouth landed on mine as he let his weight fall forward, toppling us back onto the mattress.

I reveled in the hard press of his naked chest against mine. Almost instantaneously, my nipples perked up, and my heart started to pound with excitement.

It wasn't like we hadn't been making the most of our dwindling time together the last few weeks, but there was something about the way we touched each other right now that was a little more reverent. We'd been spoiled by having unlimited access to one another. Now, we were going to have to make every kiss, every sigh, every brush of naked skin last.

Huck braced his weight above me on one of his elbows, arching away just enough that I could get a hand between us to wrestle with his belt and the fastenings on his jeans. I could feel that he was already hard, and the way his stomach muscles tightened when my knuckles skated over his defined abs.

The hand he had resting at the base of my throat tightened slightly, making my eyes widen. Huck lifted his mouth from mine and dropped a kiss on the smooth surface of the scar on my cheek. I told him time and time again that the spot was mostly numb, but that didn't stop him from always pausing to pay a bit of attention to it. It was kind of like he was trying to kiss the boo-boo away the way he had when we were little kids. Like he was trying to kiss away all the bad memories and the years of bad choices etched into that tiny spot on my face.

I pushed his clothing out of the way as he kissed his way down the side of my neck, pausing to nip at the place where my pulse was fluttering erratically under my skin. The bite was a bit harder than it had to be, and I knew it was going to leave a mark. It didn't surprise me. Huck had been more and more aggressive the closer it came to the day he had to leave. I had little love bites and bruises in the shape of his fingers littered across my skin. Most were only visible when I was completely naked, but there were a few embarrassing ones that couldn't be hidden. I was pretty sure it was his way of staking his claim, of letting anyone who dared get too close know I was already spoken for. That kind of highhandedness should rub me the wrong way, but I was also feeling my possessive side rear its ugly head knowing he was about to be going to a new school full of new people, all of whom at least shared the same interest in the law as he did. If we hadn't been to hell and back together, jealousy would eat me alive at the thought of all the new girls who were going to be in his world.

It was a good thing we were fated to be together. I had zero doubts anyone who crossed his path would ever mean as much to him as I did. Our journey was from friends, to enemies, to lovers. We'd been everything to each other, and no one else could ever say that.

Huck lifted his head as he skipped his fingertips across my collarbone, moving to the strap of my tank top, and slowly slid it down my shoulder. His heated gaze skimmed over the curve of my breast, and his lips lifted into a satisfied grin.

"You're a quick learner when the subject is something you're deeply invested in." He grunted out a low, pleased sound when my hand found the rigid length that was pressing between us. He always pulsed excitedly in my palm, and I was still blown away by how soft and hard he was at the same time.

I gazed up at him, surprised that I could still form coherent thought considering his mouth was now moving over the tight, aching point on the tip of my breast. I felt the tug right between my legs and shifted restlessly beneath him.

"Maybe that has more to do with the student than the teacher." I was always eager to learn when it came to him. His lessons always felt like something I would carry throughout my lifetime. "I'm always shooting a perfect score when we're together. And I don't mind having to go the extra mile for extra credit."

Huck laughed lightly and switched his attention to my other breast. As sad as I was to say goodbye, this way was so much better than the rushed, angry words he'd thrown at me when he left as a teenager. Back then, our parting lingered in my mind like a bad dream. Now, I would feel him and remember his touch and kiss each time I moved.

"Just keep following my lead, Ollie. I won't lead you astray." His raspy voice drifted across my overly sensitive skin as his hands moved to strip the rest of my clothing out of his way.

I arched against him and whispered, "I'd follow you to the ends of the Earth and back, Huck." It was the truth. One I could only ever give to him. No matter how far off the beaten path I might wander, Huck was always the home I returned to.

Just like Goldilocks, who was lost and alone until she stumbled upon an unlikely refuge deep in the dark woods, I magically found the place where I fit in perfectly.

That spot was right next to Huck, no matter how near or far he happened to be.

THE END

Keep reading for a preview of Fortunate Son, a next-generation Marked Men novel, featuring Rule's son and Jet's daughter. Coming very soon!

FORTUNATE SON

Prologue

66 I don't think we're a good match."

The softly spoken words echoed in my head for hours.

It wasn't like the breakup came out of nowhere. The girl I loved with every fiber of my being had been acting strange and distant for weeks. I'd known her my entire life. We grew up together and had been the best of friends before we fell in love. I knew her almost as well as I knew myself, and I could tell something between us was off, but I refused to believe the end of what we had was near.

I told myself she was just stressed out and worried about the fact we were going to different colleges. Young love was already unreliable and tricky to navigate. When you added the hurdle of a long distance to the mix, it seemed almost destined to fail. I tried to reassure her everything would be fine; after all, I was older than her and had already been in college a year. Nothing changed between us while I waited not so patiently for her to finish high school. I foolishly thought she would apply and get accepted to my school so we could stay together. It never occurred to me that she was only going to apply to schools out-of-state. I was unaware that for years she'd had her heart set on leaving not only me but also our hometown. When she finally came clean and let me know she was moving to California in the fall, I was stunned but optimistic that our relationship would survive. After all, she was my first love. I was willing to sacrifice whatever it took to keep her in my life.

Aston didn't feel the same.

I felt blindsided by both the breakup and the revelation that she was always planning to move halfway across the country. Suddenly the adorable little girl who grew up following my every step, and who had effortlessly stolen my heart with her sweet, cheerful, innocent demeanor seemed like a total stranger who never cared about me the way I cared about her.

It was easy enough to argue with her when she said we weren't a good match.

It was impossible to fight against her when she told me she wasn't happy being with me and needed a change.

I wanted to tell her we just needed some time apart. I had faith in my ability to change her mind and prove to her that we belonged together. But the look in her eyes when she ended things was definite. This wasn't a rash decision on her part. It was something she had clearly given a lot of thought to and her mind was made up.

She didn't want to be with me anymore, and I was left adrift and discombobulated.

I didn't have a lot of experience with heartbreak.

I was the kind of guy who typically got what I wanted and excelled at whatever I put my mind to. I graduated at the top of my class in high school. Got into my first choice college and was in the starting line up my first college football game. My parents had a wall full of trophies and accolades I'd earned over the years. They were always proud of what I'd accomplished, even though they had never pushed me to be perfect. All they wanted was for me to be happy, so they supported me regardless of how hard I pushed myself.

I was popular and well-liked among my peers, and as one of the oldest members of my tight-knit inner circle of relatives and longtime family friends who were all about the same age, I was often the voice of reason and most responsible member of the group. I never had a problem getting close to members of the opposite sex, but there was only one I wanted to call mine.

But she no longer wanted me, and I wasn't sure what to do with myself now.

It was my first time being rejected, and I could admit I wasn't handling it well... at all.

I glanced down at my phone, which had been ringing and pinging with messages nonstop for the last several hours. I wanted to turn the damn thing off, but there was a part of me that refused to believe I'd been dumped, and I waited for each call to show my ex's info. She never popped up on the screen, but my mom called no less than twenty times. My dad no less than ten, and my best friend, who also happened to be my cousin, was sending a text every fifteen minutes like clockwork.

I ignored them all, but eventually, the one and the only person I couldn't ignore even if I wanted to called, and I finally caved and answered the phone.

"Ry Archer, where in the hell are you? Mom and Dad are worried sick about you." My little sister's voice was shaky and sounded like she'd been crying. She was normally a pretty tough cookie, but she tended to be overly dramatic and emotional about most things. Part of that was because she was a teenage girl. But a huge chunk of it was that she took after our father in pretty much every single way other than her appearance. She looked just like our mother, with her white-blond hair and pretty green eyes.

However, she was as reckless and rebellious as our old man. She was as outspoken and opinionated as he was. She was as bold and colorful as he was. She was fearless in everything the same way he was. And she felt everything in extremes the same way he did. Both of us grew up knowing without a doubt how much we were loved and cherished by our parents, but especially by our dad. The opposite was also true. Whenever we disappointed him or did something he didn't approve of, we felt his displeasure down to our bones. It was a lot to balance, but luckily our quiet and mostly even-keeled mother kept our household and our father in check. I wished I took after her the way my little sister, Daire, took after Dad, but I was kind of the odd man out in our family.

I'd heard more than once from my grandparents and my uncle that my personality and behavior were almost a mirror image of my dad's twin brother, who was no longer with us. It was a sore spot with my dad whenever someone made the comparison, but he didn't deny that there were times I reminded him of his twin brother. No matter how much time had gone by since he lost his twin, my dad still very much missed his other half and felt his loss. Sometimes my mom told me stories about them when they were growing up, and I could sense the similarities. It sucked he had passed away so young for so many reasons. Only one of which was that I really had no one to relate to in my family. I was kind of the black sheep in a flock that was already pretty dark.

I sighed and squeezed the steering wheel between my hands.

I loved my little sister with everything in me. We were extraordinarily close and rarely kept secrets from each other. We were close enough in age that it had often been the two of us against the world no matter what. She was my favorite person and my most trusted confidant. But she was also my ex's best friend. They were only a few months apart in age, and where one went, the other often followed. When I first started showing interest in my ex, my sister was totally against the idea of us being anything more than good friends. She told me she never wanted to be caught between the two of us. She never wanted to have to pick a side or have to keep something from either one of us. I waved off the concerns because I was sure my ex and I were meant to be. I'd grown up surrounded by true love and examples of young love maturing into happy, healthy, long-lasting marriages. I thought staying with my first love through thick and thin might be the only way in which I took after my parents.

I didn't want to think that Daire knew what would happen to my relationship before I did, and she kept something so huge from me. Any way I looked at it, she had to know things were going south before I did.

"I'm going for a drive right now. Tell mom and dad not to worry. I'll be fine." I knew I would be. Eventually.

My sister sighed on the other end of the line, and I could hear her pacing around. She was the type who was constantly in motion. She never sat still, and her mind was always going a mile a minute. I knew if I didn't convince her that I was okay, she would venture out aimlessly into the night trying to track me down, even though she had no idea where I was or how long I'd been in my truck.

"You've been driving for the last four hours? Are you even in Colorado anymore?" Daire's voice rose sharply.

I looked at the clock on the dashboard and blinked when I realized how much time had passed. I was still in Colorado, but just barely. I was almost at the southern border. I didn't have a plan when I climbed in my truck and started to drive, but subconsciously I started heading toward the one person no one would ever suspect me of turning to when I was hurting.

"Give me some time, Daire." I wanted to close my eyes and make the world disappear until I could fully deal with the empty ache in the center of my chest. Since I was driving, that wasn't an option, so all I could do was shake my head and blink my eyes, which alternately felt like they were hot with tears and dry as the desert. "I have to get my head on right before I try to talk to anyone, but especially you, about what went down today."

She made a distressed sound, and I could clearly imagine her putting her brightly painted nails to her mouth. She always wore a bunch of rings and bracelets that clinked and banged together, making so much noise. My little sister was anything but subtle, and you could always hear her coming. She knew how to make an entrance, but she also knew when it was time to back down and fade into the background. She knew all my buttons and when to push them. I would *always* answer her when she called me, but I had limits to how much I would let her poke and prod me when I was hurt.

"I didn't know, Ry. I honestly had no idea Aston was going to break up with you. She's been weird lately, but I thought it was because we were graduating, or maybe because Royce left with his mom last year when she moved to New York. You know how close she was to her brother. She never mentioned anything about being unhappy with you to me. I promise I would've told you." I could hear that she was starting to cry, and it made me feel like shit.

I should've listened to her at the start when she said dating my buddy Royce's little sister was a terrible idea. We were all too close, our families too connected for it to end any other way than tragic.

Aston Wheeler was the daughter of my mom and dad's extremely close friends. All my best friends were actually in my life for the same reason. We were a close group brought together by our parents, but we stayed together because we all genuinely liked each other and had various things in common. Aston's dad worked with my uncle, operating several custom car and motorcycle garages across Denver. And both Royce's real mom and Aston's mother were ridiculously tight with my mom. Aston had been pretty sick when she was young, so her parents often turned to my mom, a doctor, for advice and guidance. My cousins Remy and Zowen, along with me, my sister, Royce and his sister, as well as a couple older kids we didn't see much, Joss and Hyde, and my dad's coworker's daughters, Glory and Bowe, all spent a lot of time together growing up. Not all of us lived in Colorado during the course of our friendship as our families grew and the world around us changed. But we always saw each other during the holidays and made it a point to be present for any major life event of the others.

Some of us were closer, like me and Zowen and Daire and Aston. Bowe and Remy were also super tight, even though the younger girl had lived in Austin the entire time we'd known her. It was fun to have a big network of diverse and interesting friends, but there were a few of us who sometimes rubbed each other the wrong way and had to work at playing nice with one another.

Well... really, that only applied to Bowe Keller and me.

She and I were the nearest in age out of everyone, but that was the only similarity between the two of us. We never particularly got along. Starting from the time we were figuring out how to walk and talk. I always thought it was a good thing she lived in Austin with her folks and I only had to see her on holidays and during the summer.

But today, I wanted her to be closer.

I wasn't certain why she was the one I wanted to share my heartache with. I just knew that I wanted to see her right now when my whole world felt like it was upside down.

I blew out a breath and tried to reassure my sister, "I believe you. I know you wouldn't stand by and let me be blindsided like that." But I also knew she would fight to the death for Aston, so she had to be in a tough spot right now. "Just give me some space right now. I'll call Mom and Dad when I get where I'm going. Tell them not to worry too much. Let me catch my breath and calm down for a minute."

My little sister sighed again, and I heard her knock something over—her sadness and frustration palpable through the phone. "You don't have to run away from home in order to hide your emotions from everyone, Ry. As hard as you try to convince everyone otherwise, we know you're human. Stop trying to force yourself to be so perfect all the damn time. You're allowed to be sad and angry right now. You're supposed to be upset when your heart gets broken. I know you don't really know what losing feels like, but this is it, and you shouldn't go through it alone."

I did tend to strive for perfection, but obviously I missed the mark or I wouldn't have gotten dumped so mercilessly.

I cleared my throat and tapped my fingers on the steering wheel, squinting as a semi-truck passed me on the opposite side of the road. "I'm only going to be alone for a little bit."

She was correct when she said I was running away to hide my feelings.

That was something I always did.

But there was one person with whom I never put on the pretense of perfection, mostly because she saw right through it and never failed to call me out on my bullshit.

"Ohh... okay." Almost instantly, my sister's tone changed, and she seemed relieved. Like I said, we were super close, and she knew me better than I knew myself some days. It wouldn't take her too long to figure out where I was going, even if the destination would be considered highly unlikely to anyone else. "Well, drive safe, and don't forget to check in with Mom and Dad when you have time. I'll try to hold them off for a little bit. For what it's worth, I already gave Aston a piece of my mind. I even called Royce to ask him if he knew what was going on, but he was as clueless as I was. About the college thing, and about you. I don't know why she was making all those decisions in secret, but I honestly think she's hurting as much as you are right now."

Impossible.

She walked away, and I could hardly move. She took me down to my knees, left me breathless, and hadn't bothered to spare me a backward glance. There wasn't an ounce of the kind, caring girl who had me wrapped around her finger for so long as she ripped my heart out. I definitely didn't recognize her. Worse than that, though, was that I didn't recognize myself either. I wasn't familiar with failure, so losing the most important thing in my world forced me to react in a way that was totally unlike me. I was behaving like the kind of people I tended to loathe.

Unreasonable.

Irrational.

Unpredictable.

The reason I disliked people who acted in such a way was because I never allowed myself the freedom to be so chaotic and carefree. I was jealous, and the envy ate away at me.

Fortunately, I had a thirteen-hour drive to pull the frayed edges of my ego together and to slip back into my role of the golden boy who was unnaturally blessed.

I drove through the night and into the very early morning. I only stopped for gas and the occasional bathroom break. I silently cursed at how big Texas was as the miles added up. I made a quick stop to shove a greasy fast-food breakfast in my face when my stomach started growling. Because I was an athlete, I normally avoided anything that came in an oil-stained paper bag. But right now, the usual rules didn't apply. I was alone, so I didn't need to pretend to be perfect for anyone.

I took a moment to shoot a couple texts off to my sister and my cousin. Zowen was pissed it took so long for me to respond to him and warned that my dad had already shown up at his house looking for me. We were all home from school for summer break, so it made sense that my folks figured I would hit up my uncle's house first when I disappeared. My uncle Rome was even scarier than my dad when it came to discipline and order. He was the last person, next to my father, I wanted to come looking for me, especially while I was all caught up in my feelings. My uncle was a former military man who was now a successful entrepreneur. He didn't take shit from anyone who wasn't his pint-sized wife or his wild, mouthy firstborn. My cousin Remy was even more of a handful than my little sister, and twice as rebellious. She was always in one kind of trouble or another, but she was probably the most loyal and passionate person I'd ever encountered in my life. Both Daire and I idolized her when we were growing up. Now, she was often the one we turned to when we needed help managing our relationships with our parents and general life advice. She was one of our group who left Denver relatively young when she ventured into the real world. I think we all expected as much from her.

Remy was a wanderer. A free spirit. She was also irrevocably in love with Hyde Bishop-Fuller, the oldest guy in our inner circle. Unfortunately, Hyde had never returned her adoration, and when he enlisted in the military a couple of years ago, Remy really saw no reason to stay in any one place for too long. She left her shattered heart in Denver and never looked back. I missed her like crazy, and I knew Zowen worried about her endlessly, but she always seemed happy and as carefree as ever when she finally materialized. I always envied her easygoing attitude. Nothing seemed to ruffle her feathers. Well, nothing other than Hyde.

I'd never been that relaxed and unaffected. I took myself far too seriously.

It was still early enough in the morning that I didn't have to fight traffic when I pulled into Austin. It was hardly a surprise that the girl I came all this way to see was just now getting home when I parked my truck at the end of her driveway. She didn't even blink when she saw me climb out of my truck and make my way toward her.

Her black and purple hair was piled on top of her head in a messy ponytail, and her dark eye makeup was smeared around her honey-colored eyes in a way that I couldn't tell if it was deliberate or not. She had on a pair of skintight red leggings that looked like they were made of leather and a pair of shiny black boots that were laced up to her knees. Her t-shirt had the logo of an obscure band scrawled across the front, and the bottom was chopped off so that it skimmed her pierced belly button. I always thought she looked like she had just climbed out of the pages of a comic book, and today was no exception.

Instead of walking into the cute but tiny mid-century modern home that sat just off South Congress Street, she waited until I was standing directly in front of her before she crossed her arms over her chest and glared up at me.

I was waiting for her to demand an explanation as to why I was suddenly standing on her doorstep. I was ready for her to pick a fight. I'd spent the last hour of the very long drive bracing myself for her to rip me apart and ask all the questions I didn't want to answer.

Instead, I whispered the words, "It hurts so bad," and almost immediately lost all the composure I'd tried so hard to build. I aimlessly made my way toward the girl who was my sworn enemy.

She didn't push me away or make fun of my complete and utter breakdown.

No. She didn't do anything I expected her to do.

Bowe Keller never did, which was why I never knew what to do with her or how to handle all the conflicting ways I felt about her.

All I knew was that she was the person I needed the most at this moment.

Chapter 1

Bowe

The last thing I expected to encounter after dragging myself home from a band practice that lasted way longer than it should have was a heartbroken, seemingly devastated Archer. The only time I crossed paths with any of the Archer family was on holidays or during summer vacations when my parents dragged me to Denver for a couple of months each year. Since that one fateful summer, the amount of time I spent with my childhood friends was less and less. I loved my life in Austin and often resented being dragged into all the memories and relationships that made up my parents' past. I was very much a live-for-the-moment type of girl, and I didn't enjoy being pulled away from my friends and the interests I had at home. I'd skipped the last trip to Denver for Christmas, and I fully planned on staying in Austin for the summer, even though my parents had heavily hinted they wanted me to tag along for their upcoming annual trip. I was living on my own now and trying to make my own choices without feeling guilty or ungrateful. It was a struggle I'd yet to master.

I had twin sisters, Yves and Zola, who were significantly younger than I was. Neither one of them had stopped texting me and begging me to go with the family since I flatly refused. So far, I'd managed to stand firm in my determination not to make the trip, but if the twins kept hounding me, I knew I was going to cave. My mom and dad struggled to have more kids after I came along. It was something they were very open about. They were transparent with me when they decided to pursue in-vitro fertilization. It hadn't been an easy process for anyone in our small family. It took more than one attempt before they were successful. As a result, my little sisters were often viewed as the miracles they were. We all treated them like they were precious and special. They might be the only soft spot I had. Or at least, the only one I would ever admit to.

The other tender, sensitive spot in my icy heart, I would rather die than acknowledge to anyone, but especially myself. Unfortunately, that secret spot had been blown wide open and was aching because the boy who claimed it was currently standing in front of me looking like a zombie.

Even as young children, Ryier Archer and I were always on opposites sides of any situation. We bickered endlessly and never saw eye-to-eye on anything. Fighting with Ry was as easy as breathing, and our endless conflicts, big and small, played a pretty big part in why I didn't want to pull myself out of my own life just to play the reoccurring villain in his. We were old enough now; there was no need to force each other to endure the other's company. There was no reason either of us had to suffer.

I didn't have to let his perceived perfection irk me. And my absolute lack of conformity no longer needed to bother him.

And he didn't need to be bothered by my blatant disregard of rules and regulations.

Things were never easy between the two of us, but over the last few years, while he'd been dating Aston Wheeler, they'd become unbearable. There were several reasons for the discontent between the two of us, but I only let myself think about them when I was alone and feeling particularly melancholy and introspective.

None of that mattered at the moment, though, because Ry looked like he was on the verge of tears. I grabbed his stupidly attractive face and looked into his icy blue eyes. It might be the first time since knowing him that Ry Archer allowed himself to show any kind of weakness or vulnerability. So, while a big part of me wanted to turn him back around and send him on his way, I knew I couldn't kick him while he was down. Instead, I practically dragged him inside and situated him on my second-hand couch before he crashed and burned.

One minute he was looking at me with his broken heart bleeding in his eyes; the next, he was knocked out and oblivious to the world around him. I was stunned when I took a good look at his sleeping face and noticed he had dried tear tracks on his ridiculously chiseled cheeks. The Ry I knew was so emotionally repressed, I wasn't sure he even knew how to cry. The boy who was currently unmoving in my living room was not the same Ry Archer I knew how to handle.

The Ry I knew and loathed was the top student. The best boyfriend. The decorated athlete and super reliable teammate. The beloved older brother. The steadfast cousin. The revered son, and the always unwaveringly loyal friend. He had no flaws and allowed for no mistakes. His stringent dedication to put on a picture-perfect front was one of the main reasons we never got along. I had no time or patience for the pretense of perfection.

Even though it was frighteningly early in the morning, I pulled my cell out of my pocket and called Daire as I went in search of an extra blanket to toss over my unwanted guest. As much as I didn't like Ry, I adored Daire. We were enough alike that she was one of the few friends in Denver I stayed in touch with no matter how chaotic or busy life got. We chatted a couple of times a week and kept each other in the loop. She kept me up-to-date on what her brother was up to, even though I would rather pull my own teeth out than ask her anything about him. She never divulged just how much she knew about the secrets Ry and I shared, but she was intuitive and knew her older brother better than anyone. I was pretty sure even if Ry never said a word, Daire would know there were reasons beyond our differences that caused us not to speak for a length of time.

"You couldn't call and give me a heads up that your brother was going to show up on my doorstep? Do I even need to ask how he got my new address?" I asked the questions without saying hello as soon as Daire picked up my call. I'd only moved into the South Congress house a month or so ago. The rent was outrageous, but fortunately, my folks were helping me stay afloat until the two roommates I had lined up moved in. They were coming closer to the start of the next semester of school, so I was supposed to have the place to myself for most of the summer. I regretted giving Daire and Remy a ritual tour and my new address when they asked about it.

The younger girl snorted, and I could hear her shifting around in bed as she snapped back, "If I told you, you would've left him sitting in his truck after he drove through the night. Plus, I didn't know where he was going until he was already out of Colorado. Is he okay?"

I cast a look over my shoulder where his huge body was taking up every inch of my couch. He looked pale, and his black hair had clearly been the victim of his agitated hands. His jeans had what looked like a grease stain on one thigh, and there was a hole in his faded t-shirt near the neck. All in all, it was the messiest, most disheveled version of Ry Archer I had ever seen.

"He's here, but I don't know that I'd call him okay. He looks like he's been put through the wringer." I finally found a quilt that my mom had made for me a couple of Christmases ago. It was made of a bunch of my dad's old band t-shirts that featured all the different logos and designs from different tours and performances he's put on through the years. It was totally nostalgic and personal. Even my dad had gotten choked up when he saw all the work and memories that had gone into the gift. I kept meaning to find somewhere in the new house to display it, but I always seemed to get distracted by other things. It was the story of my life. I had a hard time balancing my priorities and everything, even the most important things, tended to lose out to my music and the songs in my head and heart.

I tiptoed back to the couch and carefully placed the soft material over the prone body of the boy I told myself I wanted nothing to do with now that I was living my own life.

Daire sighed heavily on the other end of the call, and I could almost visualize the cute and concerned face she was making. The girl looked like a literal angel with her almost white hair and super pale skin. However, looks were very fucking deceiving in her case, because Ry's little sister was a devil in disguise. She lived for mischief and fully lived up to her name. She wasn't afraid of anything and often let her curiosity lead her into trouble. She was fearless and fierce in ways I was both scared of and admired.

"Aston broke up with him. I think it's the first time in Ry's life he's ever faced any kind of rejection. He's going to see it as an epic failure. I'm not surprised he's falling apart. He can't stand to lose, and I know he's going to figure out a way to make this all about him and whatever he's lacking. He won't take two seconds to think about the fact that Aston is probably going through something pretty major or that this is just as hard for her. He'll take all the blame and beat himself up forever."

I sucked in a startled breath and made my way through the tiny house to my bedroom. I wasn't planning on playing hostess tonight and practice had worn me out. I just wanted to crawl under my covers and sleep the whole dawning day away. "I can't believe she dumped him. Those two are so much alike, I thought they would stay together forever. It took him forever to get Royce to agree to let him date his little sister. Ry put the work in."

Aston Wheeler was as much of a perfectionist as Ry. The girl was literally flawless, which was why I didn't really care for her. Or rather, it was just one more reason I was annoyingly jealous of her. I was too stubborn to admit that was really why I was standoffish and abrupt with her. I much preferred spending time with her older brother. Royce was an artist. He was quirky and sensitive, but also a badass when it came to protecting his little sister. He was a bit messy and irresponsible with everything in his life, including romance, which made it easy for me to relate to him. There was absolutely no reason rigid and unyielding Ry Archer was the boy I had a problem forgetting. If the universe was fair, I would've fallen for Royce all those years ago instead.

Daire sighed again. "She didn't just break up with Ry; she also told him she's going to college in California. She told him she wasn't happy, and hadn't been in a long time. It's totally out of character for her. They've been together for two years, and he had no idea she was planning on moving out of state after graduation. She didn't tell him anything. I think he was blindsided by that as much as the breakup. She didn't even tell me she was applying out of state. All of this was news to me as well. I want to shake her."

I let out a low whistle as I wrestled my boots off my feet. "I didn't know she had it in her to be so secretive."

Aston seemed like such a sweet girl. I couldn't imagine her keeping something so huge from not only the guy she was seeing, but also her bestie.

"She doesn't. Which is why I'm sure there's gotta be a reason behind her actions that neither Ry nor I know about. I'm worried about her, but my brother takes priority. He comes first, no matter what." She made an amused sound that made me glare into my empty room before she asked, "Want to explain to me why, out of everyone he knows, and all his friends that live way closer than you do, he picked you to run to? Why did he go looking for you, Bowe? He ran from the girl he supposedly loved more than anything right to you."

I threw myself back on my bed and practically growled, "I'll talk to you later, Daire. I'll make sure your brother calls you once he wakes up and gets back to his regular self."

I hung up the call on the sound of her knowing laughter.

I tossed my cell toward the empty side of the bed and lifted my hands to rub my tired eyes. I was going to smear dark eye makeup all over my face, but couldn't muster up the energy to care or rouse myself to wash it all off before bed. Instead, I pulled my comforter around me and stayed sideways across the mattress as my eyes drifted closed.

I thought I was finally breaking free from all the complicated relationships that had haunted me throughout my teenage years. I loved my parents. My dad was my hero, and I wanted to be just like him when I grew up. He'd had a guitar in my hand and taught me how to play and write songs since the time I could understand what made music so magical. I had always known I wanted to pursue playing music instead of enrolling in college, much to my mother's horror. Eventually, we'd come to a compromise after I failed my entire first semester. I only went to make her happy, which we both realized was a *huge* mistake.

It wasn't that my brilliant mom was against me following in my father's footsteps. It was more that she'd been with him through all the ups and downs of being a professional musician. She stayed with him when he had nothing and when pretty much everyone on the planet recognized his face. She knew how difficult it was to have a family and to keep a relationship together when one of the people involved gave half their heart to music and melodies. She reminded me repeatedly that I had to share my dad with all the people who made it possible for him to do what he loved for a living. I knew she just wanted my life to be a little easier than that. She wanted me to have a secure future. She didn't want me to sacrifice, or go without the way she had when my dad was on tour for long stretches of time. She often reminded me how often it was just me and her, and the twins later on, when my father was away. I hated it growing up, but I understood the sacrifice now that I was older.

Music meant everything to me, and I was willing to do whatever it was going to take, to give up whatever I had to sacrifice, to make my mark the way my father had. I wanted to make both my parents proud, but more than that, I wanted to chase after my dreams and accomplish great things because they mattered to me, not because I just happened to have a famous father.

I often butted heads with my more pragmatic and reasonable mother, but I never doubted for a second that she would love and support me regardless of the path I chose for myself. She was actually the more understanding parent. Like when I started to put my foot down about being dragged to Denver. My family loved to get together with the friends and found family that had helped them not only get together, but stay together when times got tough. My parents were inexplicably close to the friends they'd lived and worked with when they were the age I was now. I understood they wanted the next generation to have the same kind of bonds and support system they had, but it wasn't something that could be forced.

The twins and I had our own friends here in Austin, and while it was nice to know there was a whole group of people we could rely on in a pinch, regardless of time and distance, they couldn't be a part of the challenges and solutions that made up our everyday lives.

Plus, Ry was the epicenter of the relationships that connected everyone. He was the one we all circulated around and gravitated toward, whether we wanted to or not. He was either related by blood to half of them or was the one who welcomed the new additions into the fold with open arms. There were a lot of us kids from the second generation running around. He was friendly and charming. He was levelheaded and calm. He was the one they turned to for advice, and the one they looked up to as a role model. The fact he and I had always rubbed each other the wrong way forever made me feel like the outcast. It made it harder to get close to the others who did nothing but sing his praises and fall for his false portrayal of perfection. I felt like I was the only person on the planet willing to call out Ry on his bullshit time and time again. I felt like I was the only one who could tell he was putting up a front, and that underneath that very pretty mask he wore, he was as much of a mess as the next conflicted kid.

I couldn't believe he was sleeping on my couch right now.

I couldn't believe his dream girl dumped him and had been hiding something as big as leaving the state from him.

I couldn't believe she found the courage to tell him to his face, that he didn't make her happy.

I couldn't believe I was the one he turned to for comfort after all the harsh words and ugly accusations we had slung at each other the last time we were in the same room together. I was pretty sure we'd reached the mutual agreement to never speak again after that big blowout.

The only thing that wasn't a surprise was that he still looked as good as ever.

All those damn Archers were blessed with some pretty fucking superior genetics.

They were all tall with outrageously striking looks. Both Zowen and Ry took after their fathers with dark hair and inexplicably pale blue eyes. Both boys were in really good shape from playing sports. Ry played football, while Zowen preferred soccer. Ry was far more serious about his chosen sport than his cousin. Ry was still playing college ball, while Zowen had given up the game to focus on school when his grades started slipping. The Archer girls, Remy and Daire, looked more like their mothers, who were fair and delicate. They were no less impressive than their siblings, even though they lacked the hulking height and bulging muscles. Any one of them was a headturner on their own. When the four of them were together, it was like they created their own magnetic force that made everyone around them unable to look away or focus on anything but them. The Archer effect was no joke.

Ry had always been astoundingly good looking. He had also always known it.

It wasn't that he was the conceited or egotistical type. More like, he'd always been the best at whatever it was he did, so of course, he would also be the guy who was the best looking wherever he went. I wanted to be irritated by his self-assurance, but he wasn't wrong.

Honestly, today was the most *real* I'd ever seen him. All of that polish and shine he wore like armor had finally tarnished, but he was still better than the average person. His hair was still thick and shiny, even when it was a ruffled mess. His body was still unbelievably ripped and gorgeously toned, even when he was dressed down and looked like he'd shoved his dinner in his face while driving eighty on the interstate. His face still looked like it'd been carved by a master sculptor, even when it was tearstained and slightly haggard. An unkempt Ry Archer was still the best looking guy I'd ever seen in person. I liked him better when his human side was showing, especially since it was so rare.

I had to remind myself he was absolutely not my type. No matter how quickly he softened my hardened heart.

I never understood how a guy whose father owned and operated one of the biggest and most well-known tattoo shops in the US could be so clean cut and proper. It wasn't that Ry didn't have any ink, but he definitely didn't embrace the form of self-expression the way a lot of the older kids had who had grown up running around the different tattoo shops our parents either worked in or frequented. He could be covered in beautiful, colorful designs that made him stand out even when he was covered up in a football uniform. Instead, he only had one complicated, black and gray image covering one of his muscular arms.

I thought it was boring. My dad, who was covered in ink from all over the world, reminded me it was just as bad to judge someone for how normal they looked as it was to make assumptions based on how they decorated their body. It wasn't my place to question why Ry did or didn't let his father put his famous and highly sought-after work all over him... but I did it anyway. Mostly because I felt like I needed to question *everything* Ry did.

The boy was beyond confusing.

So was the way I felt about him.

Because while Aston Wheeler might be his first love and the one he picked as his perfect match... I was his first everything else... and he was my one and only.

Chapter 2

Ry

Iwasn't sure what time it was when I finally managed to open my eyes the next day. I felt a little like I'd been hit by a two-hundred-fifty-pound linebacker or one of the semi-trucks I'd passed on the interstate. My head hurt the same way it did when I had too much to drink and was forced to get up early the following day for practice. I rubbed my eyes and swung my legs off the unfamiliar and seriously lumpy couch. I had no recollection of anything that happened after I fell apart as soon as I saw Bowe. It seemed like she somehow hauled me inside her home. That couldn't have been an easy task considering our size difference.

Looking around her space, one thing became immediately clear. Even if you didn't know a thing about her, you would know you were standing in the home of a musician. There were various types of guitars, both electric and acoustic, hanging on the walls and leaning against other furniture. There was an electric keyboard taking up one whole corner of the small living room, and the computer set up took up space where a dining room table should be and had all kinds of gadgets for mixing and tweaking sound, as well as an array of expensive-looking headphones. The place wasn't exactly homey, but rather looked like the inside of a recording studio, and very much reflected Bowe's number one passion.

The girl had been telling anyone who would listen that she was going to be a superstar since she started talking.

I dragged my hands down my face and got an unpleasant whiff of myself when I lifted my arms. Now that I was no longer operating in a haze of heartbreak, I slightly regretted my rash decision to take off in the middle of the night with zero plans or forethought. I hadn't even packed a bag or brought anything that would make a few nights away from home comfortable.

Fortunately, I was the overly prepared type and kept a loaded gym bag in my truck, so I should be able to get by until I hit up a big box store for essentials. After collecting my duffel from the truck and cleaning out the trash that lingered from the drive, I picked my way through Bowe's tiny house until I found the bathroom. Obviously, she was preparing to share the space with someone since the other two rooms were mostly empty but incredibly clean. It was clear she was still living her days and nights mostly backward, because I could see she was sound asleep, lying horizontally across her bed when I accidentally opened the door to her room.

She'd always been a night owl. She was the one who wanted to watch movies well into the middle of the night or party until the sun came up. She was impossible to

wake up in the morning, and swore she was at her best
once the stars came out at night.

If this were a normal visit, I would have given her
a load of shit for just getting home when dawn was
breaking, but the truth was, nothing had changed. I was
up with the sun for practice, or to study, or to help Daire
with her homework when I still lived at home. When
Bowe was in town for any length of time, my schedule
inevitably got all screwed up and out of whack. I used to
blame my constant irritation with everything she did on
being tired, but I doubted the assertion fooled anyone. I
was still cranky and irritable where she was concerned,
even when I got a good night's sleep.

Once I found the bathroom, I started the shower
and climbed under the spray. I turned the water to
scalding hot and scrubbed what was left of the sleep out
of my eyes. I let the discontent that nearly swallowed me
whole last night wash down the drain. I needed to get my
head on right and figure out what I was doing in Texas
instead of staying in Denver and smoothing things over
with Aston. I was logical enough to know it wasn't easy
for her to tell me we were over. I was also smart enough
to know if she'd kept her college choice not only from me
and Daire, but her brother as well, there was a deeper
reason behind it. She might not want to be with me in a
romantic way any longer, but we'd been friends forever,
and I cared about her immensely. Even if she didn't love
me anymore, she should still trust me. I was sure she
was hurting just as badly as I was, just in a different kind
of way. And she should know it wasn't like me to ditch
anyone who might need me, even if that someone had

ripped my heart out and handed it back to me bloody and battered.

It made no sense that instead of being there to assure Aston everything would be all right; I ran to the one person who was going to have zero sympathy for my dumb ass. I vaguely remembered feeling like I couldn't breathe all night until I finally saw Bowe. I was choking on my own unfamiliar emotions, but as soon as she touched my face and those honey eyes locked onto mine, the invisible claws shredding my insides didn't seem nearly as sharp. What sense did it make that she was the only person who could rile me up and calm me down with no effort? I always felt like she was playing with me, that I was nothing more than a toy she could wind up and send spinning when she was bored. She put me on a shelf and forgot all about my existence when it was convenient for her. It was one of the main reasons our relationship hovered close to being contentious.

I was just stepping out of the shower when I heard the doorbell followed by a series of rapid knocks on the front door. I waited for a minute to see if Bowe would wake up, but there wasn't any movement from the end of the hallway where her bedroom was. Like I said, she was impossible to wake up, no matter how insistent her visitor seemed to be.

Swearing under my breath, I pulled on a pair of track pants and scrubbed a towel over my wet hair while stomping toward the door. According to my phone, it was already late into the afternoon, which would explain why I felt so discombobulated, and why my stomach was suddenly growling. I never slept this late, regardless of circumstances.

I pulled the door open without checking who was on the other side; I was sure there was no way Bowe's dad would let her live alone without all the possible security measures. She was bound to have one of those recording doorbells and an alarm system, so it was unlikely I would get murdered once I opened the teal door.

If looks could really kill, the way the dude on the other side was glaring at me would have me six feet under.

I flicked the towel around my neck and lifted an eyebrow at the heavily tattooed visitor. "Can I help you?"

He looked like the typical kind of guy who always circled around Bowe. He was tall and skinny. Both his arms were tattooed down to his fingers. His shaggy hair was an odd mix of jet-black roots and lilac strands cut in an intentionally messy style. He had several big, heavy earrings dangling from each ear, and more rings on his fingers than a repeat Super Bowl winner. He wasn't bad looking by any stretch of the imagination, but he was such a cliché 'band dude' that I wanted to laugh. He looked like every other guy Bowe played around with since she'd been old enough to date. Half the time, I wondered if they were just trying to cos-play as her dad since so many had a similar style. She got mad when I asked her why she kept going after the same type when none of them ever seemed to stick around for very long.

"Who are you?" The question was barked at me in a cold tone as I used one corner of the towel to clean some residual water out of my ear.

I tilted my head a little and tried to knock it out when the towel didn't work. I watched him watch me, his angry gaze sliding over my half-dressed form that was as different from his as night and day.

He was tall, but I was almost a giant. I definitely got my Uncle Rome's height. Both Zowen and I were a couple inches taller than all the men in our family, except for my dad's older brother.

I'd never been skinny. I'd played sports since I was young and was blessed with really good genes. I'd always been fit and in good shape, but as I got older and more dedicated to football and my health, I was ripped. I knew it. Anyone who looked at me with or without clothes on knew it.

He had me beat when it came to ink in terms of quantity, but no one could touch me when it came to quality. I didn't have a body full of ink, I didn't want to relive all my memories through images on my skin, but I did have one intricate, detailed piece my father worked on over a period of time once I was old enough. It started out as a way for me to try and relate to him, to understand him and figure out what made him tick, and turned into one of the few experiences we shared where I felt like we finally got closer. It was something he gave me that I would have with me forever. So even though tattoos had never been as big a part of my life as they were for so much of my extended family, I felt like I had a good grasp as to *why* they were so special and important to so many people, and why they could show the world who someone was without words.

He cleared his throat and shifted his weight on his feet as we continued to stare at one another. Again, he demanded to know, "Who in the hell are you? I've never seen you before, and I spend pretty much all my free time with Bowe."

I straightened my head and gave it a shake, sending water flying everywhere. "Are you her boyfriend?"

If so, it would explain why he was envisioning tearing my head from my body and not bothering to hide it.

I saw him start to nod just as a raspy voice with a soft Texas twang drifted up from behind me.

"No. He's not my boyfriend. But he is my friend, and we're in a band together." I felt Bowe put her hand on my bare shoulder as she shoved me to one side to peer out the open door. "Why did you answer my front door half-naked, Ry? And what are you doing here, Nyle? We don't have plans today."

Bowe's bright hair was a tangled mess on top of her head. She was still wearing the same outfit she'd had on last night when I showed up unannounced. She was always a little rough around the edges, which was annoying because she was such a pretty girl, but it was pretty cute when she was rumpled and sleepy. It reminded me of another time and place when I was the reason her hair ended up wild and snarled. I could clearly recall just how soft and silky it felt in my hands and how fucking sexy it was when the neon strands dragged across my skin.

The edge of her elbow caught me right in the gut, making me cough in surprise as she glared up at me. I lifted the towel back over my head and turned on my bare heel.

"I was just getting out of the shower when someone started knocking and wouldn't stop. It seemed important, so I answered the door." I shrugged a shoulder. "Had no clue it was just one of your many admirers anxious to see you. So boring."

I heard her swear under her breath at the slight dig. It was true, though. Everywhere she went, it seemed like she had different boys falling at her feet. It was partly the edgy, hot girl in a band thing she had going on. But a big chunk of it was her whole unattainable vibe. Everyone wanted what they couldn't have, and Bowe was a master at playing the 'you-can-look-but-not-touch' game.

"For real. Who the fuck is that asshole, Bowe? I just saw you last night, and you didn't mention you were going to have a visitor anytime soon."

I chuckled to myself as I stepped back into the house and headed toward the bathroom. I kept the door open a crack so I could unabashedly listen to their conversation.

This guy had to be a new addition to Bowe's circle of friends. Otherwise, he would know one thing she absolutely hated more than anything was being questioned or pushed into a corner. She liked to think she didn't answer to anyone. Especially not some guy who wasn't even her boyfriend... even though he clearly wanted to be.

"Exactly. I saw you last night. So why are you out here pounding on my door? Like I said, we don't have practice today, and even if we did, it would be hours and hours from now. You and I don't have plans together either. There's no reason for you to be here." Her raspy voice was cold, and even though I couldn't see her, I could clearly picture the way her spine would snap straight with irritation and her shoulders would square off. Bowe Keller wasn't a pushover by any stretch of the imagination, and the girl always gave just as good as she got.

I heard the tattooed band dude nervously clear his throat. The various chains and accessories he was wearing jangled loud enough for me to hear inside the house as he shifted his weight.

"I thought it would be okay if I dropped by. I wanted to see if you maybe wanted to go get lunch with me or something. We've been practicing nonstop lately and putting in a lot of hours. This is our first real break in weeks. I thought I could treat you. I didn't know you were going to have company." I heard him make an annoyed sound as he switched from conciliatory to confrontational. I wanted to warn him he was about to reach the point of no return if he kept trying to guilt-trip her about having another man in her house—but it was more fun to listen to him dig his own grave. "How do you even know a bland meathead like that? He's not the kind of guy you usually hang out with."

I tossed my head back and laughed at my reflection in the mirror. Driving like a madman through the middle of the night was insane, but getting to lurk on this moment where Bowe was about to explode all over some overly confident punk might have made the whole trip worthwhile.

"First of all, we are nowhere near the 'just-drop-by' stage of friendship. Second of all, why would I want to spend my first day off in forever with someone I see all the damn time? Third, and most important, who is and isn't allowed to stay at my house is no business of yours.

I don't owe you an explanation about anything in my private life. We play music together, and we're friendly with one another because of the band, but that's it. You don't get to question me about anyone I know or how I might know them." I knew if I could see her that her dark eyebrows would be dipped down in a severe V over her tiny nose, and her intense eyes would be shooting amber sparks of annoyance. She was pretty when she was mad. She was also a little bit scary, even though she wasn't very big. She seemed a lot taller than she was because her attitude and charisma were so huge and infectious. When we stood next to one another, the top of her head only reached my shoulder, and that was after a late growth spurt she had after she turned sixteen.

"And he's not a meathead. Who are you to judge someone you don't know anything about? I hate judgmental, critical people the most. I have things to do today, Nyle. I'll see you at practice. Don't invite yourself over to my house ever again. I won't be as nice as Ry if I answer the door and find you on the other side of it."

The door slammed shut with a thump of finality. I slipped my t-shirt over my head and stuck my head into the hallway just in time to see Bowe march toward the small but tidy and very modern kitchen. My stomach growled again, reminding me it had been hours since I'd indulged in the greasy food on the road. I needed a real meal and a stop to get some provisions.

I followed Bowe into the kitchen, grinning as she angrily swiped her hair out of her face as she chugged milk directly from a carton she grabbed out of the fridge.

"Comb your hair and put on clothes you didn't sleep in. I'm hungry and need to stop by a store to grab some stuff, including underwear. I didn't bring anything with me when I left Denver."

She glared at me over the milk container, making me laugh because she had a bit of a white mustache leftover before she wiped it with the back of her hand. "Why do I have to go with you? I didn't invite you to ruin my day off either." She winged a midnight-colored eyebrow upward and asked, "How long are you planning on hiding out here anyway?"

I shook my head. "Dunno. But I'm not in a hurry to head home."

She sighed and closed the fridge with more force than necessary. "You have to head back and face her eventually. Do you know how shitty you'll feel if she leaves for school or something and you don't get the chance to say goodbye or clear the air? I get that you're mad and confused. I totally understand that you're hurting, but you guys have been in each other's lives for too long to just let everything go without closure."

It was my turn to lift my eyebrows in question. "Really? Because I've known you just as long as I've known Aston, and the last time we were together, you left without a word and refused to come back or even see me again. You only text back if I threaten to tell your parents you're out of communication, and you never answer me if I call you. How come I owe Aston some kind of closure, but you don't owe me anything?" It forever lived under my skin that she'd written me off so easily, regardless of all that we'd been through together, both good and bad.

A heavy silence settled between the two of us as we stared at each other without blinking. There was so

319

much between the two of us, often there didn't seem like there were enough words in the world to encompass it all, but the way we looked at each other spoke volumes.

My mother once told me that someone could always hide what was in their heart, but what they were really feeling was always reflected honestly in their eyes. I wondered what Bowe saw when she looked at me because I knew what I saw when I looked at her.

Longing.

Regret.

Confusion.

Frustration.

And not too long ago, I could've sworn what was in those molten depths was love... and hate.

"You owe Aston because you love her and she loved you. I don't owe you anything because you and I are nothing to each other. We aren't friends. We aren't family. And we aren't lovers. All we are is two people who can't seem to escape each other because our parents keep forcing us to spend time together. It's so annoying." She huffed out a breath and flounced by me, but I could see that it was all bravado. My question had shaken her a little bit. "I'll go with you, but only because I want to eat, and I want to make sure you don't buy too much stuff that indicates your stay will be extended. You aren't welcome here, Ry. I'm not going to be your safe haven indefinitely."

I watched her disappear into the bathroom, leaning back on a counter in the kitchen as I told only the walls, "But you've always been my safe haven."

Even if she didn't realize or acknowledge it, she was always the person I turned to when I needed someone to make me feel better. When I had nothing left to give, she was the one who filled my tank back up. Sometimes she topped it off with poison, but I'd grown accustomed to the bitter taste.

It was uniquely hers and stood out from the sweetness that everyone else brought to the table. It's why she lingered the way no one else did.

ACKNOWLEDGEMENTS

First and foremost, thank you to each and every one of you who picked up this book. (Especially if this is your second round with this particular title.) I know most of my readers are waiting on the edge of their seats for the next-gen of the *Marked Men* since I dropped that info in the back of my last two books, but it's the readers who picked up both *Goldilocks* and *A Righteous Man* who I decided to write the kids' books for.

YOU! Yes, you, the one reading this right now, are the reason I'm jumping back into a world I swore I would never, ever revisit. Your loyalty and support mean everything, and I honestly feel like I owe you those stories as a small thank you for making sure I'm still here, even though I stopped writing what most of my original readers wanted a very long time ago.

And an extra heartfelt thank you to anyone who has or will take a few minutes to leave a review. I hate sounding like a broken record every time I release a book, but reviews really do help, and leaving one is the very best thing you can do for a new release and an author. And in case you hate the book and worry about a bad review being unwelcome, that isn't the case. Any honest review is helpful and super encouraged. Never trust a book with no bad reviews...lol.

Of course, there would be no book, good, bad, or ugly, without my creative team. One of my favorite parts of publishing a book independently is getting to handpick the folks I want to work with. I think I have the best of the best and cannot recommend Hang, Elaine, and Beth enough. They are worth every single penny. You can find their info at the beginning of this book.

I owe my beta team the world. I think I finally have this author thing figured out nearly a decade into it, with over thirty books published. But without fail, I learn something new and figure out a way to be better and write better books each time they hand a rough draft back to me. I appreciate them so much. It's such a huge deal for anyone to offer their time and talent for the benefit of someone else. Seriously, they show up regardless of how tight the turnaround time is or how awful my initial draft is. My beta team really is the best. Pam, Teri, Alexandra, Kelly, Cheron, Sarah, and Karla all bring something invaluable to the table. I couldn't imagine putting out a book without having them be the first eyes on it.

Last, but certainly not least, is my undying gratitude to my assistant Melissa. She takes on any challenge I throw her way, usually with a smile and the occasional curse word. She's southern, so she excels at the first and is adorable when she does the second. She forces me to see the glass as half full, even on the hardest of days. I feel like we've accomplished so much and grown together. We've worked together for a long time, and I think all the best parts of both of us have rubbed off on one another. She remains one of the kindest, most compassionate humans I've ever met, even when the world feels like it is constantly on fire.

Below is a list of all the places
you can find me if you want to reach out:
Facebook.com/groups/crownoverscrowd
Bookbub: bookbub.com/authors/jay-crownover
Website: jaycrownover.com
My store: shop.spreadshirt.com/100036557
FB page: Facebook.com/AuthorJayCrownover
Twitter: twitter.com/jaycrownover
Instagram: instagram.com/jay.crownover
Pinterest: pinterest.com/jaycrownover
Spotify and Snapchat: Jay Crownover
Email: JayCrownover@gmail.com

ABOUT THE AUTHOR

Jay Crownover is the international and multiple *New York Times* and *USA Today* bestselling author of the *Marked Men* series, the *Saints of Denver* series, the *Point* series, the *Breaking Point* series, the *Getaway* series, and the *Loveless, Texas* series. Her books have been translated into many different languages all around the world. She is a tattooed, crazy-haired Colorado native who lives at the base of the Rockies with her awesome dogs. She can frequently be found enjoying a cold beer and taco Tuesdays. Jay is a self-declared music snob and outspoken book lover who is always looking for her next adventure, between the pages and on the road.

If you're interested in my other books,
you can check them out here:
The *Marked Men* Seiries:
https://www.jaycrownover.com/markedmenseries
The *Saints of Denver* Series:
https://www.jaycrownover.com/saintsofdenver
The *Point* Series:
https://www.jaycrownover.com/welcometothepoint
The *Breaking Point* Series:
https://www.jaycrownover.com/thebreakinpoint
The *Getaway* Series:
https://www.jaycrownover.com/thegetawayseries
The *Loveless* Series:
https://www.jaycrownover.com/copy-of-stand-alones
Standalone Novels:
https://www.jaycrownover.com/standalones

Made in the USA
Monee, IL
10 July 2021